THE
ASTONISHING
THING

SANDI WARD

KENSINGTON BOOKS
www.kensingtonbooks.com

KENSINGTON BOOKS are published by

Kensington Publishing Corp.
119 West 40th Street
New York, NY 10018

All Kensington titles, imprints, and distributed lines are available at special quantity discounts for bulk purchases for sales promotion, premiums, fund-raising, and educational or institutional use.

Special book excerpts or customized printings can also be created to fit specific needs. For details, write or phone the office of the Kensington Sales Manager: Kensington Publishing Corp., 119 West 40th Street, New York, NY 10018. Attn. Sales Department. Phone: 1-800-221-2647.

Kensington and the K logo Reg. U.S. Pat. & TM Off.

First Kensington Books Trade Paperback Printing: November 2017

First Kensington Books Mass Market Printing: May 2020
ISBN-13: 978-1-4967-3029-9
ISBN-10: 1-4967-3029-1

ISBN-13: 978-1-4967-1112-0 (ebook)
ISBN-10: 1-4967-1112-2 (ebook)

10 9 8 7 6 5 4 3 2 1

Printed in the United States of America

Books by Sandi Ward

THE ASTONISHING THING

SOMETHING WORTH SAVING

WHAT HOLDS US TOGETHER

Published by Kensington Publishing Corporation

For Michael, Hunter, and Summer

1

A Sweet Life

Let me tell you about my mother.

Mother is soft curves and encouraging coos. She gives careful scratches to my head and is cautious with my whiskers and ears. Mother holds me calmly and never yells. Her hair is long and dark and curly, and I love to chew on strands when I can get close enough.

Mother has many names for me: Sweetie, Cutie, Pretty Girl, Fat Fat, and Lovey. When she calls, "Here, Boo!" I run for her, because that means food.

Mother is my life, my constant companion, my soul mate. But she has not said my name in several days. Mother went out, and I am waiting for her to come back.

I don't have clear memories of the day she picked me out, but I have a recollection of being one among hundreds of cats in dark cages along a very long wall. When Mother lifted me out of my cage, I hung limp in her hands and felt secure as she pressed me gently against her chest. Her scent was instantly pleasing to me, like fresh milk. She was so confident that I was the right one that she passed me around, first to Girl, and then to Boy, who would become my sister and brother. I was a perfect fit, not just for Mother's shoulder but also for this family.

Mother is kind. She feeds me the food I like, on time, morning and night. Mother is home all day, and I sit in her warm lap if she is watching the television. If I choose to lie right in the middle of the kitchen floor, my long, cream-colored fur sticking up with static and my tummy fat spread out over the tiles, she carefully and considerately steps over me.

Best of all, I nestle with her at night, first right by her head for a good purr and then down by her feet. In the morning, I push the comforter aside with my head and extend my claws to gently scratch her hand so she will get up and feed me. And she always gets up. Always!

Of course, we are not alone in this house.

My brother, the oldest child, is tall and lanky. He is friendly to me but sometimes trips over his own feet, so I watch out when he comes running. Brother spends a lot of time at his desk in front of a big machine, pressing buttons and occasionally giving a cheer or cursing his head off. Sometimes I sit and paw at the little things moving on the screen. He always laughs and doesn't seem to mind.

My sister is good with me, and I will sit in her lap if she is reading. She stays in her room a lot, where it is warm and the light is welcoming. She has a poster tacked onto her wall that she touches or kisses when she enters or leaves the room. There are boys on this poster, and she seems to worship them. Sister also taps and talks into a small phone, mostly about things that sound very, very exciting and dramatic.

Sister has a child, a strange fluffy brown creature who is Not a Cat. He sleeps with her, like I sleep with Mother.

Not a Cat will try to get me to chase him, but I have no interest. He chirps and barks, spinning in circles. I just sit and watch, occasionally doling out a scratch with my meaty paw, which sends him running. I am bigger than him, and outweigh him by quite a bit. I am also smarter.

Then there's the man. He has silky hair on his head and a face the color of tarnished gold, and he is the biggest of all. When I was a kitten, I thought of him as the Man-Lion. He is not my father, and he does not cuddle or feed me, but he is Mother's mate. He lies down with Mother at night, and I avoid his side of the bed. I know he is strong, because I have seen him lift things. He tromps around, and I hustle to get out of his way. Not that I am afraid of him. I am just smart enough to move when I see a bull charging at me. We have a mutual dislike. But I reluctantly see why Mother likes him; he is handsome in his way, and proud, and speaks with a low tone that commands respect.

Still, I'm not sure why Mother needs him. She is the hunter and feeder of this family.

I have a nice home. This house is in a cold place. Summers are short. During most of the year, when the humans come in from the outside they are surrounded by a cloud of chilly air. Not a Cat comes in with ice and snow caked onto his paws. I know what snow is, even though I am never allowed outside, because the humans track it in and down the hall. I'll bat it with my paw and lick any ice until my tongue turns numb.

I don't mind being kept inside. This house is more

than enough for me. And when Man gets the fire going, it is very cozy.

I don't know what Man does most days when he leaves the house, but I have heard the children say that he fights with fire. Occasionally he gets up in the middle of the night when a loud horn is sounding from somewhere outside. He comes back smelling like the fireplace, but much stronger, so acrid that it makes my eyes water, and I realize he must have walked through fire. It puzzles me, because I know that fire gets very hot and I cannot sit too close to the fireplace before it starts to feel uncomfortable. I wonder how he can stand it.

The family avoids him until he has washed off the black dust and bitter scent, and they know to stay away if he broods after that. Sometimes he seems sad or exhausted, and he avoids my siblings, finding a seat away from them for a while.

He acts no differently toward me, because to me he is neither kind nor unkind. It is just as if I am invisible, as if I do not exist.

Man calls Mother "Carrie" when he is being serious. Maybe because she carries this family with all of the work she does. He calls her "Care" when he is pleading or he wants something. It seems he always wants something.

She calls him "Tom" or "Tommy." Or "Stupid," when she is mad at him.

Mother has the right touch, and I am her constant companion. She gently caresses the space between my ears and very carefully tickles my nose. At night, things get busy, but she doesn't forget about me. Late at night when my brother and sister are in bed, I have her to myself.

If Mother stops petting me and decides to touch the man, I don't get upset. I sit on the back of the couch above their heads waiting my turn. He likes a scratch behind his ears too, and she'll run her fingers through his hair like she does to my fur. We all must share Mother. I understand.

Sometimes at night when Man gets into bed I have to jump down for a little while, because he moves around too much. But I always return. Sometimes I catch him staring at me, only for a second. I cannot interpret his intentions. I ignore humans that I don't understand. As I said, we don't like each other, but we are stuck with each other.

And now I have lost all happiness, because Mother has gone out and not returned. Days and nights have passed. And yet the rest of the family is here. They are unusually quiet, and only mention Mother's name in whispers.

This has never happened before.

2

The Baby

I think the baby is the source of our problems.

I have not mentioned the baby yet. He is the newest member of our family. We had a good life before the baby came.

This is a big, old, drafty house. When I sit by a window, I feel a cold wind leaking right through the wall. I like playing in the dusty corners and padding up the creaky stairs. At night, there is often a blazing fire in the fireplace, and there is nothing I love more than sitting on a pillow placed near the hearth.

Before that baby arrived, we often enjoyed quiet evenings in the living room, with the TV playing. I found it amusing to watch Man sneak in and tickle my siblings from behind, reaching over the couch. Even though they are older children, as tall as he is, they would laugh and shriek.

"Nooooo, cut it out," my sister begged, doubling over while giggling. "Daddy, stop!"

"You scared the crap out of me," my brother would

yelp, jumping away with a grin. "I'll get you for this. I'm too fast for you, Pops. You'd better watch your back."

When she was here, Mother liked to sit apart from the others, and as much as I loved the warmth of the fire, I often joined her. I could see how she valued me above the rest of the family, but they pretended not to notice. I was always Mother's favorite. She preferred being with me to being with the humans.

I realized something was different about Mother when I noticed how slowly she waddled around the kitchen. I thought perhaps she was putting on weight due to the fact that she rarely left the house. I have put on extra pounds over time myself. So that alone wasn't a cause for concern.

I cuddled with her at night as she grew, and her expanding belly gave me a nice pocket of warmth to snuggle into, right by her chest. I didn't think about it too much, until one night something in her stomach jabbed me in the ribs. It hit me all at once.

Of course, a baby! She was pregnant. I couldn't believe I hadn't figured it out earlier.

Mother has always taken comfort in my purring, but she began hugging me in bed tighter than ever. I was happy to help out.

At the same time, I was a little confused, because my brother and sister are much older. I guess I just wasn't expecting another sibling. I thought I would always be the baby of the family.

Around the time I recognized Mother was pregnant, Man began acting erratically. He seemed excited and eager to make preparations for the baby. While sprawled out on the wood floor, taking an afternoon catnap, I watched him pull down the attic door. He made many trips up the ladder, sweat coating his face. He worked hard carrying down all sorts of strange things, including a giant, ridiculous baby cage. Man was up half the night, banging and cursing and putting the thing together. But his energy was interesting to watch.

Mother, on the other hand, grew very still. She stayed in bed, even during the day. It seemed difficult for her to get up or roll over. Brother and Sister came to her with all sorts of complaints. I scowled at them, and hissed when they flew at her too quickly. I didn't like them bothering Mother when she was tired.

Most worrisome, sometimes Mother didn't even have the energy to lift her head. I was so worried about her. As much as I loved to lie with her, I started to wonder if something was seriously wrong.

In fact, the only thing that consistently got Mother out of bed was my dinnertime. She padded her way downstairs and filled my bowls. Once in a while she would feed the other children, but not always. I was flattered and grateful, but also puzzled.

I could see sorrow and disappointment in the faces of my siblings as they watched our mother head back upstairs. I felt sorry for them.

But I also thought that perhaps the humans just didn't understand what Mother was going through. I decided that maybe she was sick, and needed a doctor. I tried to get everyone's attention, but I am limited in what I can communicate. I wanted to ask, *Why aren't you helping her?*

When I meowed, Not a Cat would bark and try to play with me. Sister would talk to me and pet my head. But I was upset and not playful.

When I was desperate, I got right up near my brother's big machine and pushed my head into his elbow. I licked and groomed his bare arm, tasting the salt on his skin. I yowled as loud as I could. But Brother seemed to think

I was looking for attention. "Hey, Boo," he said to me. "You're a good girl. You're a sweetie pie. You're a big, fat meatball of lovey-dovey fluff." He scratched my neck and kissed my head, but that wasn't what I wanted at all.

I wanted him to help Mother.

I grew frantic, and wondered if I could get Mother to help herself. I jumped up to Mother's bed and pawed at her hand, then pushed the blanket down with my head. She did not get up, but she did eventually stroke my back, and I purred as loud as I could to show her how much I appreciated it.

Man didn't have much luck with Mother either when he tried to comfort her. He seemed to sense, as I did, that she was in some measure of distress. Man would lie behind her and try to put his arm over her, but she pushed him away. At one point, she began slapping his hand, as if his touch burned her skin.

"But Carrie, I just want—"

"No." She cursed and railed at him: "Stop. Leave me alone, Tommy."

I could see she blamed him for the whole situation.

One night, when Mother's belly was enormous, she had a bad fight with Man. They were on the couch in the living room, with Mother sitting up but slumped over as if she was having trouble staying awake. I lay on the floor, watching.

Man spoke to her very intensely. He grabbed her arms and forced her to look at him. "Carrie," he begged her. "Please. Listen to me. You can't lie down all day. It's not good for you, or the baby. Just try to get up once in a while and eat something." More talking and more talking. I could see Mother was sick of it, but he just kept on talking. It amazes me what Man does not see and does not understand. I guess he is proud and strong

and thinks he knows best. He kept it up even when she
winced and hung her head in exhaustion. Man kissed
her cheeks and forehead, and tried to hold her, but she
just squirmed and protested and turned her face away. I
could see she had had enough. Enough of him, enough
of the pregnancy. Mother is my best friend, and I could
see how she felt about things.

Eventually Man left the room. *Good riddance,* I
thought. I jumped right up to comfort poor Mother.

Sister was good at distracting Mother in those final
weeks. She'd come in and sit on the bed, talking excitedly, filling Mother in on what was clearly very important information. "Ma," she'd start, flipping her hair
over her shoulder, "you will never believe what happened to Sarah today at the beach. You know Ted, who
works at the snack bar? He's the cute one, whose older
brother is a lifeguard. . . ."

Mother listened patiently, up to a point, but eventually waved her away. "Okay, honey," she'd say with a
sigh. "Let me rest now."

Sister often carried me to her room during this time,
which is no easy task. I am heavy and floppy and quite
large, but she'd get one hand under my haunches and
squeeze me to her body with her other bony arm.

She held me up to her poster. I came to realize that
the boys on the poster must represent a religion, or a
cult. Holding me in one arm, she placed my paw up to
the face of one of the boys on her poster and made me
tap him repeatedly. She chanted, "Harry, Harry, Harry,
Harry." I found this boring every time, and eventually
meowed to be let go.

But I never scratched my sister. As I mentioned, I
am very tolerant of the humans.

My sister is fourteen years old. I know this because

she had a big party that she planned and talked about for weeks. It got a little out of hand. Man had expected Mother to help him with the party, but she didn't feel well that night so she didn't come downstairs. He had to roar ferociously to get all of those kids out of our house at the end of the evening.

Brother liked to come into the bedroom and put a hand, or his ear, to Mother's big stomach. He did this for long stretches of time, eager to feel or hear something, his mouth open as if just waiting to be surprised. I was glad he took time away from his machine to visit her. But every visit ended in a plea for Mother to do something—make him food, usually. "Ma. Can you please just get up and make me a grilled cheese? I'm freaking starving." Even though he is my oldest sibling, my brother seems incapable of fixing his own meals.

As am I. So I am sympathetic.

Once in a while, he brought her the "funnies" from the crinkly newspaper, and Mother would smile. Sometimes my brother carried me away with him to his own room, calling me "Big Fat Crookshanks" or "Minerva McGonagall," and Mother would even laugh.

I don't know what's so funny about that.

When the weather grew warmer and the days were long, it was finally time for the baby to be born. The day came when Mother began to moan and breathe heavily, and two strange women came to the house to help deliver the baby. I hid away from the noise and bustle. When it was done, these women left. And Man put the crying baby into the crib.

Mother did not always respond to that baby. I snuggled up to Mother to make her feel better. She was very, very tired. Man urged her to get up. Sometimes she did, sometimes she did not. Even during the day when Man was out, there were times when the baby screamed and Mother didn't get up from the bed.

It was the height of our short summer, that brief time of year when the children come in and out of the house with bare feet and it gets humid during the day. The humans were sweaty and cranky most of the time. The baby seemed uncomfortable too, even when Man turned on the big floor fan that he placed in the nursery.

Mother still caressed my head and smoothed out my fur and held me tight against her. I never loved her more than in those times when she needed me so much.

One day I thought I'd try to help out. I jumped into the baby's cage from a high dresser. I snuggled down near the baby and purred. The baby shook spastically from screaming, but eventually slept.

When the sun went down, Man came home. I could hear him downstairs tromping around. After a few minutes, he came into the baby's room. I was half-asleep but sensed him sneaking in, and then saw him looking down at us in the darkness. I was right up against the baby, my fur covering his little head and face. I was doing my best, trying to keep the baby quiet so he wouldn't bother Mother. But Man's eyes grew very hard. I did not understand what I was doing wrong, but I could see he was very angry.

I did not expect it: Man grabbed me up with his big hands, as if I were a pile of trash, and threw me down onto the rug. It was the only time Man was purposely violent against me, and he is very lucky I am both so nimble and so fat! I came away with just a few sore spots.

I might have fared worse. But for all he was mad at me, he was more angry at *her*.

"Care, Care, Care," he raged against Mother. "God-damnit. You have to pay more attention." The baby screamed, but still, Mother didn't get up. Sister was upset and ran into her room with Not a Cat. I heard her start to cry. Brother slunk away and stayed out of sight. I hid under the bed most of the night.

I will tell you this. I don't know anything about babies, but something I could sense—even before I got into his crib—was that something was wrong with the baby boy. He cried too much and his reactions were not right.

And I came to see that even though the pregnancy was over, something was still troubling Mother, and getting worse.

3

An Ominous Phone Call

Whereas the pregnancy slowed Mother down, the baby seemed to drain her energy completely. He is a helpless creature and demands attention.

Stupid, stupid, stupid baby.

Those first few months with the newborn after Man threw me out of the crib, the baby continued to cry and cry, all through those long, hot days. Everyone took turns getting up and making formula. Sometimes Mother got up, but just as often she sank back down on the bed and rubbed her feet. Some nights Man hollered for my sister, and sometimes he silently got up and comforted the baby himself. I'd watch Man cradle that baby and stare at him in the darkness of the nursery. He'd had two babies already, of course, but that was a long time ago, so maybe it all felt new to him again.

If the baby wouldn't stop screaming, Man would wince like it was painful to him. And it *was* painful, believe me. This baby screeched with the strength of one twice his size.

Sometimes if the baby just wouldn't settle down, my brother got up and took the baby from whoever was holding him. He seemed to have the right touch and eventually got the thing quiet. Brother has a confidence about him in these situations that I find comforting.

I wish I could have held the baby. I would have helped out.

But I stayed far from the crib since Man lost his temper. Apparently, he didn't want my help.

The rest of the family continued to bother Mother. When my brother came home from wherever he spent his summer afternoons, he ran up the stairs without wiping the sand off his legs. He'd tear off his wet things in his bedroom and leave them on the floor before going to see Mother.

He would go and grab the baby and hold it in his arms while telling Mother about his day. Brother smiled at the baby and rocked him while talking. If the baby was asleep in his crib, my brother would bring in a large orange ball instead and twirl it on his finger.

But just as he did when she was pregnant, he would always end his visits by asking for something. "Ma, make me *this*. Ma, make me *that*." He was always asking for food. Brother is taller than Mother, and he eats a tremendous amount. He is old enough to drive the truck that takes the humans away from the house. He is not quite an adult, but almost. Mother calls him Jimmy. Or, "*Jesus,* Jimmy," when she is frustrated, and she rolls her eyes.

Poor Jesus Jimmy. He was hungry.

Frankly, I was too. Mother had stopped feeding me regularly.

Sometimes Jimmy would finally go down and eat sliced ham right out of the package, and he'd throw some on the floor for me. Not a Cat would come running, but I could keep him at bay with a sharp hiss and then eat the scraps. They were mine, and I was desperately hungry.

Thinking back on it, I realize Not a Cat was hungry too. He always looked at me with those round, brown eyes, hoping I would share with him and then expecting me to play with him.

He didn't understand the situation at all.

My meals started coming at odd times, from whomever I could force to get up. Usually that was my brother. Once in a while Man noticed I was hungry, and he made my sister feed me. Then I'd go curl up on Mother's bed, my belly full and my heart content. We would fall asleep as if nothing was wrong, and it was a great relief.

There was one night Man took Mother out, and she got dressed up like she used to. She was so beautiful!

Back when she got up in the morning, I liked to sit on the toilet and watch Mother get ready for the day. I did the same on the night she went out. She drew black lines around her eyes, to look like a cat. She put red on her lips. Her hair was glossy and her teeth very white. And she didn't forget me, filling a small paper cup with water and setting it beside me so I could lap it up with my tongue.

That night, when she came out of the bathroom, Man was so happy. He held her and pushed his face against her cheek and ear just like I do. I know he was marking his territory.

Cats are very territorial, and humans are too.

Mother put her sweet, gentle hands on his big arms and looked at him like maybe she did still appreciate him. Sometimes I thought they were right for each other. He was not such a bad mate. As I said, he was tall and proud, and I never saw him chase her away the way she often did to him.

Sometimes he ignored her, the way he ignored me, especially if he was in a bad mood. But if she insisted on having his attention she would sit in his lap, and he always watched and listened to her carefully. It's just that she didn't insist very often.

But late that night, when they got home, she was upset again and went straight up to the bedroom. They were both a little off balance, their words somewhat slurred. When he tried to hold her, she was already protesting. "Stupid, stupid, stupid Tommy." I don't know what he said or did, but I'm sure Mother was right and he was wrong. Man glared at her, and I didn't like that look in his eye. He watched her go into the bathroom and shut the door. Man gave up and went to another room, and I had Mother all to myself when she came out and crawled into bed.

I lay by her side, spread out on the cool comforter, my head resting on her arm. I loved her so, so much. Why couldn't the others leave her alone? Why should she have to meet their demands? Couldn't they see how special she was?

One day, a young woman who was dressed in a suit came to the house and looked at the baby. She held the baby and talked to him and seemed to be testing him. Her name was "Missus Davenport," and she was all big, big smiles and had a chipper voice. Man eyed her warily, but Mother made an effort and came into the baby's room to watch her.

After that, Missus started coming to the house twice a week to work with the baby for a couple of hours. Mother sat in the rocking chair, mostly observing, but on occasion reading a book. Sometimes I'd curl up in Mother's lap, or if it was too warm I would just watch from the floor near the fan.

Missus Davenport was mesmerizing, dangling pretty toys on a string or laying out objects on the rug for the baby to look at. She didn't seem to mind me, and even encouraged the baby to look at me. I couldn't believe she was sitting on the floor in those nice clothes. Silly! This woman was so silly. A perfect playmate for the baby, I guess.

When Missus wasn't around, Man sometimes tried to get my siblings to take the baby out in the big pushcart. Jimmy didn't mind it, but my sister had no interest. She fought it, pointing to fluffy Not a Cat and shaking his leash. She had enough to do, just like Mother.

Sister is called Mary, or "So Smart Mary" by Mother. Mary sometimes came in and talked to Mother in a very hushed voice, so no one else could hear. Mother sat up and smoothed down her hair when Sister came in to talk to her.

"Ma . . ." So Smart Mary would coo in her seductive voice, batting her eyes and leaning in, and Mother couldn't resist her. Mother often pulled green papers out of her bedside table for Mary. So Smart Mary got very excited and hugged her mother, then jumped up and twirled around, waving the green papers in the air. And then she'd be off.

Sister wasn't home very much. And when she was, she was in her room with the door shut.

I could see Man was growing afraid of my sister as she got bigger and taller, the way he looked at her with worry on his face. I was starting to see she was someone powerful, with her important things to do and her fervent religious beliefs and her exciting talk. Man sometimes stood outside her closed bedroom door, listening to her music, looking like he wanted to knock on that door . . . but he hesitated.

He may stand tall, but his eyes give him away sometimes. With his forehead creased into a frown of confusion, he stood with his hand frozen in the air, unable to knock.

It amused me.

I also suspect So Smart Mary thinks Man is not too intelligent, just like Mother does. One night, he suggested Mary make the family dinner.

She whirled to face him. "Why is that suddenly my job? Because I'm a girl? That's dumb. You're the parent. I don't have time for that."

Man didn't get angry with her. Without another word, he quietly made everyone ham sandwiches. I realized Mary was growing more powerful as Mother stayed upstairs most hours of the day.

I didn't know if that was a good thing or not.

The weather grew cooler, and I was more comfortable every day as the humidity eased. My winter coat started to come in, thick and sleek. My brother and sister went back to the work they call "school" once the hot days were over.

One day Man brought home a big, orange pumpkin and placed it on our front step. I watched through the window screen as squirrels tried to sneak up to that pumpkin and take a bite out of it. I yowled when they got too close, scaring them away.

The baby grew plump. The black hair he was born with faded over time until a thin coating of light blond hair appeared on his round head. His eyes darkened to gray blue, and he began to look more like Man.

One day, Mother got up and put a few things into a bag. She waited on the living room couch for Jimmy to get home.

I know what packing is. I know it means someone is going away for a while. But her bag was so small. I didn't give it much thought.

When Jimmy walked in, Mother talked to him quietly on the downstairs couch. He nodded a few times and then followed her to the kitchen, where she showed him the baby formula. But of course he already knew where that was and barely paid attention, glancing occasionally at the little phone in his hand. She pointed to some food in a pan in the refrigerator. And then Mother kissed him and went out. I heard the car outside start up, and I knew it would carry her away for a while.

Jimmy sat Man down on that same couch when he got home, and they talked. Nothing much seemed out of order. Man stroked his short beard as he sometimes did when he was thinking about something, and my brother imitated him on his own smooth chin, which he likes to do. They both laughed about something, and all seemed normal.

Until supper, when the phone rang.

There was something so ominous about the ring of the kitchen phone that I jumped and scampered to the doorway. I watched and listened as Man stood and picked up the phone. My siblings froze, their forks in the air, and they listened too.

At first Man stared at the floor, his mouth hanging open, his eyes wide. He was astonished. "Carrie," he whispered. His voice shook and he asked something about who was going to take care of the baby. My siblings and I fled the room and ran right up those stairs, as we knew some kind of bad news had come to this house. I hid under Mother's bed.

Late in the night, I finally found my courage and wandered down the hall to Mary's room, hearing muffled noises emerging from the darkness. When I jumped up to her bed, I was upset to find her crying, a little hand covering her eyes. Her whole body shook, as if rejecting whatever news was trying to sink in. I sniffed at her face and licked her cheek, finding it savory. After I nestled against Mary's chest, she finally settled down, her arm curled around me. She drew in one deep breath after the next, tickling my neck as she sighed in her sleep.

But as for me, I could not rest. I had a terrible vision. I know there are creatures lurking in the woods behind our house, because I have seen them through the sliding glass door, and my sister has named them for me. Squirrel, woodchuck, rabbit, deer, wild turkey, and once a fox. Most horrible is the huge, masked raccoon with long claws, who eats anything at all.

I was sure that one of these vicious creatures had attacked Mother and dragged her away.

4

Ghosts

I am especially worried about Mother now because the weather has changed and the evenings are cold. The humans call this October. It does not seem to be a good time for Mother to be lost in the woods, if that is what has happened to her.

The first day she was gone, everyone slept late and spoke in whispers. No one left the house, and no one came by. The house phone rang a few times, and Man spoke to several people. Mary spent a lot of time in her room talking quietly and rapidly into her small phone. The words just seemed to fly out of her mouth.

Jimmy stayed in his room too, pacing and twirling the orange ball on his finger. Unlike the others, he spoke to someone on his phone only once, and he closed the door when he did.

I wonder who he talked to.

It was strange to me at first that the family did not go out and look for Mother—or what was left of her. I realized that my first assumption that she'd been attacked or killed by a wild animal was just a foolish, childish thought.

But there were still evil things that could have happened.

Later in the day, everyone went in and out of the kitchen like ghosts, scavenging for food. But they didn't seem particularly hungry. Man went out the back door and a crisp wind whipped in and down the hall. He returned carrying an armful of wood. He took his time making a fire and sat by it, silently staring into the heat. When the baby cried, Man brought him downstairs and held him while sitting on the floor, not too close to the fire, looking pensively into his son's tiny face as if looking for clues to some great mystery.

I sat on the windowsill. Many of the leaves outside had already turned blazing orange and fiery red. Some were knocked loose by the wind and lay on the ground. Where we live, autumn arrives quickly, with a fierce determination. I enjoy watching the leaves flutter in the air and the squirrels outside scurrying back and forth. The air that moves through the screen is crisp and rich, while the sun feels hot on my fur.

But nature is just teasing me when that happens. We're always in for a long winter.

By the end of that first day, it occurred to me that maybe the family knew where Mother was but for some reason weren't allowed to go to her. Otherwise, why wouldn't they be out looking for her? That thought put me in a dark mood. I sat under the stairs all night, thinking it over.

The next day, an older woman came by. She'd been to the house many times before. I'd figured out from previous visits that she was Man's mother. I knew this from the way my siblings ran to her and hugged her. "Mahmee!" They sighed, holding her, as if it was a great relief.

I also knew it was Man's mother from the way Man didn't make eye contact with her when she was in front of him, yet stared at her when her back was turned. He seemed desperate to get her approval and hear what she had to say but couldn't admit it to her face.

Mahmee's attitude made me wonder if this was all Man's fault, if perhaps he was to blame for Mother's disappearance. Mahmee scolded and pointed at him while he sat at the kitchen table and stared guiltily at his hands. My siblings drifted upstairs, as if they knew the adults needed time alone. "Tommy. *Tommy*. It was just a matter of time." Mahmee seemed to be frustrated, and Man sat, not responding to her. She took a book out of her large bag and pressed it into his hands, which he accepted and stared at, but I could tell from his glazed expression that he was not in a reading mood.

"Ma." That was all he had to say. He was too upset to talk.

Mahmee marched upstairs and took the baby into her arms, then sat with him in the rocking chair. I followed her and watched from under the crib, curious, as Mahmee frowned at the baby, shaking her head. "Now, now." She held that baby tight. Later, she went home, and I was sorry to see her go.

That second day, all was strange and too quiet once again. I was lying on a pile of stuffed pillows on the floor in Mary's room when she came in and slammed the door, long blond hair flying behind her. She threw herself down on her bed and stared at her favorite poster. Just as quickly, she jumped up on her knees, then touched and kissed the face of each of the boys on the poster.

Mary's movements were always quick, dramatic, decisive. I had to be careful around her, never knowing when she would suddenly spring up.

She was like a cat, in that way.

My sister didn't see me on the floor, and I was startled when she jumped down from the bed and tore across the room. She grabbed scissors from her desk, then ran back across the room to stab her poster with their sharp end.

The poster with her Gods on it! I was shocked, and felt my eyes widen, the fur bristling down my spine.

Again and again she stabbed the poster, jamming the scissors into the wall. She then tore down the poster and took her time cutting it up into a hundred little bits. "Good-bye, boys," she said calmly. "Good-bye, Harry. Good-bye." Once there were many little pieces of paper in front of her, she threw them out all over her green rug, as if it were snowing inside.

She buried her face in her pillow a long time. I stayed right where I was, watching her.

Eventually, Mary sat up and wiped her eyes, and her mouth twisted into a half smile as she observed the paper-snow all over the place. I imagined that she found something satisfying about making a great mess.

Mary pouted at the gouges in the wall. I wondered if she was thinking what I was thinking: Man might not be pleased. Suddenly, Mary looked over—probably my twitching tail caught her eye. Sometimes I have no control over my stupid tail. It goes crazy when I'm nervous.

Sister smiled at me, but her eyes were still sad. I soon came to see her plan: cover it up. She went over to her bookcase, slid out some papers, and unfolded them. She tacked a few pictures to the wall to hide the mess.

I think we both felt better after that.

I wanted to join Mary on the bed, but little, precious, fluffy "Jasper" (the creature that is Not a Cat) was up there, and he and I can't share a bed. It's fine. I know he's Sister's baby.

I used to be Mother's baby.

Where is Mother? I mused again. I was as frustrated as Mary.

At the end of the second day, Man and Jimmy went out and brought back hot food. The scent of the steam got Jasper and me worked up. We paced under the table, rubbing against legs. Jasper jumped up to beg. I meowed, begging too, though I prefer to think of it as vocalizing my needs rather than begging. My family didn't seem to know what I needed, so I had to tell them. Only Mother anticipated my hunger.

Our bowls got filled, and for a short while it was almost as if everything was okay again. There was a fire in the fireplace, the way Mother liked it. There was clean, cold water and food in our bowls. But the family didn't talk. Until suddenly Jimmy did.

I was just starting to doze off when I heard Jimmy start to mutter something in a bitter, hostile tone. My ears pricked up.

"What did you say to her, Pops?" Jimmy asked, breaking the silence. "I mean, come on. What the hell did you *do*? You must have done something really stupid this time."

There was a long silence.

The next thing I knew Man was on his feet, and Jimmy was looking up at his father, mouth hanging open. A *bang* filled the room as a chair tipped over and slammed against the floor. I ran out, turning to watch from a corner of the living room.

The baby, in a basket on the floor, started screaming. Man whirled around and, seeing that his chair had fallen close to where the basket with the baby lay, grew even more enraged. "You need to GROW UP," he shouted at Jimmy. "Do you think that attitude helps the situation? Don't open your goddamn mouth if you don't have something helpful to say. DO YOU HAVE ANYTHING ELSE TO ASK ME?"

He was so angry. I'd seen it before, his face red and fists clenched. The humans are so big, and I am so small. It frightens me when Man is in a fury. But there was something in his eyes that made me realize he was also very sad.

Jimmy shrank back from Man, his face pale. He shook his head no.

I ran upstairs and hid under Mother's bed. I was grieving too. I missed Mother.

I just wanted to disappear. I thought I could possibly run out the front door and take off into the cold wilderness. Maybe find Mother, dead or alive. I wondered if that would be possible, to find her scent and follow it to her.

I curled up between two boxes in the darkness under the bed, and I didn't come out for a very long time. I didn't want to get in Man's way.

On the third day, my siblings rose early and got dressed and went out, grabbing shoes and apples and pastry and gloves. There was a loud flurry of activity, music playing and water running and mumbled comments, and then with a slam of the door they were gone.

They were going out? Back to school? I was confused. Were they going to look for Mother? It didn't seem so. They had packs on their backs, just like any other day.

Man sat on the couch, bleary eyed. The baby had been up for hours but now slept again. He carried the baby up the stairs and put him down in his crib. "Finn," Man whispered as he stared at him and stroked the baby's fine hair, and I understood that Finn was the baby's name.

I followed Man back to Mother's bedroom. He fell back into the bed and pulled the covers up to his chest. I jumped up to the edge of the bed, watching. Man put a hand over his eyes. I love the smell of the quilted comforter, and I padded quietly up to sleep on Mother's pillow. I started to purr, loudly. I couldn't help it. I was so happy on her pillow!

Man swatted me away with a heavy hand. I jumped and scooted to the end of the bed. But I didn't leave.

How dare he push me! I squinted at him, bristling with indignation. This was my bed too. If he was going to kick and prevent me from sleeping on the bed at night, I had the right to sleep on it during the day.

It was only fair. It was Mother's bed too. And my bed.

I gave him an unhappy yeow.

Man leaned up and looked at me. And I mean *really* looked at me, making eye contact. He didn't look irritated. He seemed upset.

"Boo. I'm sorry."

I stared at him, and it dawned on me that *he was speaking to me.* He was looking and talking and saying my name. That never happened.

For a moment, I froze. But as I watched him, I realized he meant me no harm. He even slid his hand out on the bedspread, inviting me to come toward him.

Why would I ever interact with him? I'd always had all I needed with Mother.

I didn't approach him. I didn't trust him yet. He had done nothing to earn my trust. And he didn't deserve my friendship.

Man lay back down and pulled the sheet up right to his eyebrows so I could no longer see his face. We both fell asleep.

A few hours later, a loud knocking and ringing of the doorbell startled us both. We sprang up. Man grabbed jeans and a belt and tucked in his shirt, then hurried downstairs.

It was Missus Davenport. She was all great smiles and enthusiastic nods, and shook Man's hand with energy when he opened the door. Her suit was a very striking blue, the color of a bird that I cannot name. Man followed her up the stairs, straightening out his hair.

The fact is, he didn't look so good.

When the Missus picked Finn up out of his crib and had him securely in her arms, Man stood with his arms crossed and explained things to her. I watched from the hallway, my tail twitching, too nervous to go into the room.

I couldn't hear Man because he spoke quietly to her and his back was to me. But I could see Missus had a happy demeanor that faded, as first her eyes grew wide in surprise, and then I watched her struggle to quiet her facial expression. Her cheeks grew pale, and her eyebrows knit together as she squeezed Finn tighter against her chest. She listened and nodded, until finally Man finished his little speech and left, walking past me to go into Mother's bedroom. He closed the door.

I stayed, to see what the Missus would do. She was

young, and usually spoke to the baby in a chipper, sing-song voice. Missus was all fluttery hands and oversized gestures and loving touches.

But now, she placed Finn back down in his crib. I got up and padded my way into the room, watching her stare at the baby as Man's words sunk in. At first, she didn't move, as if puzzled about what to do next.

And then her eyes teared up. Her hand flew to cover her mouth.

Her face convinced me that whatever had happened to Mother was something horrible.

But Mother could still be alive. I fear I cannot survive without her. She's my one true partner who feeds and cares for me, who strokes my head and holds me all night. I worry that the stupid baby needs her too, even if it may somehow be his fault that she left.

I am determined to find out exactly where Mother is.

5

Halloween

Get up, Jimmy.

Get up, get up, get up.

I bat his chest with my paw. I try to push the comforter down with my head. These are tactics that used to work with Mother, and I hope they'll now work with Jimmy.

Many days have passed since Mother left, and still no one thinks to get up and feed me breakfast. My stomach growls in desperation until someone finally opens a can and dumps wet food into my bowl.

Jimmy's hand is tucked under his head, and I nuzzle my wet nose against his bare upper arm. He has a funny scar that looks like a big crooked X on the soft underside of his arm. Usually the scar is hidden by the sleeve of his shirt, but he sleeps with no shirt on, so now it is exposed. I push my face right into the X.

Jimmy stirs. He grins at me, then scratches my head. My brother doesn't get the connection between my persistence and food though. He rolls over and goes back to sleep, even though sunlight peeks through the blinds.

I give up. Forget breakfast. I guess it's time to roll right into my midmorning nap.

I fall asleep on the dark red flannel sheet, right by Jimmy's hand. I have a wonderful dream in which I am between Mother and Man on the bed. My back is pressed up hard against Mother's stomach, and in my dream I know it is the time before Finn came, back when I was still the baby of the family.

Mother has her head on her pillow, and she's telling Man a great story. Although my back is to her, I can hear the wonderful, excited sound of her voice. And from my vantage point I can see Man's face. He is propped up on one elbow, staring at her, hanging on her every word. He is so amused by her. I can see it in the way he tips his head, a small smile curling his mouth. I am sure she's told this story before, but she keeps going, and Man doesn't interrupt.

I imagine what he is seeing: the dark curls falling around her face, spread out over her pillow. Her big eyes, full of excitement. The curve of her lips and her open mouth and her funny expressions when she is reenacting a scene. Mother is so dramatic. She smiles a lot and laughs easily, and my brother is the same way.

Man is different from them. He is still with his body, always watching. Listening. My sister is more like her dad; she studies people.

My dream is spoiled when Jimmy rolls over and sits up. But I don't mind. Maybe now I'll get food!

I follow him downstairs and meow repeatedly. *C'mon, Jimmy. Feed me.* He looks at me, puzzled, his hair—black like Mother's hair—sticking up all over the place. Thankfully I see him head to the cabinet and pull out a can of food.

Now all he has to do is pop open the can! I think he can handle that. Maybe.

Mahmee has been coming to take care of the baby every day. But she doesn't always make supper, so Jimmy has become an expert in opening cans and making sandwiches. Mahmee seems very tired by the time Jimmy and Mary get home in the afternoon, and sometimes she just leaves. I think taking care of Finn is hard for her.

Watching Mahmee walk down our steep wooden stairs, one step at a time with Finn in her arms, makes me verr-rry nervous. I can tell she is frightened too, the way she stays right up against the railing. The stairs are slippery.

I never sit on a stair when Mahmee is coming down.

Earlier this week, Jimmy made himself supper when Man had to work late and Mahmee had already left for the day. He put a can in the machine they use to heat up food. It created great sparks and a popping noise and foul-smelling smoke. An alarm sounded. The high-pitched whine was unbearable, and I ran to hide under a chair in the living room.

Mary came running downstairs and helped Jimmy air out the kitchen by opening a window, thank goodness. She shrieked at him, and he cowered from her. She ended up making five bags of popcorn in a row to get rid of the rancid smell.

"What the hell?" she growled at him. "Seriously, you forgot you can't put metal in the microwave? What is wrong with you?"

"Sorry. Really." Jimmy frowned as he stood in the corner, wringing his hands. "I just . . . I don't know where my mind is lately. I can't think straight. I can't get anything right."

I'm glad Jimmy did not start a fire while Man was

out and burn our kitchen down. That would have been a disaster for all of us, but especially embarrassing for Man, who is an expert on fires.

Mary had a bad week. I kept catching her with those big, silver scissors again. She'd sit on her bed and place the sharp blades right up against her sleek blond hair, as if she intended to cut it. She'd also take one of the blades and hold it right up to her knee, as if she wanted to stab herself. Each time I watched her, alarmed. My little heart beat hard in my chest. When I saw her playing with those scissors, I jumped up to the bed and plopped myself in Mary's lap. I knew it would force her to put the scissors down, because she wouldn't want to accidentally snip off a piece of my delicate ear or my unpredictable tail. Sure enough, she gave me a kiss and relaxed her hold on the scissors.

Not a Cat frowned at me, grumpy and jealous. He didn't like me up on Mary's bed. But I had to do it.

Now it's finally the end of the week, and today is the holiday the humans call Halloween, when they dress up in fantastical costumes. I know my brother and sister are excited. They have worked on their outfits all week in great anticipation, and they have been very talkative all day.

Mary dresses poor Jasper up in ridiculous hats and capes every year. You'll never see me in a costume. Mary once tried to put one on me, but I kept wiggling backward to prevent it. She got the message. It was uncomfortable for me. Jasper will tolerate anything to please his mother, but Mary is not my mother.

Plus, I was too fat to fit into that costume.

I watch from the landing at the top of the stairs, curious. Jimmy is in his room, talking to someone on his small phone. When he comes out, his clothes are torn and his face is streaked with what looks like, but doesn't smell like, blood.

Jimmy smells, in general. His underwear and socks on the floor interest Jasper and me a great deal. We love the smell of the humans, and we enjoy sitting on piles of dirty laundry. Jimmy is a big human, and he gives off a strong scent, a chemical that lets me know he is looking for a mate. I don't know if the humans can sense it.

The problem is, he adds on a terrible, pungent scent from a bottle that makes my eyes water.

When he steps out of the bathroom after taking a shower, Mary moans, "*Jesus,* Jimmy, too much," while holding her hands over her delicate face. He just ruffles his wet hair with a towel and snaps it at her. If she runs, he chases her.

She is right. Jesus Jimmy puts on too much of that stuff. It's disgusting.

I am surprised when a girl comes to the door for Jimmy. I have never seen her before. Just as there are different breeds of cats, there are different breeds of humans, and she does not look quite like anyone in our family. Her skin is a little darker and her eyes rounder.

No matter. What interests me most is that she is a female, which means she will probably point to me, and crouch down, and make baby noises at me. All of which she does, just as I expect. Sometimes I run from a stranger out of caution. But this girl is patient, waiting for me to come to her in my own time.

I see why Jimmy likes her. She has good instincts. And she's very pretty, despite the fact that she is dressed in torn clothing to match Jimmy, fake blood all over her.

She asks Jimmy a question. Jimmy picks me up, and

I let him, my fat draping over his big hands. He carries me to the kitchen, and the girl follows. He hunts in the refrigerator and pulls out a little piece of ham. He hands it to the girl, who holds it out toward me.

Really? More food? I thought the can Jimmy gave me this morning would be all I'd get.

I grab it from her fingers with my teeth, being careful not to accidentally bite the girl. I like her. By the time they start to gather their things, I am happy and purring and sorry they have to leave. Man comes up from the basement and gives the girl a handshake. I guess he approves.

But when Mary comes downstairs, dressed all in red, Man is waiting for her and blocking the door. He points at her bare legs and shakes his head no. It is cold out, after all, which I think must be his concern. Mary pouts and stamps her foot but finally tromps back upstairs. She comes back down wearing bright red tights that match her very short red skirt. Man's arms are folded and his face is creased, but he doesn't say anything this time.

When Mary's friends arrive they don't come in the house, but I can hear them talking excitedly on the front steps, and they squeal when they see her. She hugs them all. Man watches her walk down the path to the street and then closes the door. He moves into the living room and I follow him, jumping up on the back of a chair. He waits and watches from behind a curtain, where she cannot see him.

When they get to the corner of our yard, Mary and her friends stop. Although her friends form a loose circle around her, I can still see Mary as she reaches up under her skirt and wiggles out of the tights. The girls are all laughing as she flings the tights up over her head with a flourish and then sticks them deep in the middle of a hedge. They walk away, giggling hysterically.

Man frowns, but I know he won't go out there and yell at her in front of her friends. His arms are still crossed tightly.

Without Mother here, he is at a loss as to what to do.

I know that special days are a busy time for Man. He is often called to work, I assume to help people with their fires. Before Jimmy leaves, Man pulls him aside and points to his watch. I understand. Jimmy *must* get home on time, because chances are very good that at some point tonight Man's little phone will ring, or the horn outside will sound, and he will have to go out.

But unlike every other year, Man is now alone with a baby. He can't go anywhere until Jimmy gets back. I suspect he could tell Jimmy not to go out, but I think he doesn't want to ruin Jimmy's holiday, considering Mother isn't here and that's enough of a disappointment by itself.

Man spends the evening watching TV and getting up to hand out candy to the many children who ring the doorbell. I watch from the middle of the stairs, not too close. One woman with a toddler in hand asks brightly, "Where's Carrie tonight?" Man just answers that she went out. He gives that child extra candy and closes the door. When he turns back around, I can't read his expression.

Every time Man goes back to the living room, he anxiously glances at the clock. But he worries for nothing. I can see the relief on his face when his son walks in on time, Jimmy's smile in contrast with his pale, painted face, which still scares me a little bit.

It turns out Man never gets a call to go work with a fire. But he tosses and turns all night.

And Mary is good. She does not stay out too late and get into trouble. I realize why the next day.

The family wakes up early, and they each take their time getting dressed, looking at one shirt and then the next. Mary changes her pants. Jimmy combs his hair. They are not getting into fancy clothes exactly, but just seem to be taking care with themselves. Even the baby is put into a new outfit. Man struggles with the baby clothes. He is mean to Mary and snaps at Jimmy as he tries to pack the baby's things into a bag.

Mary clicks Jasper's red leash on his harness. And then, they are gone.

In the late afternoon, when the sun is sinking low, Mahmee arrives. I perk up. She is carrying many bags, which I think means "Sunday supper," the one meal she sometimes makes for us.

I'm not disappointed when I see what she pulls out of the bags!

I sit on a kitchen chair to watch her prepare the food. Mahmee plucks big, plump, juicy white scallops from a tray one at a time and places them in a pan. She grabs a red box of crackers from the cupboard, puts some crackers in a plastic bag, and then smashes them up with the base of a heavy glass. She sprinkles the cracker crumbs over the scallops and then melts butter in a pan to pour on top of that.

Deliciousness.

"I see you," she teases me. "I see you." Mahmee points a blue spatula at me with a devilish look in her eye. She dabs a finger in the butter—quickly, as I suppose it's hot—and then approaches me. She puts her hand right near my nose, and I happily lick the butter off her finger.

"Wicked good, huh?"

Wicked good, indeed. I am loving Mahmee right now.

I hear the front door opening, and I run to greet my family. They look tired, and stay quiet, but seem relieved when they inhale the warm scent of the food cooking. Even the baby is calm, up on Jimmy's shoulder.

We've always had fish a few times a week. I know we live near the place where the fish come from, because on some days I can smell brine in the air that wafts through the screen door. But we haven't had fish lately, because Man doesn't cook.

Standing in the front hall, Man closes his eyes and takes a deep breath. He's been eating ham sandwiches all week.

When he opens his eyes, he and I are alone in the hall. My siblings have already gone into the kitchen.

I don't know what to think. I wonder if he has seen Mother. I search his face, but I just can't tell. I wish he could tell me. I think he wants to.

Have you seen her? Have you seen my mother? Is she okay? Please I wish I wish I wish I could just ask you this one question.

And then he looks right at me again, like he did a week ago. It catches me off guard, but I stare back and tip my head. He scratches behind his ear and his eyes water up.

"I'm sorry, Boo," he says to me. He's said that to me before. I don't know what he means.

I walk back into the darkness under the stairs. I'll get my scallops later. I'm really not in the mood to forgive Man, considering I have no idea what I'm forgiving him for.

6

We Are Alone in This

I think she's alive!

I have no proof. I have not seen her face or heard her voice. But the clues are there.

I have been listening very hard. Before Mother disappeared, I often ignored the other humans. Their comings and goings were not of very much interest to me. But now, little by little, I am starting to pay more attention.

Jimmy has never spent much time talking into his small phone. In the past, he has used it for watching moving pictures and listening to musical things.

But lately he's been talking. To two people.

One is the girl who came to the house on Halloween. Her name is Aruna, and she has been here a few times since then. I know when Jimmy is calling her, because he smiles as he presses the buttons, and he closes his eyes when he greets her.

"Hey, beautiful," he says to her through the phone.

His eyes pop open and he grins when she responds.

Even from across the room, I can hear Aruna squeal with delight at hearing his voice.

Personally, I don't think Jimmy is as handsome as Man. But he certainly has a nice, easy way with people. Just like Mother does. He practically shines with confidence. My brother is always smiling, and humans gravitate to him. Nothing embarrasses him. He's an open book.

Man has never had those qualities.

And then sometimes, when he's getting ready for bed, Jimmy closes the door and speaks with someone different. I perk up from where I lie on his bed and listen hard. He talks quietly. I cannot hear the voice on the other end, but I have heard him call her Ma. When I first heard that, I didn't believe it and thought I misunderstood him. But it's been a few times now.

They never speak for very long. Sometimes after he hangs up, Jimmy buries his face in his hand, but always just for a minute or two. And Jimmy doesn't mention it to the others. I always jump up to rub my face into his elbows, trying to distract him and help him feel better.

It has been a long time since Mother left. It has been so long, I have lost track of the time. But if Jimmy is speaking to her, then she is alive. And that gives me hope, and great relief.

But if she is alive, why doesn't she come to visit us? Why has she stayed away for so long?

And why didn't she take me with her?

Lately, I have been worried about Man. For my siblings, days are busy and life goes on. But Man seems to be in a dark place. He was always a loner. It occurs to me he has always been content with our family and never had many friends, other than one man called Sean, who comes to visit him. In this way, he is unlike

Mother, who always had her phone on her ear or at her fingertips and, when she was feeling energetic, parties and visitors.

Right now, no one comes to visit him or help out. Maybe he hasn't really explained the situation to anyone. Or maybe there's no one for him to tell.

I've seen him sitting on the edge of his bed at night, and that is the worst time. He sits with his back to Mother's pillow and won't look at it. Sometimes he flips open the book Mahmee gave him, but closes it without finishing the pages. Other times, he picks up a little wooden cross from the bedside table, but just holds it and then puts it back down. Nothing interests him.

Maybe he and I are alone in this.

He pushes back the covers, and although it is cold and our house is drafty, he lies there in just his T-shirt and boxer shorts and stares at the ceiling. Lately, more often, he'll look at me, and it is in a friendly way. He is lonely. So am I. My siblings have important things to do, and Mahmee is wonderful but she doesn't love me fiercely like Mother did.

I have started to approach Man on the bed. He doesn't caress my face and scratch my ears like Mother did, but his hand is warm and not too heavy, and he'll rub down my silky fur. He's putting his scent on me—and that, I know, is a protective gesture. In return, I knock my head into his fingers, to put my scent on him.

"You are so, so fat," he tells me. This is something Mother used to say all the time, when she was admiring me. It makes me purr.

One day, Man comes home with a new book. And the day after that, yet another book. Eventually there is a stack beside his bedside table.

I imagine what these books are called.

There is probably one called *How to Hunt, Capture, Kill, and Prepare Food*. The whole family is failing miserably at this.

For breakfast this morning, Mary had water and string cheese. And she had to cut the mold off with a knife before eating it.

There is also probably one called *How to Take Care of a Baby*. Man seems comfortable with the baby, but I don't know if he did much baby care the first two times around. He gets especially confused and frustrated by the diapers and clothes. And the bottles and the formula. And the thermometer.

One book could be called *How to Fix Your Damaged Baby*. Because, as I've said, something is not quite right with ours.

Another book might be *Ways to Make Your Girl Follow Directions*. I have seen Mary snarl at Man when he asks her to carry out a task. He barks right back when she growls at him, but all the noise doesn't seem to make her move any faster.

One might be *What to Do If Your Mate Goes Out and Does Not Come Home*. That would be the most important one of all. If he could just fix that problem, I think the other problems would go away. And we could go back to life as it was before, when I was always fed on time, and brushed every day, and held all night.

I think Missus Davenport is feeling frustrated lately too. When Missus first came to visit while Mahmee was caring for Finn, Mahmee was always happy to see her. Mostly because she then hustled to the kitchen to make hot coffee and spread out her deck of cards on the table for a game.

After a week or two of this, Missus Davenport came downstairs and had a few strong words with her. Mahmee seemed surprised and rolled her eyes at me after

Missus had left the room. But Mahmee got up, switched off the radio, left her coffee on the table with a loud sigh, and followed Missus up the stairs.

Now she sits in the rocking chair and watches Missus Davenport play with the baby on the rug. Missus tries to get Mahmee to come down and work with Finn, but Mahmee just presses her lips together and shakes her head no, pointing to her knees.

If Mahmee sat down on this rug, I predict she'd never get up again.

Tonight, the doorbell rings around suppertime. Man answers, and there is Missus Davenport. I guess she wants to speak to him, rather than Mahmee. She is not in her work clothes. Instead she wears clothes for exercise. She is even springier than usual in her sneakers.

Standing in the foyer, I hear her say "*Miss* Davenport, not Missus" and "Charlotte" a few times, and I gather that it is her first name. Charlotte is passionate and enthusiastic about something, but Man just stands there frowning, arms folded, as if he doesn't like what she is saying.

Relax, I want to tell him. *She's on your side.* I even get up and welcome Charlotte to show Man how it is done, walking right up to her. Charlotte gives me a gentle pat on the head.

She presses Man, but he resists what she is asking for. Charlotte goes on and on, and I realize she is telling him that she wants the whole family to get more involved and work with the baby, and it seems very important to her. Something about her expressive way of moving her hands reminds me of Mother, and maybe it reminds Man of Mother too, because he finally says okay.

Charlotte melts into a deep smile and rests her hand

on Man's wrist. He still hasn't uncrossed his arms. "Thank you," she says to him, before running out.

She has to let herself out, because Man is still staring down at his arm where she touched him. I guess he is thinking about what she has said.

Man's best friend, Sean, has been here a couple of times since Mother left. About fifteen minutes after Charlotte leaves, he knocks on the door.

Bang, bang, bang.

The most important thing to know about Sean, from my perspective on the floor, is that he wears big, heavy boots. I get out of his way quickly, the same way I hustle away from Man. I wouldn't want to get my tail crunched under that boot.

Sean is a dominant male, with a loud voice and a barrel of a chest. He makes Man laugh, but Man hasn't been laughing so much lately. Sean has short whiskers on his face just like Man and weighs several pounds more.

Sean always wears hats and shirts with the letter "B," which doesn't make sense to me because his name is Sean, not Billy or Brendan.

I know what a B is, because Charlotte uses these little books with Finn that contain photos of baby faces and sometimes symbols. It's ridiculous. It can't possibly mean anything to that baby. But I have figured out that Charlotte is some kind of healer and that she is here to help, so I guess it's okay.

When he is not wearing his B hat, Sean has a flat cap that he wears at an angle. I keep waiting for that cap to fall off his head, but it never does.

I believe Man has known Sean for a very long time. They talk about the same things all the time. The Sox and who is the best closer. The Bruins and how badly they beat the Flyers. Who is the biggest asshole down at the fire department. How many roast beef with cheese-sauce-onion they need to get. And whether or not Sean needs to run to the packy and get more dark brown bottles of beer.

Sean also seems to have a lot of trouble with women. He has his own mate, and four pudgy, sweet, lovely daughters who have visited here before. He's not particularly good-looking in my opinion, with a face like a bulldog. Yet he goes on and on: *Why did Marlene tell me her bra size? Why does Jenny want a ride in my new truck? Don't these ladies know I'm married? These girls are killing me, Tommy.*

Man is always highly amused. He likes people who entertain him. So do I.

When Sean walks in, he wipes his boots over and over compulsively on the front mat. He has a big, brown paper bag in one hand. The first thing he says to Man is, "Jeez, Tommy-boy, you don't look so sharp."

Mary is there, and she always makes fun of the two of them. "Yeah, Pops, you don't look so *shap*."

Sean grins and calls her a "whippasnappa."

Mary smiles back and sticks her tongue out at him. Jimmy comes downstairs and shakes Sean's hand.

Sean points at Jimmy's smooth face. "Nothin' yet, huh?"

Jimmy pushes Sean's hand away with a smile. "Don't remind me. I'm working on it."

This is the way many men are around here, with the short beards. I think they look magnificent, like lions. They all go into the kitchen to talk.

But after Jimmy and Mary leave and go upstairs, Sean hunches over the kitchen table and leans toward Man. I see the way Sean folds his hands under the table, and I know he feels nervous and stressed about something.

"How's Carrie?" he asks, almost a whisper, like he is afraid to ask.

I freeze, pinning my ears back. That's Mother's name.

I don't quite catch the answer. It's hard to hear the men when they are talking softly.

But that's it. Now I know. She's alive. And if she's alive, then maybe I can find her.

From across the kitchen, I can see Sean has already drained two of his brown bottles and has started on a third, whereas Man is still on his first one. The truth is, Mother is the one who drinks with Sean when he comes over. The two of them together sometimes have a very jolly time, laughing and telling great stories. Other times they fight bitterly, but they always apologize the next day.

But now I sense a betrayal, because Sean is using words like "crazy" and "abusive" and "nasty." At first I think he is criticizing Man and talking some sense into him, but the more I listen, the more I realize that doesn't make sense.

Man and I are not good friends, but Man is not those things.

And then I realize I know who he is talking about. My whiskers start twitching, and I am furious, because that is . . . that is not like my mother at all. Sean has known her for many years, so I don't understand. Isn't she getting rest somewhere? Isn't she coming back soon? Why is Sean saying these horrible things?

Man doesn't respond, which makes me even angrier. He just holds his bottle and stares at it. He doesn't join in the criticism. But he also doesn't defend Mother.

Stupid, stupid, stupid Tommy. Sitting there with that dumb look on his face. Mother is right.

But the worst part is—in a way, he and I are alone in this. And we need to figure out how to get her back.

For the first time, I realize that while I am small and limited in what I can do, Man is not. Even if he is to blame for Mother's disappearance, perhaps I could help him in some small way as he tries to get her back.

But how?

I am afraid that he and I will never really understand each other, not the way Mother and I did. I may have to go out and look for her on my own. I just need to wait until the right time and then dash out the door.

I can do it. I will if I have to.

7

Trimming the Branches at 2 a.m.

Sean's words haunt me for days. He seemed satisfied and relieved that my mother is gone.

I agreed with the one thing Man finally said to Sean in reply: "A little baby needs his mother." That fact is true. There is no getting around it.

For the next couple of days, I brood, skulking from one corner to the next. Now that I know for sure she's alive, I don't understand why Mother doesn't visit us here at the house. I get frustrated and angry when I think about it, because it doesn't make sense.

Maybe Mother, wherever she is, could have taken the baby with her. And maybe she could have taken *me* with her too. She should come back and get us.

But then she wouldn't really be able to get the rest she needs, isn't that right? I'd like to think she will be back any day now, relaxed and all better.

But I suspect I am wrong about that. I will go to her if she will not come to me.

It will be dangerous for me outside. There are animals and humans and machines and cold air and bright lights. Just thinking about it makes me shudder. To put it out of my mind, I jump up on the soft, familiar couch and huddle in a corner, feeling like a coward.

In the middle of the week, the neighbor from next door comes over and interrupts supper.

Supper is ham sandwiches. With cheese. Again. It's one of the only meals Man knows how to make, and even Jimmy can make it in a pinch. Jimmy holds down little strips of white cheese under the table, which I snatch greedily from his fingers. The cheese is bland but milky. I'll take what I can get. I'm just happy that someone is remembering to feed me.

I watch from the hallway. The neighbor is a little older, with hair that is graying on the sides. He's red in the face and agitated. He has loud words for Man, pointing at a tree on the side of our house. I've seen this person from the window, coming into our driveway to talk to Man more than once. Man isn't much of a talker, and he usually starts walking away while the neighbor is still yapping behind him.

Now, Man scowls, raising an eyebrow, and listens to the neighbor. Man starts closing the door before the neighbor seems quite done. The neighbor is still talking and strenuously pointing off to the side yard. The door clicks shut.

"Calm down," Man mutters to himself after he closes the door.

Good riddance, I think. *We have enough to deal with.*

But in the middle of the night, after he has tried reading his books and has been tossing and turning for
hours, Man sits up in bed. He turns and stands up, pulls
on his jeans, throws on a sweatshirt, and heads down
the steep wooden stairs in the darkness. He gets one of
his big, heavy-lined coats out of the closet and slips
into his boots. And heads out the door.

It is not long before I hear a loud machine whirring
outside. I walk over to the dining room window, the
pads on my feet sinking into the soft carpet. I jump up
onto a chest of drawers, skirting between two dishes,
to see if I can view anything out the window. It's very
dark, but I can *feel* the buzzing, and it's somewhere
very close.

Jimmy comes running down the stairs, and Mary is
soon behind him.

"Where's Dad?" Mary asks. "Dad. DAD?"

"Oh. My. God." Jimmy has his face right up against
the glass, above me, breathing a fog onto the window.
No one has bothered to turn on the lights, and we stand
there in the dark. "Dad is OUT THERE. Jesus Christmas."

Mary is already rushing toward the coat closet. She
pulls out a lined flannel coat and helps Jimmy get into
it, and then she hands him gloves so he can run out
there and help his dad. The air that rushes in when my
brother opens the door is bitter cold.

Mary and I return to the window, and we can hear
people talking. I think I hear not only Jimmy's voice
but also the neighbor's, and clearly this is unusual. Man
does not generally go out and trim branches or do yard
work of any kind in the middle of the night. I can hear
Man yelling, and he is fierce when it happens. I get the
impression that you do not want to cross him. I have

seen people shrink away from him when he loses his temper. And then there is no more talking. Just buzzing.

They're out there awhile, and I assume they finish the job.

For a moment, I think about darting out the door when they come back into the house so I can go look for Mother. The humans will certainly be tired and distracted. But Mary picks me up and holds me to her chest, and I lose my chance.

When Man and Jimmy enter, they quietly take their coats off. Mary has a pink blanket wrapped around her shoulders, and I feel very warm in her arms as she carefully asks them a few questions. Pretty soon Jimmy is getting into his story—*really* getting into it, the way Mother would, imitating the neighbor—and soon he has Mary smiling, and then laughing. Even Man looks pleased.

I know Jimmy reminds them of Mother. Jimmy reminds me of Mother, so much that it hurts sometimes.

When they go to bed, Man sleeps hard, like a rock. He gets his rest for a few hours anyway, until Finn starts screaming just before dawn.

The next day, Man looks tired but at peace. He goes to work but comes home early because Charlotte is coming today. She still visits twice a week, but last week something changed. Early in the week, Charlotte came in the morning and Mahmee watched her work with Finn. But at the end of the week, she came in the afternoon when Mahmee was gone and Man was at home.

I am starting to see that Charlotte can't just teach Finn by herself. She wants to teach others how to work with Finn. And maybe, a little bit, teach Man how to be a mother.

Most of the time, they use toys and pictures and books down on the rug. But sometimes there is also a lesson on diapers or bottles, because the baby naturally needs these things sometimes when Charlotte is here. She doesn't do these things for Man, but watches and instructs as he does them. She is very patient with him.

At first I worried that Man would be insulted that she was helping him with these things. He is a proud Man who already has two older children.

But he doesn't seem to mind. He seems relieved.

Charlotte seems relieved too. Perhaps things are not so hopeless. She pulls Mary or Jimmy into the nursery once in a while and gets them working with Finn. Finn is a happy little human, when he's not screaming with discomfort. But he's getting bigger fast. He can push his head up and move around. He is very active. I wonder when he will start walking on two feet, like a human child.

We need to do something about those steep stairs.

On a cold but sunny day when everyone is home, Aruna stops by in the late morning. She looks bright-eyed and is wrapped in a red coat, her hair pulled back in a ponytail with a matching red ribbon tied around her dark hair. Jimmy gives her a hug, but I have not seen him kiss her yet. Aruna turns her collar up against the wind, ready to go back out, but sees me out of the corner of her eye. I receive a friendly pat on the head, and when I rev up the purring, I get scratched between my ears and she picks me up.

Aruna is soooo sweet. She makes me shiver with delight.

Suddenly, I have a thought. When Aruna puts me down, I start to meow, over and over. She frowns. And then she tells Jimmy to go get something for me. He comes out of the kitchen with a spoonful of something that he hands to her.

Aruna leans down to present me with a bite of tuna. Mother always bought the most delicious, fresh tuna, but I can tell this is from a can. It has a slight metallic taste. No matter.

If you had told me this past summer that Jesus Jimmy and a girl (a complete stranger to me then) would become my heroes, I would never have believed it.

But now, here they are. My saviors. Keeping me fat and happy. I didn't think anyone would ever remember to feed me the way that Mother did.

After they leave, Man sees that Jimmy accidentally left his little phone on the kitchen table. He holds it in his hand for a moment as he sits eating a bowl of cereal.

After a minute, Man turns it on and starts scrolling through something. He is only half-looking when something catches his eye.

Man works with the phone for a few minutes, pressing buttons, listening. His mouth opens and then shuts. He squints at it, and I think he is reading something on the small screen. It is very puzzling to him, whatever he has found.

I know that Jimmy has been talking to Mother, but he doesn't.

I jump up on the chair next to him to get a better look. Absentmindedly, Man strokes my back. I arch to lean into him.

After staring at the table a long while, he finally clicks something and puts the phone to his ear.

"Care," he says. I lift my head to stare at him. He

must be talking to Mother. His face doesn't give anything away. I watch, wide-eyed, crouched on the chair. My heart beats hard in my chest.

They talk for a very long time.

Man asks a lot of questions, calmly. They start like, "*Why can't—?*" and "*Why don't—?*" and "*Yes, but why did you—?*"

Then the conversation turns to Finn, and Man does his best to tell her some stories. I can hear Mother laugh on the other end, wherever she is.

At the end of the conversation, Man clearly wants to keep her on the line, and she wants to go. He tries, "*But please don't—*" and "*But we all need—*" and "*But don't you think—*" and "*I thought you felt—*"

It occurs to me that Man hasn't been talking to Mother on the phone these past few weeks. And many weeks have gone by.

Perhaps Mother bought a new phone so Man wouldn't bother her. But why wouldn't she want Man to call her? I haven't figured out yet if it is Man's fault or the baby's fault that she left, but how can Man apologize for whatever he did if she won't let him reach her? He needs to tell her that the baby is getting better so she will come back and take care of us all.

Now I think, for the first time, that my mother is being foolish and stubborn.

I wish she would just let him apologize. Let him say what he needs to say.

I know Mother is out there. And I know she loves me. She loves me and Mary and Jimmy and Finn, and she even loves that yappy Jasper.

I heard Mary and Mahmee talking about the holiday called Thanksgiving. It is coming soon. Mahmee said she will make us a turkey, and I plan to eat my share. So that means it won't be long until we celebrate the even bigger and more special holiday, called Christmas. I am sure Mother will come home for that and we'll have a happy reunion.

It will be a tremendous day!

If Man can just convince her to come.

When he stops talking into the phone, he looks tired, his eyes heavy. I am not sure what it means.

Just a few short days later, Man is going through the mail and finds a letter. It is late in the evening, and the kids have gone to bed already. He brings it over to the fireplace and sits down.

He looks at it a long time, unopened. Finally, he gets up, goes into the kitchen, retrieves a dark brown bottle from the refrigerator, and brings it into the living room. The fire sparks and cracks as he drinks and stares at his letter.

Man doesn't usually drink that foamy beer when he is alone, maybe because it makes people talk loudly and he can't afford to be loud when the baby is sleeping. But now, he drinks the whole bottle before tearing open the letter.

Honestly, he has no one to talk to anyway.

I climb into his lap. It is so incredibly warm and snuggly sitting there by the fire. I have never sat in Father's lap before, and it is not too bad.

I—Did I just call him Father?

Sorry, I think I did. I don't know why I did that.

No—I take it back. I did it because he must be Father to me now. I settle in, both into the word and into his lap. I see how things have changed. He must adopt me because Mother is not here, and we are getting so tired of waiting for her. She is making us wait too long.

He holds the letter above me and reads it several times. He is so still that I relax and start to nod off.

I am startled when his body turns suddenly. I jump up and run over to the middle of the rug. I think he forgot I was there. Father puts the letter into the fire, then changes his mind and grabs it back out with his hand, which seems like a dangerous thing to do. But I guess Father knows how to handle fire. He slaps the edges of the paper with the palm of his hand, where it is singed. I worry that he is going to burn his hand.

Crouched over the letter, on all fours, he reads it again. He starts taking long, deep, shaky breaths. He stays like that a long time, trying to breathe, like his throat is closing up. His hand goes to his heart, and when he winces I know he is in tremendous pain. But he stays as quiet as he can. I believe he doesn't want to disturb the children. I am afraid to get closer, because I'm not sure when he will suddenly move.

I think Father has had more bad news. I am worried it is from Mother.

He rolls over onto his back, right there by the fire, and lays an arm over his eyes. As if he does not have the strength to get up. Eventually, he falls into a restless sleep. If I could bring a blanket to him, I would. But I cannot, so I curl up by his knee.

We fall asleep, he and I.

The day will come when I go out and look for my mother, but today is not the right day. Father needs me.

8

What Is Under the Bed

In the morning, Father wakes up early and looks around in wonder when he finds he is by the cold fireplace. I think he must be sore when he sits up, wincing and holding his back. We can both hear Finn stirring in his crib.

Carefully folding the letter and putting it in his back pocket, Father heads upstairs. I follow. He lifts Finn out of his crib and wraps him up in several layers, and I realize they are going out. He brings Finn down and puts him in the car seat that waits by the front door before he gets his coat on.

When Father returns about half an hour later, he brings the baby in first, placing the car seat, with Finn still in it, inside the door. He walks back to the car to get a few bags. When he lays everything out on the kitchen table, I see it is doughnuts and coffee and orange juice.

It takes Jimmy and Mary another hour after his return to wander downstairs, but when they do, they are happy to see the food. Father is looking through the newspaper. He usually finds a few things to show Jimmy about the Sox in the summer or the Bruins in the winter.

I think the Sox and the Bruins must be warlike tribes of peoples. From the way Father describes them, it sounds as if they are always in battle.

Everyone is quiet and relaxed. But when the whole family is seated and tucking into their food, Father asks my siblings a question that makes them freeze.

"So. You guys have been talking to your mother?"

His arms are crossed, which makes his shoulder muscles tense under his tight shirt, and he looks a little intimidating. Which he already is anyway.

I want to tell him: *breathe*.

And this: *loosen up*.

"Uhhhhhh . . ." Mary realizes she must answer his question. She opens her eyes wide at Jimmy, who gives a subtle shrug. "Um, yeah, Dad."

"You talk to her all the time?"

"Well . . ." She puts her doughnut down. "Yes and no. We don't talk, we text." Mary has a snappy way of talking. She is at a loss, so she just repeats herself, as if he is an idiot and doesn't understand the difference. "We don't *talk,* we *text.*" She lifts her eyebrows, as if to say, *Get it?*

Jimmy snorts. But then it's his turn. "Dad, I'm really sorry. Ma said not to tell you. She said you weren't going to handle it well. She said you would drive her crazy."

Father just sighs. So now we know. Everyone has been talking to Mother except for him.

He shakes his head and drinks his coffee.

Father loves coffee, just like Mahmee does. In some

ways, Father is very like Mahmee. Because of this, they get on each other's nerves sometimes. It works out well that Mahmee leaves most days before Father gets home.

Mahmee is generous, even if she is stubborn, just like Father. I believe that Mahmee gave Father this house. I have come to realize that this house is the one that Father grew up in, yet Mahmee no longer lives here. I can smell his scent everywhere, on the old, ratty furniture and on baby blankets in the closet.

Maybe this is one reason Mother felt she had to leave us to get her rest. It is Father's house. But then, where is she? Unlike Father, she has no family anywhere near here. But she does have friends. Many, many friends.

I hope she is with friends. And not injured or sick in the hospital, which I have heard Mother say is the worst place in the world to end up. That's the best I can hope for.

"Dad," Mary asks, "it's Sunday. Why don't we go to church anymore?"

"I don't really want to see anyone," Father mumbles quietly, head lowered as if he's talking to his plate.

"Dad, maybe you *should* see people." Jimmy grabs a second doughnut, rips it in half, and stuffs a piece in his mouth.

Father scowls. "I don't want to have to explain it. You know they're already talking about it anyway—"

"But Dad, of course people are going to talk. People either love Ma or hate her." Jimmy puts his hands out in front of him as if he is a scale, balancing items on his two palms. "They *love* her"—and here he drops one hand—"or they *hate* her." And he drops the other hand.

Hate her? I don't understand Jimmy's words. How

could anyone ever hate our mother? She is the sweetest, loveliest, kindest person.

To me anyway.

Maybe not to everyone.

Maybe not to Father, at least, not all of the time. But she did love him once. Of that, I am sure. I remember when she held him and kissed him and loved him so, so much.

And, I remember when she . . . Well, when she was not happy. When she was tired and moody and very angry. But we all get like that sometimes, don't we?

I need to think about it. I slink up the steep stairs and crawl under Mother's bed. I need a break.

It is dark under the big bed, and I love it. I enjoy prowling in the night, and I sometimes seek out the dark even in the middle of the day. It feels soothing on my eyes, and I feel very safe tucked tight among the boxes.

I see one of Mother's little, round red pills sitting by a shoebox, and suddenly I feel nostalgic. I bat it with my paw until it skids out of sight.

Mother has been taking the red pills every day since I met her. I am not sure what they do, but they seem to give her energy.

There was a time, maybe a year before Finn was born, when the pills stopped working. I knew something was wrong because Mother was too tired to get out of bed. I remember those days well. I didn't mind Mother being in bed, because we could cuddle. We had a wonderful, amazing time together. It was a rainy month in the middle of winter, dark and damp, and I was so glad to have Mother to warm me up.

When those pills stopped working, Jimmy finally confronted Father in the kitchen one night. I watched from where I lay spread out on the tile.

"She's gotta go back," Jimmy begged. "*Please,* Pops. You can't pretend it's not happening."

"I don't want to go back. Those doctors have no idea what they're doing. They can't even figure out—"

"Just give them one more chance. I'm worried. C'mon. Just try it."

Father rubbed his neck, listening. He finally agreed.

She was gone for a day, and when she returned, Mother was back to taking the red pills, plus some light blue rectangular ones. And Mother was full of energy once again. Full, full, full of it! Making lots of calls and seeing lots of friends. Telling lots of funny stories.

In those days, at bedtime, Father would sit in bed and watch her pace and talk, back and forth, wearing a trail into the rug. He listened to her stories until she wore herself out. When she'd finally lie in bed, he'd throw an arm over her, as if that alone would keep her anchored until morning. Father would nuzzle her behind the ear until she laughed and relaxed, and I would have to jump off the bed if she started to kiss him, because then he moved around too much.

I didn't like getting kicked in the hip or the head, which is what happened if Father wasn't paying attention.

That would be on a good night.

On a bad night, they would fight. Mother could start a fight about any old thing. She could never "let it alone," as Father begged her to do. Sometimes he just stared at her, with a wounded pout on his face as she cursed at him. After throwing his pillow and a blanket into the hallway, she'd slam the door behind him.

Other nights, he fought back, bellowing down the hallway. I would watch the muscles twitch in his arms as he clenched his fists and screamed his heart out.

Sometimes on those nights he somehow ended up back in our bed, which confused me. But when Mother changed her mind, I was in no position to argue.

Either way, it didn't make a difference to me. Mother gathered me to her chest and caressed me when she was ready to sleep, whether Father was there or not. She was always loving toward me.

I miss her. I hope she misses me too.

The other person who really bothered her sometimes was Jimmy. Oh, there was one day when she was still adjusting to those new blue pills that she really let him have it. He just messed up one thing after another. He spilled the cereal all over the kitchen floor and forgot to take the trash out, which caused the ants to march in. Then he handed her a slip saying his homework was late for the third time that month.

Mother always kept the house very, very clean. There was never a mess until the day she left. And she was extremely organized. I don't know how Jimmy got to be such a messy, careless child.

I was angry at Jimmy too, for making Mother so, so frustrated.

At first, she just screamed at him: how he was so disappointing, and how she couldn't believe he screwed up again. How he was driving her crazy. How he was making so much work for her. How he was just as stupid as his father.

But this one time was different: She hit him. More than once, on the arm and his side.

Jimmy was already bigger than Mother, but he didn't fight back. He just looked stunned and ran outside. It was a nice spring day. Believe me, he was perfectly fine.

I sat on the windowsill by the screen and watched Jimmy as he stood on the front step, talking into his little phone. "Dad. Turn around and come back. She just hauled off and started wailing on me. Yes . . . yes. But Dad, I'm late for school—okay. Okay."

When Father arrived, Jimmy got up his courage and told Mother how he felt, standing tall while she sat on the couch in the living room. I could see he felt braver with Father there next to him.

"You don't get to do that to me, Ma," he warned her, his eyes finally starting to water. He blinked back the tears. "I'm not going through that again."

I don't know what he meant by "again." I'd never seen her do that before.

Mother and I scowled at him. Jimmy caused the problem, not her.

Father looked worried and hustled Jimmy to the door. "You should go to school." He walked outside with Jimmy for a minute, talking to him quickly and quietly. "Tell them you slept in by mistake."

It was that point of the spring where the trees had just bloomed with baby green leaves and the air was heavy with moisture. They stood there on the step not noticing the beautiful day that was unfolding around them.

Jimmy whirled around. "Dad—you won't let her call the school, will you? Because then everyone will know—"

Father assured Jimmy he would not let Mother call the school. He promised he would not leave her alone all day. And Father said he would be there when Jimmy got home from school.

"You gonna call the doctor?"

"Nah. It's fine. She's just tired. I'll figure it out."

Jimmy nodded. Father put one hand on either side of his son's head and kissed him on the forehead.

I was mad at Jimmy, even if Father wasn't.

Good riddance, Jimmy, I thought. *Go think about what you did wrong. Upsetting Mother that way.*

Father came back in and went upstairs. He never went to work that day. He brought down Mother's little bottles of pills and made sure she'd taken them. When Father asked Mother if she felt anxious or agitated, she just rolled her eyes.

I wondered if maybe she had not taken enough pills, or she had taken too many, and her energy was off. Perhaps that was why Mother was so, so frustrated. Mother offered many arguments about why she didn't want or need those pills anymore, but Father was having none of it. He just kept shaking his head no. He didn't want to hear it.

Father was angry, but he didn't yell at her that day. He just counted out her pills, over and over, double-checking. Keeping a nervous eye on her. Sitting right next to her when she got tired and lay down on the couch.

So that's about all I know about the pills. I wonder if Mother has new pills, wherever she is.

I try to hunt down that little red pill under the bed, between the boxes. Although I nose around, I can't find it. When the doorbell rings, I decide to go see who it is.

Sweet Aruna has come to watch a movie with Jimmy. Jimmy is happy to see her. He helps her take her coat off and hangs it up. Winter is almost here, and they express a desire to stay inside on their day off.

I understand. I've never been outside, but after his walk Jasper sometimes comes in looking like a popsicle, coated in ice. I wouldn't want to be out there either.

Aruna sits with Jimmy on the couch. The room is dark and the shades are drawn. There's a movie on the

TV, but they aren't really watching it. They are preoccupied with the upcoming school winter social, talking quietly about who is going and what they'll wear.

"Are you going to dance with me at the social, even the slow dances?" Aruna asks, slowly blinking her big brown eyes at him. She is teasing him. She wears a thick sweater, and I have never felt anything so soft against the pads of my paws, as I knead into the material while sitting right on her lap. Lucky me! Aruna really loves me, I am sure of it. And she isn't much interested in Jasper. Which in my book makes her pretty smart.

"Yes, of course," Jimmy replies. He has his arm up on the back of the couch behind her. Sometimes he nuzzles his head against hers as if he's sleepy, although he looks wide awake to me.

"Are you going to try to kiss me too?"

"What do you mean, *try*?" A sly smile emerges on his face. "I ain't trying. I'm doing."

When Father goes out to do an errand, Jimmy tells Aruna a few stories about the many ways his dad has been "freaking out" lately. Aruna has a beautiful laugh, like the bells Mother hung on the back screen door. She laughs repeatedly, but as the stories go on, she laughs less and less.

Until finally Jimmy doesn't sound so amused. He sounds tired. And Aruna isn't laughing at all anymore. She pats his leg.

"Poor Jimmy."

"Yeah," he joins in. "Poor me."

I watch as Jimmy's hand pulls away from her and slides up to his arm, covering the X scar that is hidden by the sleeve of his shirt. I know the scar is there, but Aruna probably does not. I have seen him touch the scar before, as if he's protecting it, at times when he is upset. But I don't know if he realizes he's doing it.

That's not the only scar he has. There's another one on his leg. It is also a big crooked X. It looks exactly like the one on his arm.

Aruna slowly leans in. She kisses Jimmy once, on the cheek, just barely.

"There it is," he says triumphantly. And now he's laughing again.

Jimmy's a good boy. He always bounces back.

Aruna smiles at him. She takes his hand, and he intertwines his fingers with hers.

Now, watching Jimmy, I wonder if Mother was too hard on him. Did she need to hit him so many times for being messy and careless? It seemed right at the time, the kind of thing a mother should do, but now I'm not so sure. I don't know exactly what human mothers are supposed to do to get their children to behave.

Mother never hit me. But, of course, I'm a cat. That's different.

My back twitches, and I jump up and start cleaning myself head to toe. I lick until my neck is sore and my tongue is raw.

Aruna and Jimmy are kind, and they do feed me, but neither one is my mother. I refuse to think bad thoughts about Mother. I don't know why I suddenly feel so guilty.

I have let my concern for Father distract me. I'm determined to make my plans to go find her.

9

Ten Fingers, Ten Toes

Jimmy and Father are in Finn's room watching Charlotte do something funny that makes the baby laugh over and over. It's some silly game with a puppet. I watch from the hallway. Jimmy is laughing so hard that he is crying and holding his stomach, which makes Father laugh too.

I can see Charlotte enjoys this game. She likes the baby's funny reactions. And I think she loves having an audience.

Charlotte is tall and thin, with brown hair that falls in waves, and there is never a hair out of place. She paints her lips the color of a blushing peach, and today she wears a beautiful necklace with big, shiny white flowers on it. Charlotte smiles sweetly at Father and Jimmy.

I wonder if most of the time Charlotte works with mothers. Perhaps our house is unique in that there is no mother here. In this house, Charlotte is outnumbered by male humans.

I am glad to see that Father and Charlotte are finally relaxed around each other. At first, they were both very formal. I don't think Father even liked her.

Charlotte is a slightly awkward human, if you ask me. Her gestures are not always smooth, and she makes funny faces, especially at Finn.

But now Father lets his guard down and asks her questions, and he isn't afraid to make suggestions. Charlotte can be quite goofy, not just with the baby but also apparently with anyone. Something about her makes Father feel comfortable enough to talk. It makes me glad to hear them interacting from wherever I am in the house.

Charlotte makes dramatic faces and sweeping gestures when she's talking to Finn, and she guides Jimmy and Father so they will teach the baby in the same way. Sometimes I think that baby is making progress, and sometimes I don't. It's hard for me to figure out what's going on and how much that baby is learning.

I had never seen a human baby before, but Finn looks like what I expected. Big head, big eyes, just a few teeth. Ten fingers, ten toes.

Yet something is off. Something about his reaction to the things around him is wrong.

It puzzles me. But I am determined to figure it out.

While the others are still laughing, Mary sweeps up the stairs and stands in Finn's doorway. Her back is to me, but I can see her arms are tightly folded. It's the same stance Father takes when he is upset and closing himself off from the world.

"What are you doing?" she asks.

Jimmy explains the game, in hysterics.

"No," Mary interrupts. "No. What I mean is"—she points at Father—"what are *you* doing?"

Father looks up at her from where he is sitting on

the rug. His face is blank. His mouth opens a little as he tries to think of a reply, but he is mystified. He seems to realize suddenly that Mary is angry about something, as his face opens with surprise.

Mary whips around, her long blond hair flying behind her. She stomps off into her room and closes the door.

Jimmy sits between the two adults. "Don't get up," he says, putting one hand on Father's shoulder and the other on Charlotte's arm. "She has a bug up her butt about something. I'll talk to her. Keep working." Jimmy wipes his hands on his jeans and stands.

He comes out into the hallway, clears his throat, and wipes the smile off his face. He knocks, just once, on Mary's door before entering. I follow along, on silent paws.

Mary sits on her bed, up by her pillow. Her legs are crossed and her arms still folded.

Jimmy shuts the door behind him and stands in front of her. "What's the matter with you?"

Mary grits her teeth. "You know what," she snaps at him.

Jimmy takes a deep breath. His hair is messy, and he's chewing gum. From my angle on the floor, his head seems to nearly hit the ceiling fan because he has grown so tall.

"Good grief, Mare." Just like Father sometimes calls Mother *Care,* he and Jimmy will call Mary *Mare.* "What's the one day of the week you see Pops in a good mood?"

He waits, but she does not answer. Mary does not want to play games.

"Let's see . . . Oh, yeah, that's right. It's Thursday. Why is that?" Jimmy pauses again, arms spread in front of him as he makes everything bigger with gestures.

"Do you think it's because Charlotte visits? I do. And why is he happy? Because she's really nice. It's that simple."

Mary squints at him, looking even angrier.

"You know, Mare . . ." He sighs. "Sometimes people need visitors to remind them how to act. We're not having a party in there. We're working with Finn. Pops has had a rough time of it lately, if you hadn't noticed, and Charlotte makes him happy." Jimmy shrugs. "Charlotte makes me happy. And she makes Finn happy. She makes us feel like Finn is going to be okay. So you need to get over it."

"She's not Ma. Don't pretend like she is, as if this makes everything better."

"Of course she's not Ma. Of course we're not pretending she's Ma. It's got nothin' to do with Ma."

Mary frowns down at the bedspread.

"Listen. We all love Ma. But Ma's not here. And Finn is growing every day. That kid needs help, and Pops needs help. Even I need help. And I'm not afraid to admit it. So leave us alone."

Mary huffs. "Give me a break. This is all about *you* now?"

"Mare." Jimmy sighs. "Yeah, I need help. Why am I not allowed to say that? Ma always loved you best. She thinks you're perfect. She never took it out on you like she did me and Pops. We need a break, so cut us some slack."

I see Mary's hand move slowly toward her bedside table. And then I see the sharp, silver scissors sitting there. I don't know what Mary is planning to do, but I'm alarmed. Jimmy is still talking, unaware. "Ma always said you got the looks and the talent and the brains in this family, that you're just as smart as she is."

"I'm not as smart as she is," Mary hisses. She grips

the scissors now, her hand turning red as she squeezes them in her fist. "*I don't want to be like her at all.*"

I leap into action. With one swift push, I am airborne and then land just in front of Mary. She is startled, and then her shoulders relax a bit when we make eye contact.

Jimmy sits next to me on the bed and calmly reaches over me to put his hands around the hand holding the scissors. He pries Mary's fingers loose one by one. Mary lets him take the scissors without a fight.

Jimmy looks into his lap and thinks about it. He's a calm soul, in general. He has taken sharp things out of Mother's hand before too. Once, it was scissors. Once, it was a kitchen knife.

"Then don't be. Don't be like her." That's his only answer. He drops his head, as if guilty that he doesn't have a better answer for her. When he leaves the room, he takes the scissors with him.

I peer up at Mary. She is as still as a statue, mouth pressed into a grim line. I climb into Mary's lap. It's warm and comfortable. I hope I can help her feel better.

I start purring as loud as I can, and finally she rubs me down. I feel the tension draining out of her hands and into my fur.

When Charlotte's time is up, Father walks her down the stairs. I leave Mary and sit on the landing to watch him say good-bye. He is carrying Finn, and they are still talking about a few things. Just before opening the door, Charlotte automatically extends her hand to shake his, but his arms are full of the squirming baby. "I—" He can't quite manage it. "I'm sorry. I—" I can see they both feel embarrassed for a moment.

Just let her go, I think. *Shake her hand next time.*

Father stands in the doorway, watching her walk to her car.

After Charlotte leaves, we have supper. We're having turkey sandwiches tonight, instead of ham. I'm so proud of Father for trying a new food! I get a little in my bowl, thankfully.

Later that night, I am lying on the soft flannel sheet on Jimmy's bed when Father comes in. Jimmy is doing homework, lying back flat and holding the book above his head. Now it's Father's turn to shut the door.

"Is Mary okay?" he asks my brother.

"Yeah," Jimmy says, rolling his eyes, making light of it. "She's just being Mary."

"All right." From the way Father scans the room, his eyes glazed, I can see he has other things on his mind. "Did . . ." He stops midsentence.

"What?"

"Did your mother say anything about coming here for Christmas? To visit?"

Jimmy now closes his book, laying it aside. He looks up at Father, a little confused. "Um . . . no. Do you want me to ask her?" Before Father can answer, Jimmy scrambles up. "Never mind. Stupid question. Let me ask her. I'm sure she wants to. Right?"

They stare at each other. Maybe they don't really know the answer to that question.

I get up, stretch my legs. When Father sits on the bed, I rub my head against his back. I'm glad Father asked. It's a great idea.

Father looks down at his feet. "Do you think . . . ?" He can't seem to finish his question.

"Yeah. I'm sure she'll say yes, Pops. Don't worry. I've got it all taken care of."

Father opens his mouth, but closes it again. He rubs

his knees with his hands. "Does . . . Does Mary know where your ma is living now?" he asks quietly, leaning slightly toward Jimmy.

"Nooooo," Jimmy says, shaking his head slowly, raising an eyebrow. "I don't think so. Mary would've said something."

"Let's not tell her yet," Father suggests. "Do you think?"

"Yesssss." Jimmy nods in slow motion. "Agreed."

When Father leaves the room, I follow him. He takes a shower for a long time, puts on his underwear and a T-shirt, and then comes in to lie on the bed with me. "Move over, Boo," he says.

He lets me knead my claws into the comforter. When Mother was here, he would give me a swat if I started up with this. But now I have taken over her side of the bed, and he allows it.

Later that night, when Father is in bed reading one of his books, Jimmy comes in quickly and jumps on the bed. Thank goodness Jimmy sees me just in time, or he might have landed on me. His huge grin tells the whole story. His hands are balled into fists, as if he is about to explode with excitement.

"She's coming?" Father looks very surprised. He sticks his book on the bedside table so quickly that it falls onto the floor.

"Yeah. She'll come by. Not this weekend, but next weekend."

"She said yes, right away? You didn't have to convince her? She wants to come?" Father reaches down to pick up his book and sets it on the table as he's talking. He rarely talks this fast, shooting out questions one after the next. "Is she going to stay all day? Is she coming for lunch? Is she staying for dinner?"

Jimmy sits close to his dad and rubs his chin. "Uhhh,

I don't know about that. I wouldn't make any assumptions. Because, you know, it's hard to say. We're talking about Ma here. Who the hell knows what she'll end up doing."

They look at each other, both buzzing with anticipation. I can feel it, even just sitting on the edge of the bed near them. I rub my head repeatedly on Jimmy's knee, and he runs a hand down my back.

The next morning, Jimmy and Mary come downstairs first, to pack papers and food in their great scramble to get to school on time every morning. Jimmy loads up his backpack with an apple, an orange, and two bananas, because Mahmee went shopping yesterday and I suspect he wants to stock up before they run out of everything again. Jimmy eats enough for two humans. Mary is just putting orange juice back into the refrigerator when her eyes open wide and she gasps.

We all turn. Jasper pivots, and gives a *yip!* We are all shocked by what we see.

Jimmy cranes his head. "What the—?"

Mary does a double take. "Dad!"

Father has shaved. His face turns red as we all stare at him, and without the beard the flush on his cheeks is easy to see. He comes into the kitchen and reaches up to get a coffee cup from a high shelf. Jimmy and Mary exchange a look when his back is turned.

We all continue to look. Father has lost several years off his appearance, easily. Easily!

I see now, for the first time, how much he looks like sweet Mary. How could I not have seen it before? The sandy hair, the light eyes, a gentle face.

Mother likes to say that Father is a "handsome devil"

and Mary is a "beautiful angel," and I never understood what she meant. But now I see that devil and angel must be the same thing, because Father and Mary have the same looks.

"Oh. My. God. Seriously, Pops." Jimmy reaches forward, his mouth hanging open, and rubs down his father's cheek. "What did you do?"

"Knock it off." He pushes Jimmy away, but gently.

I have never seen Father without his beard. I barely recognize him. He is like Father's younger brother come to visit us.

"Daddy. *Who are you?*" Mary wails.

Father rolls his eyes and shakes his head. He pours a full cup of coffee and starts to drink it, standing against the counter. I think he is still embarrassed. Mary rushes up to him and gives him a pinch on the arm. She is grinning and can't stop staring. "Look at you, look at you," she repeats in an easy, singsong voice.

Mother is coming.

That's what I heard. That's what Father heard. So now we must all get ready.

Maybe I don't need to run away and find her after all! My relief is overwhelming. The outdoors is big and wild and scary.

But once Mother gets here, it is important that she stay. If she walks out again, we may never get her back.

10

Getting Ready for the Big, Big Holiday

The big, big holiday is almost here. And Mother is coming to visit. Everyone is excited.

Especially me!

But it seems like my family is just not ready. There is not enough time to prepare. Everything feels very rushed, as if time is accelerating. There is a general feeling of anxiety in the house.

One night, Father and Jimmy walk in the front door together, letting in a cold draft and peeling off their coats and gloves. Mahmee was here babysitting Finn, and he was being good, so she had a little time to bake. I watched Mahmee work in the kitchen, and she rewarded me with a dab of soft butter. I licked it right off of a spoon.

Incredibly good, that butter. Incredibly good, that Mahmee.

A sweet scent warms the air. "Mahmee, what'd you

make me?" Jimmy asks as he passes Mahmee in the living room. Mahmee just smiles and kisses her boys hello and good-bye.

Father and Jimmy exchange a look. They walk into the kitchen and see a blueberry pie sitting in the middle of the kitchen table.

Jimmy quickly goes to the silverware drawer and pulls out a fork. He grabs a carton of milk from the refrigerator, sits down at the kitchen table, and pulls the pie toward him.

"Hey," Father objects in a sharp tone. "What are you doing?"

Jimmy's fork hovers in the air above the pie. "Uh, seriously, unless you have supper ready, Dad, and it's not a ham sandwich, this is what I'm eating." And Jimmy digs in, shoveling forkfuls of pie into his mouth. No plate necessary. No glass for the milk either, which he chugs from the container.

Father just stares at him for a moment before striding over to the silverware drawer, sliding it open, and grabbing his own fork. He sits opposite Jimmy and starts eating the other side. They eat without talking, until the pie is finished.

Jimmy pushes back from the table. "I think I'm gonna puke."

Father holds his stomach with both hands. He winces, and I can see he doesn't feel so good either.

When Jimmy lurches for the kitchen sink, Father jumps up and heads for the living room couch. Jimmy is sick and Father is not, but Father lies on the couch a long time before getting up.

This is the kind of week we've been having.

Mary walks in not long after. Her hair is wet, and she smells of soap. She's carrying Jimmy's big, orange ball.

Mary is athletic, like Father. Jimmy is more like me, inclined to spend a lazy afternoon lying about.

The wonderful scent of the pie still hangs in the air, and Mary comes into the living room, curious. Jimmy is now lying on the rug, and Father is sprawled out on the couch. Mary asks what Mahmee made.

"Nothing," Jimmy lies.

Mary raises an eyebrow.

But Father backs Jimmy up, swearing that if Mahmee cooked something, she took it with her.

Neither of them wants to get in trouble with Mary. They're lucky that Jimmy thought to hide the pie plate before crawling out to the living room floor. But this is what we do in our family lately, all of us: We grab food wherever we can.

The next day, the whole family goes out, including Finn. There's plenty of snow on the ground, so they bundle up tight with hats and gloves and boots. When they come back, they carry a big pine tree into the house. They set it up in the living room. It takes quite a few adjustments until it stands up perfectly straight.

The annual pine tree! It smells soooo good. So fresh and crisp. I love to hide under the branches and smell the wonderful outdoors. And I enjoy batting the bright things they usually hang on the tree.

By the time they get the tree up, everyone is exhausted. They all do this every year. But there is a pause in the action. The thing is, Mother usually decorates the tree. Honestly, the rest of them don't seem to have a clue where to begin.

By the end of the day, all they have managed to do is get some tangled wires out of the attic. Finn has been difficult and fussy all day, grabbing and chewing everything he can reach. They've had their hands full.

After supper, I sit by the blazing fire. Father sits on the living room rug near the tree. He tries to untangle the wires, and he works on it a very long time. Jimmy comes into the room to find his father with wires all over his lap.

"I don't think I can do it," Father says quietly.

"You mean . . ." Jimmy stands in front of him, assessing the situation. "You mean, literally?"

"What?"

"You mean, literally, you're bad with the lights? Or do you mean you just can't deal with it?"

Father gives him a look and shrugs. "Both, I guess."

"Well . . ." Jimmy takes one end of the wire and plugs it in. A hundred tiny white lights flash on. It is beautiful. "To start, Ma always plugs it in. That might help."

Jimmy takes the wires away from Father and gets them untangled in no time. Father seems tired, his shoulders slumped, looking down at the rug with no expression on his face.

Jimmy clears his throat. "You know what, Dad?" His voice gets louder. "You gotta prepare yourself. Because if Ma flakes out and cancels on us, then Christmas is going to suck."

Father looks at Jimmy.

"You heard me. And then Christmas is going to roll right into Valentine's Day. Which is going to suck too. For you anyway." Something else occurs to Jimmy as he carefully lays the wires out across the floor. "And then we're going to run smack into Mother's Day. If she's not home by then, that's going to suck for everybody."

Father scowls, and finally nods.

They all agree that they will get the lights on the tree but forget about the decorations, just this once.

I'm afraid it is true what Jimmy said, that they are reluctant to decorate because they're nervous that Mother will not show up. If that happens, we won't be able to stand looking at this tree at all. The bright lights and baubles will just remind us of our hopes, easily shattered.

Jimmy puts the wires on the tree, with Mary assisting him. The tree glows and twinkles. Then Jimmy carries the boxes of decorations right back up to the attic without putting any of them on the tree. I'm disappointed.

The next day there is some game of sport on the TV all day. Mary makes popcorn and they watch on and off.

Sean comes over late in the day with hot roast beef sandwiches for everyone. He also has cookies that his wife made.

"Thanks," Mary says, taking the cookies from him. She looks disappointed. "We don't have anything for you. I'm so sorry. You know Mom usually—"

Sean stops her. He tells her not to worry about it, that he knows Carrie used to do all of the shopping.

Father comes out of the kitchen.

"Here he is," Sean greets him. "Clean-shaven. You're like a new man. I still don't recognize you. What'd you do with my friend Tom?"

Father offers Sean some coffee. Mother used to make the coffee every morning, but Father has finally figured out how to do it himself.

I'm proud of him. The contraption that makes the coffee looks very difficult to master.

Mary beats Father to the kitchen, and she swings a cabinet door open to grab a coffee mug. She asks Sean how he likes his coffee.

Sean raises his eyebrows at her. "Very sweet. The way I like my ladies." Mary rolls her eyes and opens a cabinet to find the sugar.

Jimmy, who has just entered the kitchen, groans.

Sean shrugs. "Speaking of ladies, how's it going with your girl, Jim?" Sean now sits at the kitchen table with Father. He turns to Father, tapping him on the arm. "What's her name again?"

Father pauses, caught off guard. "Um, it's . . . Anya? Or, Anna . . . something?"

Standing in the doorway to the kitchen, Jimmy's face darkens. "Don't forget her name. Don't do that, Pops." Jimmy is clearly upset. "Aruna. It's not that hard."

Sean frowns. "It's an unusual name, that's all," he says. "Give your Pops a break. He's got a lot on his mind."

"I don't care. He should know it by now. We've been going out for two months."

Father apologizes and stares at his hands.

Sean hits Father on the arm. "It's okay, Tommy. You've got a lot on your mind." Sean turns in his seat. "So, Big Jim. What are you gettin' Aruna for Christmas? It is kind of a romantic holiday, as my wife likes to remind me."

Jimmy pauses, and he sticks his hands in his pockets, looking sheepish. I think he's embarrassed because Father probably won't be having a "romantic holiday." Or maybe Jimmy is just not good with shopping and gifts.

"Uh, well, actually, you know, Aruna's not Catholic.

She's not Christian at all. She doesn't celebrate Christmas. But I'm still planning to get her a gift."

"So?" Sean is on the edge of his seat, waiting for the answer.

"Um, well, I noticed her favorite color is red . . . ?" Jimmy is obviously on one of those rare topics outside of his comfort zone, because he glances at the floor as he talks. "So, maybe, a red scarf?"

"But isn't her coat red?" Father asks.

Sean slams the table triumphantly. "You see? Your Pops *is* paying attention, after all."

Jimmy's lips purse as he thinks it over. "Yeah . . . Yeah, so you think maybe . . . blue?"

Father hesitates, but just for a moment. "Call your mom and ask her."

I have never heard Father talk like this before, so casually about Mother. As if she is just *someone,* who lives *somewhere else.*

They all agree, that's what Jimmy will do. He will call and ask Mother for advice. Mother will know the right thing to do. Of course she will.

Just as he's about to leave the kitchen, Jimmy turns. "Wait, Pops. I need to get something for Ma too, don't I? Are you getting her something?"

Father looks stunned, suddenly panicked. Sean glances over and sees the look on Father's face. "Nah, Big Jim," Sean says in a hurry. "Your ma doesn't want your pops to do that. Not . . . Jimmy, just ask your ma about your girl. Ask her about the scarf."

Sean turns to face Father and speaks emphatically, to make sure Father understands: "Carrie wouldn't want you to do that."

It makes me sad, to see how Father goes from normal to grieving in a heartbeat.

I can't believe Mother is coming here. We're all flustered.

When my family has days off, they have too much time to think. I prefer the days when everyone is out working and Mahmee is here, with her radio on. She doesn't seem as stressed out as the rest of them.

And, of course, when Charlotte visits, things are better. Early in the week, Charlotte still works with Mahmee in the morning. But later in the week, she comes in the afternoon and works with Father. I am convinced she helps to distract Father from his misery, at least for a short time.

When Charlotte arrives, she walks in without knocking because Father has told her to do that. "Hello!" she calls out, stomping the snow off her boots. When Father comes down the stairs, her mouth hangs half-open for a moment as she assesses Father's new look, clean-shaven.

Compliment him, I think. *He's had a really hard week.*

But she surprises me and doesn't say anything. Usually she has something positive to say.

Maybe this is a little different. Maybe it would be too personal for her to comment on how he looks.

While Father never likes being the focus of attention, he also doesn't run away when she stares at him a beat too long. He waits, leaning on the banister, and just looks back at her.

"Okay!" Her smile is chipper and bright. "Let's go get started."

I like Charlotte. I give her a quick wink.

She sees me sitting at the bottom of the stairs and gives a brief stroke to my head before hurrying to catch up with Father. I stand up and lean into her touch. Her movements are not graceful, but she always acknowledges my presence with a light touch, which I appreciate.

Once they've gone up the stairs, I wonder if there is more I can do to help my family get ready for Mother's visit. I jump up on the table that sits by the front door and pick out a framed photo of Mother with Mary when she was little, cooking together in the kitchen. I bat my paw at the dusty photo until it falls over and onto the floor.

Surely Mary will see this and fix it, move the photo to the front. When Mother sees this photo, she will remember the wonderful times she had with us. And then she will want to stay.

I will make sure Mother remembers. Maybe she just needs a little help.

11

What I Think You Have Already Figured Out

I hear a car in the driveway. Mother is here. She is here! She is here! My little heart is beating fast. I have missed her so much.

While I cannot wait to see her, I am also incredibly angry at her. She has put us through so much stress and anxiety. Why did she leave so suddenly? Why didn't she tell Father she was planning to go? It seems unnecessarily cruel to have left without warning. But maybe she knew my family would never let her go if they realized her intention to stay away for so long.

Father and my siblings spent a while getting ready for her visit. Father has many button-down flannel shirts, and this is what he would normally wear. But he does not wear one of these. Instead, he has on a new black sweater.

I wonder where the sweater came from. Did Sean or Jimmy or Mary help him pick it out? As he's standing by the bed, I rub my head against his arm, and he strokes my back. The sweater is very soft and fits him perfectly. He looks comfortable, and I think he made a good choice.

We have to make an effort to get Mother to stay. I hope she's coming home to stay. She has had plenty of time to take a break and rest herself. I need her to come back to take care of me—to take care of all of us. We have been struggling without her. I haven't forgotten the days when the house was clean, we were all fed on time, and Mother and I were the best of friends. I can't wait to take a long afternoon nap with her, the way we used to. Mother can climb under the wool blanket, and I will lie on top of it. I look forward to flopping down against her stomach and nuzzling my wet nose into her hand.

When she walks in the house, Mother is beaming, and she stares at everything around her. No wonder—she has not been here in months. Her eyes sparkle, and I can see she is so much better. So much healthier. Just like the old Mother I used to know. And I am so, so happy for her.

Everyone hugs Mother and smiles, and Jimmy hands Finn over to her. It is almost Christmas, and my family has decorated the best they could, and lights are twinkling on the tree. For a moment everything seems perfect.

I can't believe what I am seeing! My sweet Mother. I forgot how beautiful and bright her face is. How everyone who sees her gets excited just looking at her. How her shiny black hair turns almost blue in the light. How she stands a good half-foot shorter than Father, and he towers over her. I am astonished at the little details I have already forgotten.

Yet I hang back, on a middle stair. Mother sees me and gasps with happiness, coming to the bottom of the stairs to coo at me. I just stare. I realize that I don't want to approach her right now. She abandoned me. It wasn't right, and it wasn't fair. I am disappointed at how quickly I have lost all of my resolve to make her want to stay. Instead, I want to punish her. When she takes a step toward me, I get to my feet to make it clear that I will run away if she pursues me. I know she will have strange scents on her, and I can't deal with that yet.

Mother pouts, but that's the way it is.

And then I notice for the first time that she has no suitcase with her. Mother is wearing new clothes and has not brought back her old clothes.

On top of that—and I am so surprised about this, but—there is a man with her. It is Robert, and I know him. He is a good friend of Mother's, an old friend. He works with plants. Through the window I have seen his truck driving by, pulling a trailer with equipment on it. Not many homes on this street have grass because it is rocky and the woods are dense. But people need bushes trimmed back, and flowers planted, and that is what he does in this neighborhood. Father shakes Robert's hand as if he was expecting him and does not look upset.

But I wasn't expecting it, and I find it strange. I feel the fur on my back start to stand on end. Something is not right.

Robert stands next to Mother like he belongs here. Robert has kind brown eyes. Sometimes he wears glasses, sometimes not. He is a little like Father in that he is usually soft spoken and he is a good listener. And Mother has always looked at him fondly.

He is different from Father in that he has short dark hair and his skin is always tan from working outside. He is more wiry than Father, yet looks strong enough.

Father does our yard work himself. But Robert has stopped by many times over the years. Mother usually gave him water, and sometimes he did a small job that she requested, and he refused to take money for it. He came by a few times to visit the baby, and Mother always appreciated his gifts and his advice.

I always thought he was a sweet person.

But now, when he squeezes Mother's hand as he says good-bye to her, my stomach drops.

Because suddenly I understand something I didn't before.

Jimmy and Mary go out with Robert, leaving Finn with Mother and Father. They promise to be back later, when they will all open gifts.

Father and Mother go to the couch to talk, which they do for a long while. I sneak down and watch from under the rocking chair. Finn has fallen asleep in his car seat, so they leave him there on the floor by their feet. Mother can't stop admiring the baby.

"Look at you," Mother gushes, turning to Father. She rubs Father's arm vigorously until he finally smiles at her. She remarks on the fact that he shaved, and touches his face gently. She says it reminds her of when they first met. She asks if he remembers when they first started dating.

I wonder now if Father knew that shaving would have this effect on her, if he guessed that it would remind her of those first years they were together. He looks at her as if he can't possibly get enough of her. But then I can tell from the sudden sadness in his face that he realizes that he doesn't actually want to hear those stories.

We have all heard the story of how they met a million times.

We've all heard the story of how she never knew

Tommy in high school, even though it is a very small town. Mother moved here right before senior year thanks to her father's new job, and Tommy had already graduated a year or two before.

But then they worked together that summer in the kitchen at the beach club. She'd had her eye on him for weeks, but Tommy never asked her out. He smiled at her, and he seemed to think she was very funny. He laughed at her stories, but he never made a move. All summer long.

Mother knew that Tommy met Sean and some other guys after work most nights, and they'd walk down to the rocks on the beach to drink beer and whatever they'd stolen from their parents' liquor cabinets. Mother dropped hints that she'd like to go, but they never invited her.

At this point in the story, if my siblings are listening, Mother pauses to remind them: *Your father was never good with new people.*

And she adds: *Nobody in this town is good with new people.*

So one night she was in the doorway to the kitchen at the beach club and she noticed some of the boys helping the chef with food prep. They were goofing around, singing and dancing to an old Rolling Stones song on the radio. Mother saw Tommy, and she was transfixed, watching him move, nodding his head, and that was it for her.

You wouldn't know it, but Father is in fact a good dancer. He has more rhythm than the others do, although Mary is right behind him with some very graceful moves.

The way Mother tells it, by mid-August things were slow at the beach club. There weren't many members around and they had a string of overcast days. So she invited Tommy to go for a walk around the club, and he said okay. They walked around the perimeter of the pool, and she ended up pulling him into the girls locker room, right into the first stall, shutting the door behind her.

Mother always was a little impulsive.

This is the way she tells the story to my siblings: She told Father she had her bathing suit on under her waitress uniform, so he suggested they go for a swim. And that's what they did, sneaking out to jump in the ocean.

This is the way she tells the story to Sean: She told Father she had her bathing suit on under her waitress uniform, and he put his hands on his hips and told her to *prove it*. And he was such a cocky asshole that she whipped her dress off immediately, which completely astonished him.

Here, Mother pauses to show how his mouth hung partway open, his eyebrow arched.

When she kissed him, he tasted like Orange Crush soda. And she really expected someone as cute as Tommy Sullivan to know how to work a bikini, but he was useless with it. The strings behind her neck somehow ended up in tight knots that he couldn't get undone without her help.

And then she laughs, and says to Sean, *He was so cute but not so bright, you know?*

I know Father whispered *I love you* before they ever left that stall, while she was sitting on his lap, which is where he always puts her when he is listening very closely to her.

And I know that she ignored what he said because she thought he was *perfectly ridiculous* and *hilarious*.

It wasn't until months later that she fully realized how wrong she was. Father might have been acting *ridiculous* but he was never *hilarious*.

He is in fact dead serious about most everything and can't tell a joke to save his life.

I've heard that story many times.

I once heard Father recall the end to that story when he was talking privately with Mother, which is that they ended up back down in the changing room stall, and Mother back on his lap, every day until the end of the summer. At which point the manager said, Thank God the season is over, or I'd have to fire you two, the way things are going.

But now, Father isn't in the mood to hear this story.

He steers her off the topic and talks about the kids instead.

Father tells her that they all need her to come home, and she shakes her head. Finn stirs, so Mother takes him out of the car seat. She smiles at the baby while she keeps rubbing Father's arm, but she still insists it won't work. She reminds him that she "wasn't happy."

Wasn't happy?

Weren't we very, very happy? My ears pin back in frustration.

Frankly, I don't care anymore that she "wasn't happy." We need her home. Don't we?

"But your medication is working now," Father argues, as if this was the only problem.

Mother has sharp words for him, reminding him of many, many things. She explains that when she says she wasn't happy, she is not just talking about being depressed. I see the hope drain from Father's face, leaving it very pale. When he keeps asking her questions and he is on the verge of tears, Mother just gets embarrassed for him and moves farther away from him on the couch.

She cuddles Finn and asks if he wants her to take the baby for a while, to make it easier on him.

"Whatever you want," he insists.

In the end they agree that Finn belongs here, in this big house, with his siblings and Mahmee and the pets. Mother knows it has been hard on Father, and she apologizes over and over.

"It's better for Finn to be here," she says finally. "Safer. More secure. More people watching him."

He can't argue with that. And I know Father wants this baby. Back before she got pregnant, he asked her for this baby so many times I lost count. I remember it well.

I wonder if the reason Father wanted the baby is that he noticed Mother loves to talk about Jimmy and Mary when they were very young. She enjoys telling stories about her babies, who are now almost adults. I think Father may have hoped that a baby would make Mother cheerful again.

Most of the time Father asked Mother about having another baby in the bedroom, speaking softly to her, where no one else could hear other than me. But Mary once heard Father suggest it, and she made a funny face. As if he was talking nonsense. Jimmy and Mary probably never expected Mother to really get pregnant. Neither did I.

I wonder how Father achieved it. He does not seem capable of tricking Mother into doing what she does not want to do. I think it is possible that he was simply very persuasive when he was whispering and stroking her hair and unbuttoning her pajamas, and Mother let her guard down just long enough to agree to it.

Mother hands Finn to Father. Father rests the baby on his shoulder and pats the baby's head. When he lifts his eyes to gaze at Mother again, she has turned away.

She leans down and wiggles her fingers, trying to

coax me to come over to her. Her cooing is sweet in my ears. But I won't do it.

Three things are so obvious that it hurts.

First: Father and I love Mother so much.

Second: Until this moment, he and I believed there was a chance she was going to announce today that she was coming home for good.

And the third I think you have already figured out.

12

Door Darter

I have never been a "door darter." That is what Mother used to call Jasper when he'd see something outside and try to scoot out the door, between her legs or under her feet.

My entire world is in this old house. Why would I want to go outside, where it is too cold or too hot and the air is overwhelming with scent? Inside, I have my water bowl, my scratching post, and lots of comfy sitting places. I can run up the steep stairs and sit on the landing, looking down to watch the humans. I can prowl under the stairs, chasing after a loose paper clip. Once in a while, I even go down to the damp basement to slink around on the cold cement.

But now, all I can think of is what I might be missing. I have this strange urge to run out the door. To see what's out there in the world.

I know I have thought a lot about going out to find Mother, and now I do not need to. I know where she is.

She is with Robert, and she is safe. But this information doesn't comfort me like I hoped it would.

Usually at this time of year, we have a warm kitchen where lots of baking is going on, creating sweet and savory smells. There are bright balls on the pine tree and crumpled paper to dive into.

This year, the house is quiet and still. It does not feel right.

I wonder if I should run away, just like Mother did. Away from this whole family. I can't help but think it is their fault she left. They didn't take care of her. They demanded too much of her. I still love my family, but the humans remind me of our staggering failure to keep Mother here. And I want to punish them somehow.

One night Father tells Jimmy and Mary that they have to go out with the baby. I think he insists they go somewhere special, because they get dressed up in fancy clothing, although my brother and sister drag their feet and complain about it. It feels more like they are in mourning than celebrating.

The next day, Mahmee comes over bright and early with coffee cake and muffins, and several loads of gifts. Good, sweet Mahmee.

Father sits on the couch and watches most of the morning, the baby in his arms. He will not put that baby down. He will not eat and he will not open a gift. He keeps repeating that it is Finn's first Christmas and it almost brings him to tears a few times.

Mary senses his distress and at one point asks to hold Finn and has Father take a few photos of her and the baby together. She puts wrapping paper around the baby's shoulders as if it were a cloak, and a bow on his head. Then she poses with her cheek up against Finn's cheek.

Finn's face looks more like Mary's face as he gets older. He has blond hair to match Mary's hair, and it is the same silky texture. Their cheeks flush the same shade of pink. They are clearly related.

Mahmee watches her son. I can see that Father is suffering. I think Mahmee is going to offer to hold the baby next, but she does not. I believe something about clinging on to Finn is bringing Father comfort, and maybe she sees that too.

I watch the steam rise from Mahmee's mug as she pours herself another cup of coffee. She gets through the day by making fresh pot after fresh pot.

Mary helps her set out a lunch. Mahmee brought a chicken to roast, along with some of those other plants that humans eat. Cooked plants don't interest me at all. It baffles me that humans like to eat such things. They eat at the kitchen table like it's any other meal, and not anything special. Jasper and I get a little chicken in our bowls when they are done.

After lunch, Jimmy surprises us with gifts. First, Jasper is presented with a giant bone, bigger than his head. He can barely pick it up, never mind get his jaw around it to gnaw on. I am given a little furry ball that perhaps represents a small mammal. It smells sharp and zesty, and makes me a little crazed. I bat the toy around, then grab and chew on it, kicking it with my powerful hind legs until it rips open, sending shreds of herbs all over the floor. My legs run a mile a minute as I zip around from room to room while Mary cleans it up. I must admit, it's all very exciting. My little heart beats hard until I calm down.

Finally, it is time for Mahmee to go home. She and Father sit in a corner of the living room, and Mahmee has a thick book open in her lap. Their heads bow over the book. Father puts a hand over his eyes and holds it there while Mahmee talks. He walks her to the door and hugs her good-bye. The children run over and thank her for everything.

Jimmy finds an old black-and-white movie on the TV and relaxes on the couch with Mary. The dirty dishes still sit on the kitchen table, so I jump up while no one is looking to lick a few plates.

Mother never let dishes sit out like this. She enjoyed cleaning, and took pride in a tidy house. Standards have dropped dramatically around here.

I feel like they may never recover.

Later, when Father goes out the back door to fetch some firewood, and leaves the door cracked open, I sit on my haunches and look into the darkness. Maybe. Maybe I'll go. Maybe I'll dart. It just washes over me, this strange impulse, this desire to run.

Tentatively, I stand up. I glance back over my shoulder, at the golden glow that bathes the entire kitchen. And then, moving forward, I dash out.

I glide silently over smooth stones and frozen dirt. Afraid, I jump behind a bush. It is very dark, but my eyes slowly start to adjust. I see a shape moving near a large pile of wood, and I see it is Father.

He tromps past me, his arms full of wood, boots crunching in the deep snow. The door swings shut as he enters the house again, and then it gets very quiet.

The first thing I notice, once I am alone, is that my mouth and eyes sting with cold. The rest of me feels okay, though, padded with fat and fur. Then I realize that the earth under my paws is damp, and icy. But it doesn't hurt, as I expected. It just feels odd.

Our backyard is woods, so there are very tall trees and large spaces under the canopy where not much grows other than weeds and brambles. A variety of granite rocks, some as small as a loaf of bread but others as big as a kitchen table, are scattered between the trees. I would like to climb those rocks one day.

Or, maybe not.

You see, huge, vicious turkeys roam around here. Tall deer with tremendous antlers. And other odd monsters that are unfamiliar to me. Sometimes I look out the back sliding glass door that leads into the dining room, and I freeze, seeing a pair of marble eyes peering in at me. Gathering my courage, I stare back. I hiss and attack the door with my paws, as fierce as I can, ready to defend my home.

But I've never had to meet any type of wild creature face-to-face. I'm not sure if I would fight or flee. I don't know what I am supposed to do, or how strong my claws are compared to those of other animals.

I wonder where Mother is. I wonder if she is sitting with Robert at this very moment. I do not know if Robert has his own children, or nearby relatives, or if he celebrates this holiday like we do. I hope Mother is surrounded by people on this day, but there is no way to know. My heart sinks a little.

I am angry at Mother. But also, today in particular, I just miss her.

For a moment, I wonder if I could find her. If I could somehow sniff out her scent. But I have been an indoor cat for so long, I don't think I have those skills. Or if I did at one time, I don't think I do anymore. It's disheartening.

I take in a deep breath. The cold sears my lungs. No, no scent of Mother. I smell only the smoke coming from the chimney and the sharp, crisp dampness of the snow. And I can smell Father. Yes, he was out here with me.

And now he's not. I am alone.

Have they even noticed I am gone? How long will it take before someone looks around and realizes I am missing?

I am feeling sorry for myself. But I cannot help it.

I sit, watch, and listen. It is still and peaceful. Yet I don't dare move from behind my bush.

Time goes by. It might be minutes, or it might be an hour. Time for me is fluid, often measured by the movements of the sun and the grumbling of my hungry stomach.

Finally, the door swings open. I see Mary stick her head out and tentatively call my name. "Boo? You there, Boo?" She looks confused. I have never gone outside before. I'm sure she thinks this can't be right. She withdraws.

Through the trees, I can see little sparks of light in the black sky. I wonder how far away they are.

Now Mary comes back outside, and this time she has on a warm hat, and coat, and mittens, and boots. She slowly treads through the snow, looking right and left. "Here, kitty." She makes kissy noises. "Sweetie. Hey, sweetie." She makes her voice soft and kind. I can see the warmth of her breath hanging as a mist in the frozen air. "Hey, baby."

Now she starts walking away from me, out toward the trees. I watch her, and feel unable to move. I can't go out there. It's dark and scary, and I would feel exposed. I'm sure a creature would attack me immediately. But I worry. I don't want anything horrible to happen to Mary.

Jimmy trudges out, pulling his wool jacket tighter around him, and then he decides to zip up. He takes gloves out of his pockets and slips them on.

Father is last, and he has the baby all bundled up. I watch him through the needles of the bush that conceals me. I am grateful and pleased that the entire family is out here. I can't believe Father took the time to get Finn dressed and bring him out here.

I realize Father is the one I've really been waiting for.

"It's a beautiful night, isn't it?" Jimmy tips his head back and stares up at the sky, blinking against the cold.

Father glances at Jimmy and then follows his gaze up to the twinkling stars. "Yeah," he agrees. "It really is."

Finn looks content. Father knows how to hold the baby tight against his shoulder. I think Father is really getting good with that baby.

I meow, as loud as I can manage. They all spin around. Only Father turns his head in the right direction, toward where I lie under the bush. Maybe this is because he is used to listening for creatures when he puts out fires. Or maybe it is just because he is a father and his instincts are sharper than the others when he hears a living thing in distress.

"Shhhh," he tells the others, and they freeze.

"Boo?" He takes a step toward me. "Hi, Boo. C'mon. Come out. It's okay. Come on. You must be cold. It's okay."

I think it's safe to emerge, now that my human family is all around. No wild animal would dare come into our yard right now. The voices and movement of the humans would frighten them. I slowly slink out from under the bush. In the shadows, they don't see me right away.

"Oh, there you are!" Mary is very excited. "Boo! Why are you—?"

"Wait." Father turns to Mary. "Don't scare her off."

He looks at me again. "C'mon, Boo. It's cold out here."

I take a step closer to them. While my eyesight is good in the dark, there is nothing about this scene that is familiar to me. The humans look like strange shapes to me, all bundled up and profiled against the deep, snowy woods. Father is right; I worry I may jump back involuntarily just from fear of getting stepped on. I have no sense of how close or far away people are against the white snow.

I meow. *Take me inside,* I want to say. I think it is as simple as walking back in the door, but I'm disoriented and not sure.

"Mary. Mare. Just crouch down and move up to her slowly." Father nods at her to go ahead.

Mary gets right down on her knees in the snow. "C'mon, Boo. Let's go. Nice treats are inside! Yummy yum yum for Fatty Fat Cat."

I walk up to her. The snow feels delicate under my paws. Mary runs a hand over my back. The next thing I know, I am being picked up. I am like jelly in her arms, melting into her chest. She carries me swiftly inside while Jimmy holds the door open. We swoosh into the bright kitchen, and I close my eyes tightly for a moment because I'm temporarily blinded. Mary sits right down in a kitchen chair, keeping me on her warm lap. She snuggles her face into mine.

"Your nose is cold. You bad thing. Bad, bad kitty. Don't go out like that again." She turns her head to look up at Jimmy and Father. "She's never done that before. Isn't that strange?"

Jimmy scratches his head. He says something in response, but I am not listening closely. I am just happy to be on Mary's lap. I start to purr. They all pet my head.

Mary doesn't need to worry. I won't be going out again. I'm not sure why I ran out in the first place. We have not been ourselves lately, none of us.

I wonder if we will ever be ourselves again.

Or maybe we will change into something else. Something better. I hope.

13

Mary's Request

It is a few nights after the big holiday, and it has been snowing for hours. Someone left the back porch light on, and from the kitchen window I watch the snowflakes drift. Millions of them. It is very magical. I wish Mother were here to watch with me.

I am still a little stunned that Mother was here at all. I'm angry at myself for not letting her pet me. I miss her gentle caress, the way she was so careful around my whiskers. I feel like nothing in my life will be the same again. I wonder if she will at some point decide to come get me.

And, if that happens, I wonder if I will still want to go with her.

Mother and I were best friends. We spent all of our time together. I was as close to her as an animal could possibly be to a human. And yet . . .

The thought of leaving Father causes an unexpected pain in my heart. I know now that he cares for me. That changes everything. We share the same heartbreak and bring some comfort to each other.

It would be hard to leave this house, the only place I've ever known. And I hate the thought of leaving Father here, as lonely as he is.

I catch the sound of padded footsteps in my big ears. Someone is walking around upstairs. I leave the view and run up to investigate.

Father is sitting in bed, reading a book. The lamp by his side throws a golden glow over him in the dark room. It is very, very late.

He is still reading his books every night. Sometimes he holds his cross, says a few words, and puts it down.

Other nights he pulls the letter that Mother wrote to him out of where it is pressed between the pages of one of his big, thick books. He lies on his stomach and reads it over and over. I believe that he is not supposed to call her, and this letter is all he has. Still, it does not seem healthy that he reads it so often. Sometimes I climb right up on his back, and he lets me. I sit there like a big loaf of bread right out of the oven, warming him.

I wonder if the letter is short and to the point, or rambling and incoherent.

I wonder if the letter is kind, or cruel.

There is no way for me to know.

Tonight, when I walk in, I see that Father is reading a book that I think has something to do with toddlers, because there are pictures of little children on the cover. Mary stands by the bed, holding a big, fluffy stuffed creature. She asks if she can get in. Father says okay.

Mary pulls back the big comforter and climbs in. Father puts his book down, turns out the light so she can try to sleep, and lies back. He puts his hands under his head.

Mary is a big girl, taller than Mother now. She takes up a lot of room in the bed.

What she doesn't know is that Father has something tucked under his pillow. Earlier he was looking through the closet, which is still full of Mother's summer clothes. I know Mother has other important things to do right now. She has not come to get her things. Father has to look at her clothes every day. He absentmindedly ran his hands over the flimsy sundresses and thin shirts. Finally his hand caught hold of a soft, lightweight sweatshirt. He pulled it out and looked at it for a moment, and now it is under his pillow.

Just for safekeeping, I guess.

I jump up on the bed to join them. I love hunkering down between two humans. It's extremely warm and cozy.

Mary's head rests on Mother's pillow and she stares at the ceiling, even though she's in total darkness. It is easy for me to make out their words because they talk slowly and sleepily, with long pauses in-between. There is no wind to rattle the house tonight. It always feels warmer when it's snowing out, as if we are co-cooned in here.

"Daddy?"

"Yes?"

"Is Ma with Robert now? Like, really with him?"

He sighs. "I guess."

"Why . . ." She is very tired. "Why didn't you and Jimmy tell me sooner?"

There is a silence as he thinks about it. "Because. We weren't sure if it would last. If it was serious."

I also think: *Father and Jimmy hoped it wouldn't last.* But maybe they were kidding themselves.

Mary's eyes flutter. She is fighting off sleep. "Robert is nice. I guess."

"Yeah." Father is also staring at the ceiling. "I guess."

I wish I knew more about Robert. I did always think he was very kind to Mother. He does not seem like the type of human who would kidnap her and hold her against her will.

So how did I not see what was going on?

I was Mother's best friend, after all. I should've known about this.

"You didn't seem mad at him. You didn't beat him up or anything."

Father chuckles. "No, baby." He scratches his ear. "Like you said, he's nice. He's nice to your mom. He's taking care of her. She needs someone to look after her. I probably wasn't the best person for that."

Mary frowns. "Daddy?"

"Yes?"

"I don't get it."

"I don't either."

A few minutes go by.

"Daddy, you know who else is nice?"

He pauses, drifting in and out of consciousness. "No. Who?"

I see her head turn a bit toward her dad. "Charlotte."

Father turns away from her and faces the wall, shifting his weight.

Mary turns onto her side to face Father, talking to his back. "Did you hear me?"

"Yeah. She's nice. I guess."

Mary puts one hand under her head. "Yeah, Daddy, she is. She's nice and smart and pretty."

There is a long pause. "If you say so."

"I do." A little smile flickers over her face. "She's good with Finn. You know, you don't have to wear the same flannel shirt every time she comes over here. It's a little embarrassing. She dresses up to come here."

I see Father's head pick up and he turns a bit toward her, puzzled. "What?"

"Daddy, come on." She gives her stuffed creature a squeeze.

"What?"

"You know, you have some nice shirts. If you'd just wear them."

He puts his head back down. I know he is thinking about what she is saying.

"I mean," Mary continues, "you could make a little effort. To look nice."

"I don't look nice?"

"Yeah, you do, Daddy. But I'm just saying . . ." Mary squints and thinks about how to put it. "I'm saying it would be okay to make an effort. That I would be proud of you."

"Oh, you would, huh?"

"Yeah." Mary snuggles down deeper under the comforter. "I'm just saying it would be okay."

"Okay, thanks. I guess."

They are both quiet a long time. The snow continues to fall.

"Why did you change your mind? I thought . . ."

"Ohhhh," Mary says in a breathy voice, "I don't know. Jimmy was right. Charlotte's okay. She's got nothing to do with Ma."

"Jimmy said that?"

"Yeah." Mary sighs, in the same way Father does. I hear the furnace cycling on downstairs. This old house leaks heat, and the furnace is always trying to catch up. A minute goes by. My whiskers can sense the slight flow of warmer air starting to circulate in the room.

"I can't sleep, Daddy." I can hear it in Mary's trembling voice: She is fighting off tears now.

"I can't either." Father scratches his ear again, and flips over to face her. "I haven't slept in months. Between Finn waking up, and my head racing . . . or my heart beating too fast . . . it's like I'm really anxious, but I don't know what about. I'm not sure how to fix that."

"I know, me too. That's how I feel too. And Jimmy, he's snoring the minute his head hits the pillow. It's *so* unfair." She sniffles. "Maybe you need a sleeping pill. You could ask the doctor."

"No, Mare. No pills."

Mary wipes her nose. "Okay. If you say so." She's pouting now. "When are you guys going to make a schedule?"

Father thinks about this. "A schedule? What kind of schedule?"

"You know . . ." Mary's hand flutters in the air between them as she tries to explain it. "You know . . . For us. For me and Jimmy and Finn. To see Ma. On the weekends or something. Doesn't she want to see us on the weekends?"

"Oh. Um . . . yeah, sweetheart. Of course she does. It's just that I haven't had a chance to talk to her about that yet. We both want to make sure that everything is settled before we start that. We both just want what's best for you guys."

Even in the darkness, I can see that Mary is biting her lower lip. I'm not sure she believes him.

"Daddy?"

"Yeah?"

"Do you think that maybe once her medication gets really, really straightened out, and she feels really, really better, that she's going to realize she wants to come back?"

Father shifts onto his back, and then away from Mary again. "No. She's already better. Also, she wrote me a letter."

"What?"

"No, sweetheart. I said no. It's not just her medication. It's everything. She wrote me a letter and told me . . . She told me that, uh, you know, all the ways I messed up. That she's done here." Father puts a hand up over his eyes.

Even in the dark, he must hide. I can see it was a mistake mentioning the letter. It's all still too raw in his heart. He cannot let Mary see how much he suffers.

"You didn't mess up." Mary fiddles with one of the buttons on her pajama top. "C'mon, Daddy, it was—"

"No, sweetheart, I did. I did."

Mary gives up on her questions. She senses something is wrong. She's in over her head.

I know there is something Father needs to apologize to Mother for. There is something he hasn't had the opportunity to say. But I haven't seen him do anything wrong. They had many ordinary fights about ordinary things, but there's something else I'm missing.

Mary knows where I am, nestled between her and Father, and her hand finds me without having to even look. Her strokes are kind and gentle, and my purring revs up. I can't help it.

"Boo," she whispers to me. "Good girl. You're my best girl. My favorite girl. We girls have to stick together."

Oh! I never thought of that before. Without me, Mary would have no other female companionship. Perhaps she needs me a little more than I realized.

We hear the clicky tick-tick of Jasper's nails on the hardwood floor. He has just realized Mary is missing from bed, and he has come looking for her. Mary tells Father she's going back to her room and leans over to kiss him good night and say "I love you" before dragging her large stuffed animal out with her. Jasper trots behind, on her heels.

I hope my purring will help Father sleep. And it seems to. He drifts off, his breathing slow and heavy.

I am still up half the night though. I wish I were large enough to guard the humans in this big house against the creatures outside. I want to help them— Father, Jimmy, Mary. Even the stupid baby. He is smaller and weaker than everyone else, like me, and he needs extra help.

I have made up my mind: I will not run away again. And if Mother comes back for me and wants to take me with her, I will not go. No matter what. I want to stay.

I have become something more than Mother's personal companion. I am a member of this family, and I have responsibilities here. We all have faults, we all have weaknesses, and we all have insecurities. These humans are not perfect, and neither am I. But together we each get a little bit stronger.

Together, we can figure out a way forward.

14

Corned Beef and Cabbage

When I enter the kitchen, Jimmy is eating his way through a giant bag of pretzels. I don't know where it all goes, the great mounds of food that he eats. When I eat well, my belly expands. But I don't think Jimmy has an ounce of fat on him. He does not have muscles like Father, and he is softer looking. Yet he holds no extra padding either.

When the bag of pretzels is empty, Jimmy hunts around the kitchen, opening cabinet doors, searching for something. He finally pulls a large frying pan out from under the sink and sets it on the stove. After finding a stick of butter in the refrigerator, he cuts off a glob and melts it until I hear a sizzle. Finally, he pulls a large, yellow box out from a low shelf and pours little, lightweight O's into the pan. He turns them over with a spatula. My mouth waters when I smell the butter browning.

Mary enters and stands over the pan, taking in a deep breath. "Ahhhh," she breathes out, enjoying it like I am.

Jimmy promises he will split the food with her, and she seems content. But when they finally sit at the table, each with their own bowl, Mary looks around the kitchen with disgust. I see her looking at the dirty dishes. I know she is thinking the same thing I am, that Mother kept this house extremely clean. And now it is always a mess.

Mary picks through her bowl, selecting the perfect O with two fingers and placing it between her lips.

I think Mary eats like a bird more than a human sometimes.

They eat in silence for a minute. "Where's Dad?" Mary asks.

Jimmy explains that he's upstairs with Finn.

Mary nods and reaches up to adjust her hairband, which is starting to slide forward on her head. Mary's hair is silky and slippery. Sometimes I'll sit behind her on the couch and gnaw on a golden strand, if I can catch it in my paw.

"Remember when Ma used to make popcorn in that frying pan?" Mary asks out of the blue.

Jimmy says he does. He talks about the time there was popcorn all over the floor. The popcorn exploded, and Mother shouted in surprise, trying to cover the popcorn with foil. Jimmy gets excited as he recounts this story, and Mary starts to smile.

I remember that day, chasing the popcorn all around the corners of the kitchen floor. We had fun, fun, fun.

I listen extra-carefully, my ears twitching, because I want to hear these memories of Mother. I miss her so.

Many times in the past when the teenagers talked to each other, I had no interest. But now I feel closer to them, and I strain to learn what I can. It is important to me that I understand.

Mary tells stories about all of the wonderful food

Mother used to cook. I start to purr, and I feel my eyes closing in satisfaction as I lie on the kitchen floor listening to the happy tone in her voice.

Jimmy tells her he remembers. He begs Mary to stop because she's making him hungry.

Mary looks at her brother. "Wait—is that your dinner? Pretzels and fried cereal?"

Clutching his bowl with both hands, Mary and I both notice at the same time that Jimmy's eyes are red. To me, he looks very weary for someone so young.

"Remember . . . remember when Ma made you that banana cream pie for your birthday when you turned twelve?"

Now Jimmy nods, and laughs.

Mary tells a story about how Mother took her out for hours and hours shopping for Jimmy's birthday. Jimmy sits with a grin, listening. He is usually the one who tells the stories around here, and I think he enjoys hearing Mary talk for a change.

Jimmy remembers aloud that Father didn't know where Mother had gone with Mary, and he was very angry. I don't remember this at all. I must have been very little then. My kitten days are all a bit fuzzy.

"It was worth it though," Jimmy says. "I loved walking in and seeing the pie with all the banana slices on top . . ."

"And the yellow tablecloth. And yellow balloons attached to your chair."

"Everything yellow, God help her. If there's one thing you can say about Ma, it's that she's organized."

"Super organized." Mary eats another O, and then two more, and then a handful, her appetite increasing as she talks. "And coordinated. And driven. A perfectionist."

"The kitchen was clean," Jimmy admits with a shrug.

"We had good food."

"Remember when she made that corned beef and cabbage last Saint Patrick's Day? With the mustard and cinnamon in it?"

"Oh my God," Mary says, "Pops was so happy. He went on and on about how good it was."

"Me too. I had three helpings. And then one more around midnight." Jimmy's mouth curls into a twisted smile. "Dad was upset there were no leftovers the next day, because I ate them."

"He loved her cooking. He . . ." Mary hesitates. "He loves her so much," she whispers. "Poor Dad. Ugh."

"Don't—don't even go there, Mare. I don't want to talk about it."

"Sorry."

I walk over and brush my face against Mary's leg. She picks me up and plops me in her lap. I continue purring, as loud as I can. I like the way her jeans feel under my paws, rough and warm. "Good Boo. Sweet Boo."

I am surprised when Mary starts talking about the day they picked me out at the animal shelter. I've heard them talk about this before. I don't remember much about my life before the day they came to take me home. Now, Mary says that Mother wanted to take my two sisters home too.

I am shocked. Two sisters? It occurs to me for the first time that I might have had another kind of family before I found my humans. I wonder where my cat sisters are now. And do I have a cat mother? It's all very hard to imagine.

"Pops would *not* have liked that." Mary smiles, remembering. "Good thing we talked her out of it. She is such an animal lover. I think she liked animals more than people sometimes."

That's what I thought! I blink up at Mary in agreement.

Jimmy just smiles. He takes an O and rolls it between his fingers before smashing it and letting the crumbs fall back into his bowl.

"What kind of cake do you think she'll make for Finn, on his first birthday?"

". . . What?" Jimmy asks, as if coming out of a trance.

"His birthday. Finn's first birthday, next July." There is a scratching sound as Mary swirls the dry cereal pieces around in the bowl with her fingers. "Do you remember that Batman cake she made you one year? A blue cake with blue frosting. And the Bat-Signal on top. I remember the blue and black balloons, and the sparklers we had out in the backyard."

"Sure." Jimmy grins. "That was a good one. I loved that."

"But who's going to make Finn a cake?" I feel Mary squeeze my middle, her fingers sliding through my silky fur. "Who's going to throw *his* party? Finn is going to need a cake."

Jimmy reaches to the napkin holder but finds it empty. He looks around for a moment before finally getting up, washing his hands at the sink with the dish soap, and reaching into the cabinet below for a paper towel to dry his hands. He looks at his little sister. "I'll tell ya what, Mare. Let's agree that just in case Ma doesn't bring a cake over, we'll go to the bakery downtown."

Now I feel Mary's hands petting me heavily, from

head to tail. It feels really good. But I can tell, from the way she firmly runs her hands down my back, that she is distressed. Mary shakes her head. "A cake from a bakery wouldn't be the same."

Jimmy tells her it would be fine.

"No, it wouldn't." Mary is getting a whiny tone in her voice. I can feel the vibration as I press up against her stomach. "It's not fair. Finn deserves a cake. I'm going to be so mad at Ma if she doesn't bring one over here."

Jimmy leans on the counter behind him. He looks down at the floor, as if examining the tile.

"Get over it," he warns, an edge in his voice. "It's just a cake." Mary and I both look up, because we realize at the same time that Jimmy is getting angry. "For Dad's sake," he continues, "you've got to knock it off with that stuff. He's stressed out enough without you making it worse. Haven't you noticed he's a little tense? Do you want him to have a stroke?"

Mary starts talking fast, launching into a long list of complaints about Father. She talks about his bad moods, his sharp words, and his inability to keep the house tidy.

She's right, I must admit. But I don't like her tone.

Jimmy glares at her. He takes a deep breath.

Pivoting right around, so his back is to Mary, Jimmy turns on the water. He lets it run and sticks two fingers under the water periodically to test it. When steam starts to rise from the sink, he picks up a glass and rinses it in the water. Grabbing a bright green sponge, he squirts dish soap on it and wipes it around the outside of the glass, and then the inside.

"What are you doing?"

"What does it look like I'm doing?"

Mary watches Jimmy for a minute. Then she lifts

me up and kisses me on the face, mushing her face right into my whiskers. She wipes her cheek on mine, knowing that this is how I put my scent on humans.

Mary is an observant girl. She's smart, like Mother.

"I'll dry," Mary offers, putting me on the floor as she gets up and grabs a towel.

"You don't have to."

"No, I will. It's okay." She takes the glass that Jimmy hands her, runs the rough towel over the glass, and puts it away. They work for a few minutes in silence.

Jimmy hands her the last plate, and Mary stacks it away in the cabinet. She wraps her hands up in the gray towel, looking defeated. Pulling her arms up to cross them over her chest, I notice the way she clutches the old towel way too tight. "Why did Dad want that baby so much? Why did he want it?"

"It doesn't matter, Mare." Jimmy sighs. "Maybe he thought it would fix things. Maybe he just wanted to feel normal, like maybe he thought he could start over. Try again. I don't know."

"Try again? Look at what she did to you. Look at all the shit he let her get away with. He wanted to put another kid through that?" Mary reaches out and grabs Jimmy's arm in a quick movement, right where the scar is, that big, crooked X. She knows exactly where the scar is.

Jimmy freezes, and the blood drains from his face. He looks down at her, wide-eyed, as if frightened for a moment. It's the same way Father sometimes pales in fear before Mary.

She is just a fourteen-year-old girl. But she is a strong, smart girl.

I see Mary flex her fingers, gripping her brother's arm tightly. As if she's afraid he'll move away.

For the first time, I wonder if that scar still hurts. I don't know much about how the human body heals.

I assume it hurt a lot the first time, when Mother made the Xs with a kitchen knife on Jimmy. I heard Father talk about it once, to Mary, when Mother was pregnant with Finn.

It happened years ago, when Jimmy was old enough to walk and talk but too young to stop his Mother. Father told Mary he wanted her to know what happened, in case Mother had similar ideas about the new baby.

Father told Mary that it was not punishment, that Mother was not angry with Jimmy when she did it. Rather, Mother was afraid that other humans were going to come into the house and take Jimmy away from her, and she wanted to know how to identify him again, her precious firstborn son. It was what Father called a "delusion," but I'm still not sure what that word means. He told Mary they could not blame Mother for what she did because she had been sick at the time.

I don't always understand everything that humans do. At the time Father explained it, I thought Mother's idea was a good one. An action taken out of love. And fear. And concern.

I heard Father tell Mary that he fixed Jimmy's cuts with soap and Band-Aids. He did not call the doctor, or anyone else. So maybe it wasn't so bad.

Or maybe he felt he needed to hide it from the world.

But now, looking at the way Jimmy's eyes are tearing up, I think perhaps Mother's actions weren't necessary. Maybe Mother hurt him more than I realized. Is it possible the scars still hurt to this day? Maybe Mother was wrong to do it.

Jimmy closes his eyes for a quick moment and

looks incredibly sad when he finally opens them. "No. No, Mare. She didn't mean to . . ." He stops, swallows, and then starts anew. "I think Pops had hope. Maybe he thought Finn would make Ma happy again and she'd stay, or he could be a better dad the third time around. I'm not going to fault him for that." Jimmy presses his lips together, and then takes in a deep breath, his shoulders relaxing as he breathes out again. "I'm glad we have Finn. But parents are idiots sometimes."

Mary agrees, nodding quickly, and lets go of his arm.

Mary is still wringing the dirty towel, and Jimmy now takes it from Mary's hands. It reminds me of when he recently took the scissors out of her hands. "I can help you make a cake. All we need is cake mix and a few ingredients, right? We'll read the box. We can do it."

Mary's face lights up with hope. "How about banana bread in the shape of a cake? Finn loves bananas, just like you. We could put cream cheese frosting and banana slices on top. Doesn't that sound good?"

Jimmy scratches his head. "Sure, Mare. That sounds great." Jimmy breaks into a crooked smile. "Maybe Aruna will help. I think we can even outdo Ma. If we put our minds to it."

When they leave the kitchen, it's very quiet. I listen to the grandfather clock chime in the dining room. I cannot follow my siblings. I feel heavy, like I can't heave myself up off the floor.

I feel terrible, like I have done something wrong. Felt something wrong.

If Mother was wrong to make the Xs on Jimmy, then maybe she was wrong the time I saw her hitting him too. Perhaps on that day when Mother was so angry, I could have meowed to distract her. I could have hissed, or knocked over a vase. I could have done something!

I miss my siblings, now that they have gone upstairs.

Later, Father and I will lie in bed and feel miserable together. We both have so much to think about.

He and I will remember. We will remember who we failed to protect. And we'll both remember what we've lost.

15

Tequila

Many weeks after the big holiday, when the pine tree has started to lose needles and Father has finally dragged it outside, Sean arrives one night looking a little more dressed up than usual. His flat cap sits at an extra-jaunty angle. He has on a new pair of boots. Mary and Jimmy let him in.

"Where are you guys going?" Mary asks, her arms folded. My siblings seem very curious about what is going on. They have already had supper, and it has been dark out for a few hours.

Sean says they are going to "Captain Dan's." I take it this must be the home of an important person in town, because Jimmy seems impressed.

"They serve fifty kinds of tequila," Sean says. "Let's be frank, kids. I'm taking your pops out to get him blasted. Because I think he needs it."

Mary looks skeptical, cocking an eyebrow. She tells Sean not to get Father sick.

"And after that," Sean continues, pointing at the two of them, "I'm taking him out to get a tattoo."

Jimmy's head jerks back and Mary blanches.

"I'm just kidding," Sean insists. "Jeeeeeez."

Jimmy challenges Sean, asking if he can really afford tequila.

"Nah, not really. But I'd do anything for your pops. We're all going."

Mary is suspicious. She asks, "Who's *we?* Who is going?"

Sean ignores her. "Captain Dan's is an institution," Sean says. "All a yiz will go there one day. Even Finn. He'll be popular with the ladies. You see that blond hair coming in on his little head? He'll be a *looka* like your pops."

I listen very carefully, now that they are discussing Finn. I want to know what is wrong with that baby.

Jimmy puts his hands on his hips. He asks Sean if what he's implying is that Finn is good-looking and he is not. "What am I, Sasquatch?"

"You already got a lady, Jimmy. You're off the market." Sean shakes his hands in front of him, as if to say, *Isn't that obvious?*

Jimmy rolls his eyes. He tells Sean he made a "good save." But, he persists, "In this hypothetical situation, where Finn is twenty-one years old and out at the tequila bar, don't you think Finn is going to have some, shall we say, *communication problems* when he talks to the ladies?"

Sean shakes his head. "That's what I'm saying. He'll be like your dad. You don't think your pops has some serious communication problems of his own?" He laughs. "But he did okay, landing your mom. It was just a matter of flashing those blue eyes." Sean opens his eyes wide and winks dramatically, to demonstrate.

Mary smacks Sean on the arm. She tells Sean, "It's not a joke. Finn's problems aren't a joke."

Sean shakes his head. "Mare, I ain't making a joke. That boy's going to be beating the ladies away with a hockey stick. You wait and see."

Father comes downstairs in a hurry and grabs his coat. It looks as if he wants to rush past the kids without having to answer too many questions. He sticks his feet in his boots and doesn't bother to stop and tie the laces. "Don't wait up," he says, giving Mary a kiss on the cheek. "If Finn needs anything, call me."

When they are gone, Mary immediately takes out her little phone and starts punching it with her thumbs. She is very important, and her friends need her advice on many things. She flops down on the living room couch. Mary twists her hair and piles it on top of her head in a bun, securing it there with two pencils, while waiting for her phone to jingle with new messages.

Jimmy sits next to her, watching a movie on the TV. He holds Finn in his arms.

My siblings seem a little apprehensive, glancing at each other once in a while. I think they trust Sean, so I'm not sure what the problem is.

Finn is subdued, chewing absentmindedly on a toy and drooling. Once in a while, Jimmy turns Finn around so he can make exaggerated faces at him, and Finn smiles. But when Mary says something, or Jimmy points at the TV, Finn has no interest and pays no attention.

Now that the baby is older, I think any day now I am going to figure out exactly what is wrong with him.

Jimmy makes some really funny faces at that baby.

Eventually it gets very late. Through the window I

see the full moon slowly rising in the sky. My siblings go upstairs, and I follow them.

I am lying on Mother's bed when I hear a truck engine. I decide to go downstairs to check on Father. I love to feel the cool breeze that swooshes in every time anyone opens the front door. It smells delicious, the smoke from wood fires combined with crisp ice and snow and bark and pine.

I pad down the wooden stairs as quietly as I can, but let's face it: I am too heavy to be silent. My full weight follows each paw on the way down. When I go down the stairs, it sounds like this: a hollow *boom boom boom boom boom boom boom boom.*

Father walks in red-faced and a little unsteady. I guess Sean dropped him off. I watch from the bottom stair. There is a woman with him, and I recognize her because she has been here a few times for parties and barbeques over the years. Her name is Jenny. She has wavy blond hair and a wide, pleasant face. She's shorter than Father and a little heavy, like me. Despite the cold, she is wearing a short black dress with just a light jacket thrown on top.

They both stand in the foyer, frozen, listening. It is dark and they don't turn the lights on. Mary is asleep upstairs, and Jimmy is in his room with the light on but the door closed.

They exhale. "Okay," Father says. He quietly takes off his coat and helps Jenny out of her jacket. He throws their coats on the stair railing, and they make their way to the living room.

I silently follow them. They don't even seem to see me.

Jenny has several demands as she sits on the couch. I watch Father go into the kitchen to first retrieve her a glass of water and then bring her a glass with ice. She pours the water from the first glass over the ice. Then she requests an aspirin. I'm exhausted just watching Father fetch these things, one after the other. They talk a little as he's doing these things, but they are whispering, so I don't catch what they're saying.

When he finally sits next to her on the couch, Jenny puts her water down on the coffee table. The table is so covered with newspapers and magazines and notebooks and homework that she has to push a few things aside to make room for her glass.

I jump up to sit on an armchair just opposite, for a better view.

Jenny inches toward Father and puts a hand on his knee. She bursts out in a loud whisper, "Tommy. I am *so sorry* to hear about Carrie."

I see he is caught off guard by her words. As am I.

Father just stares at her, his face suddenly sad. "I—" A reply catches in his throat. I realize he does not know what to say.

How could anyone from outside our family ever understand?

It would be impossible to explain.

Knowing Father, he probably hasn't tried to explain it to anyone. But I bet Sean has started to tell people that Mother has left. Sean is Father's friend, and he must want the best for him. He might feel it's better to get things out in the open.

As I've heard Mother say in the past, we live in a small town, and people like to talk. Perhaps Father is foolish if he thinks he can keep Mother's absence a secret. And the way Mother is, we all know she can't keep a secret, even if she wanted to.

Jenny scoots forward so that she is very close to Father, her face just inches away from his. She puts her hand on Father's chest and starts rubbing up and down. At first she rubs gently, and then more insistently. He is still red in the face, and his head is tipped as he studies her, impassive.

"You're *so cute*," Jenny gushes, her words slurring together. "I mean, seriously, Tommy. You are really, really cute. What is Carrie *thinking?*"

Father is confused, and frowns. Jenny is missing the point. I don't know how much Sean told her, but she must not have the whole story.

Could she? How could anyone?

Jenny stands up and smooths down her black dress. She offers Father her hand, which he takes as he stands also. "C'mon, Tommy. I'll make you feel better." She is smiling and seems very lovely, but then I see where she is leading him.

Father stops short at the foot of the stairs. Jenny takes two steps up, but Father doesn't follow. He just looks up the stairs, wary.

I know exactly what he's thinking, because I'm thinking the same thing: *That leads to Mother's bedroom.*

And this: *The kids are up there.*

And maybe also: *This wouldn't be the first time a woman got him into trouble by going too far too fast, and this is probably the wrong way to go about things.*

I run right over to Father.

Father is still wobbly on his feet, and he leans on the banister. He sees me standing right next to him.

He and I look at each other. For a good long minute.

"I don't think I . . . I don't think I can . . ." Father cannot get out the right words. "You know. I'm not quite . . . You know, Jen, I don't think I can. . . ."

Father has never been very good with words.

Father doesn't seem nervous that Jenny will be

angry, but I am. Sometimes humans surprise me with their anger. I feel my ears pull back in anticipation.

But Father obviously knows her better than I do, because she is not mad at all.

"Awwwwww, poor baby," she moans, as if this is the cutest thing she's ever heard. As if he's a little kitten that's turned up on her doorstep. She hurries down the two stairs to stand right in front of him, and she starts rubbing his chest again. Up and down. "Awwwwww."

The funny sound she is making causes Father to smile. For the first time tonight, I see a flicker of interest cross his face.

I think: *Really?* After all of the mating behavior she has displayed—leaning in, holding his knee, smiling wide, rubbing his chest, none of which he responded to—this strange noise that you would make to a kitten is what interests him?

I will never completely understand humans.

He doesn't push her away. In fact, he puts his hands on her arms and holds her elbows, which surprises me. His eyes glance down and take in her entire body before coming back up to meet her gaze again.

I think: *Good for you.* Because Father isn't much for reaching out.

Just the opposite. He usually has his arms crossed, as if he's sending the message: *Don't bother me.*

He studies her for a long moment. But he's already made up his mind. Jenny is not going to be his mate. At least, not tonight.

"Let me drive you home," he offers. And soon they're on the way back out. In my opinion, they're both too tired and off-kilter to drive the truck. But there they go.

When Father gets back, I am happy to have him safe in our bed and not out in the ice and snow in the middle of the night. We sleep well.

I dream wonderful thoughts about Mother. Of the days when she and I had the greatest bond a human and a cat could possibly experience.

I understand that Mother has a new mate now. I am still very angry with her, and I don't want Father to be lonely. At the same time, I am greatly relieved that Jenny has left the house. It somehow felt wrong to have Jenny here. And I don't want to share Father with anyone just now.

In the morning, I follow Father into Finn's room. Finn is crying, and Father brings him down to his high chair in the kitchen. Father makes coffee and takes aspirin. He puts ice in a baggie, which he then applies to his forehead as he sits down in a kitchen chair.

Jimmy walks in, sleepy eyed and hair askew. "Have fun last night?" he asks as he pours himself an orange juice.

"Yup," Father says, still holding the ice to his head.

"I heard a girl talking," Jimmy says as he sits down. Jimmy was never one for beating around the bush.

Father snorts. "Yeah. Jenny Fitzgerald. You know. From Borough Hall."

Jimmy says something to acknowledge that he does know her, as he sits in a chair across from Father. Again, he mentions that he heard her voice.

Father pauses. "She was here for, like, ten minutes. Tops."

Jimmy drums his fingertips on the kitchen table. He is dressed just like his dad, in a T-shirt that is too small and flannel, plaid pajama pants. "Ten minutes, huh?" He picks up his glass of juice and swirls it around. "Ten minutes seems like enough time to . . . you know . . ."

"*What?*" Father slams the bag of ice down on the table, harder than he meant to, and looks at Jimmy.

"I just didn't know if Sean was taking you out to get you drunk or get you *something else*." Jimmy gives him a knowing look.

Father stares at Jimmy. And then he laughs in disbelief. "Oh my God. I can't believe you just said that. Don't go there. Please. My head hurts."

"Well, Pops. I'm just saying."

"Uhhh, okay." Father thinks about it. He blinks hard as he tries to focus on the table. "Listen. I don't want you to think that going out to a bar and getting drunk is a good way to—"

"Pops. Don't worry about it." Jimmy gets back up to take a loaf of bread out of the cabinet. He insists that he was just kidding. That he doesn't need a lecture. He moves over to the old toaster and puts a slice of bread in the top. The toaster creates a burning smell when Jimmy presses down the button.

Everything in this kitchen is old, but it works.

Jimmy takes a jar of jam out of the refrigerator and sets it on the counter. The toast pops up and Jimmy turns, accidentally knocking the glass jar onto the floor. It lands with a sharp *smash!*

I am spooked, and I scamper safely back to the living room rug. Despite being fat, I am very agile when I need to be. When I turn, I see that Father has jumped up, quick as a cat, and Jimmy is frozen where he stands. They both have bare feet.

Father grabs Finn up out of his high chair and climbs on top of kitchen chairs to get him out of the room and away from the mess. Once Finn is safely upstairs in his crib, he and Jimmy put their sneakers on. They get a broom, paper towels, and the vacuum. It takes them a long while to clean up the bright red jam that has splashed everywhere, and I watch them.

But I'm thinking about Finn. I noticed something powerfully strange.

When that glass hit the floor, Finn didn't burst out crying with fear or surprise. He didn't even turn his head.

I suddenly realize I know something I did not before. That baby cannot hear anything.

Something in my heart flips over hard and fast, like the fish Jimmy used to bring home in his orange bucket.

It is so curious. I wonder how long a human whose ears do not work can survive. Perhaps Finn will be confined to our home, just like I am.

It must scare Father to death to realize that Finn would not be able to hear a predator sneaking up on him.

I remember how Father and Mother talked about Finn when she came to visit. Mother offered to take the baby for a while, and Father at first said okay, before they decided together that he should stay here. It hits me all at once that in the future, Mother might not just ask Father if she can take me with her—she might want the baby too. And that Father, in one of his dark moods, might think that it would be best if this happened, perhaps out of fear of being unable to care for us all.

But I want to help Father take care of Finn, to show him that we can do it together. Even if the baby cannot hear. I'll figure out a way.

16

Back in Black

I am lying on Jimmy's thick rug when he walks in, carrying Finn. Finn is all gurgles and bubbles, chewing on his knuckles.

Kneeling, Jimmy carefully places the baby right next to me. I roll closer to Finn so he will feel my soft fur. Jimmy crouches over the baby, smiling at him, and then winking at me.

Jimmy is wearing a soft, plaid, button-down shirt like the ones Father wears, with the sleeves rolled up. I suddenly realize that the shirt he is wearing actually *is* one of Father's shirts. It comes as a shock to me that they now wear the same size shirts. I think that in the past year Jimmy has settled into his body. He's no longer awkward or clumsy. His movements have become more assured and confident, his shoulders wider and his posture straight.

I still think of Jimmy as one of the children, but I see he has also become a young man.

Jimmy puts his hands over his eyes, and then quickly pulls his hands away, looking incredibly surprised to see Finn still lying there. The baby gasps and laughs, kicking his legs.

Jimmy plays this game over and over. I recognize it. Finn loves the repetition. The twentieth time, Finn laughs just as hard as the first time. The joke never gets old.

I get up and smell the baby, sniffing him all over. Sensing that I have inhaled baby powder into my nose, I shake and sneeze.

Jimmy lifts me up, laughing, and moves me a little farther away from Finn. Seeing his brother laugh, Finn laughs again too.

I wonder what it must be like in there, in the baby's mind, in all of the quiet. I do appreciate silence, but of course, silence is never really silence. There is the clock ticking, or water running in the pipes, or wind buffeting the house, or the panting of Jasper as he sits in the hallway. There are a hundred other little noises that make up silence.

Silence is different for that baby.

Jimmy reaches behind him, and I see there is something new on the floor in his room. I thought it was just a big black box, but now I see it has knobs that turn. It is very dusty. Perhaps Jimmy found it on one of those shelves in the basement, where Father keeps his old things.

Jimmy plugs a cord into the wall and fiddles with the buttons. I jump as loud music bursts forth.

Usually when he listens to music, Jimmy plays it from his very small, thin phone. This box is huge in comparison.

Jimmy reaches under Finn's arms and pulls the baby

into his lap. He shuffles up as close to the box as he can, and he places Finn's hands on one end of the box. Jimmy turns a button, and the music gets even louder.

My ears flatten back at the assault. I look left and then right. I have an overwhelming urge to flee.

I run under the bed, just peeking out.

Jimmy turns a knob and gets static, then voices talking, then static, then a song. He continues to turn the knob, the noise changing every few seconds, until he finds what he is looking for.

Jimmy looks up to the ceiling a moment and puts his hand on his heart, as if in quick thanks.

Finn's hands have already moved, so Jimmy takes Finn's little hands in his again and flattens Finn's palms up against the end of the box. Now I notice that the box is shaking, ever so slightly. I think Jimmy is trying to get Finn to feel the music.

"I got nine lives," Jimmy sings along, "Cat's eyes. Abusin' every one of them and running wild . . ."

My tail twitches violently. Did he just say something about a cat?

Mary comes running in. "WHAT THE—?"

But then she sees what is happening. She raises one eyebrow.

"AC/DC?" she asks. " 'Back in Black'?"

"Yeah," Jimmy yells over the music.

Mary puts her hands on her hips and frowns. "I guess you don't have to worry about blowing his ears out," she shouts.

"WHAT?"

"Never mind."

It's hard to tell if Finn is feeling the music or not, but he seems to like sitting in Jimmy's lap and touching the box.

"Your phone is ringing," Mary says.

"WHAT?"

She points. "PHONE."

Jimmy shuts off the music, lifts Finn out of his lap in one swift motion to plop him on the rug, and grabs the phone. "Hey, sweetheart." He presses the phone to his ear and looks at Mary, pointing at Finn. She sits down with Finn when Jimmy leaves the room and heads out into the hall.

Ah, the music is over. Blessed relief.

Mary reaches for the button. Have I spoken too soon?

Again, there is static, and then different types of music burst forth as she spins the dial. Finally Mary settles on a song that is much different from the last one.

I still hate it. All music sounds horrible to me.

After sitting Finn up on his bottom and leaning him on pillows so that he is facing her, Mary crosses her legs and sits up straight. She makes her hand into a fist, holds it near her mouth, and starts singing into her hand.

It's a love song, I believe, judging by the faces Mary makes as she sings. I think she looks quite lovely, and I can feel the longing and heartache she is trying to communicate, even though I can't stand the music. Finn watches her, enraptured. Mary uses her hands to illustrate some of the words, and the sadness on her face almost brings tears to my eyes, even though I realize she is acting.

A moving shadow catches my eye, and from where I sit under the crib I see Jimmy and Father standing in the doorway. Mary's back is to them, and she is unaware they have snuck up behind her. Father folds his arms, leaning against the door frame, and he looks amused. Jimmy grins.

Mary is surprised when she turns and sees them, and

she hides her face in her hands. "Were you listening?" She laughs, hard. "I'm so embarrassed." She turns back to the big black box. "Oh. This next song is beautiful too. Do you guys know this song? It's on the radio all the time."

Jimmy says something about never listening to crappy pop songs. Father just shrugs. He doesn't seem to know the song either. He's been preoccupied lately, and probably isn't aware of all of the songs that important people like Mary know.

Mary picks Finn up off the floor and holds him in her arms as she sings to him. It is a nice song, I think, not too loud. Earnest and serious and slow, Mary sings the love song right to Finn, rocking him back and forth. Finn is getting very big in her arms, and he smiles at her. Jimmy wanders away, patting his dad on the back, but Father stays and listens, tipping his head.

Mary sings a verse or two, until she turns her head to look at her father and sees the expression on his face. Her voice fades out. And then she stops.

"Oh." She looks embarrassed all over again. Mary glances down at her feet. "It's okay, Dad. I didn't mean to—"

He reassures her that he's fine.

"Sorry. You just looked so . . ."

Father tells her that he's fine again, and turns away. He walks down the hall and goes into his own bedroom. The door clicks shut behind him.

"Don't quit your day job, Mare!" Jimmy yells from somewhere down the hall.

Mary stands there. She walks over and clicks off the box.

"No worries, baby," she says to Finn. "Just a momentary blip in the program. A bump in the road." She kisses his fat cheek. "Just a little hiccup. We don't need that music anyway, do we?"

Finn seems to agree as he pulls a clump of Mary's hair into his mouth with a big smile. I blink my eyes at him.

When Mary lies down on the rug next to Finn, I approach and snuggle right next to the baby, so he is sandwiched between the two of us. It reminds me of how I used to lie between Mother and Father, and it was the best feeling in the world. It makes me happy knowing I can give this feeling to someone else, and it makes me doubly satisfied to know I can comfort the baby. He will never hear me meow. But when his little hand clumsily touches my fur, I hope he knows that I am on his side.

A tall, dark shadow appears at the doorway. It is Jimmy again, coming back to his room, and he finds all of us lying on his rug. Without a word, he lies down at our feet and stretches out.

The four of us make a good team.

I wonder again if Mother will return and want some of us to go home with her.

What if she does?

And if she does, who will go? One of us may have to go.

I wonder if it will be me.

17

Space and Energy

One night, Father stays up far too late. Just as he is about to get up off the living room couch to go to bed, he notices something that interests him on the TV. It seems to be some kind of emotional story. When he starts the show he is sitting up, and by the end of it he is exhausted and lying on the couch. Although he holds the controller for the TV in his hand, I see he is unable to turn it off until the very end.

There is no reason for him to hurry to bed. Without Mother here, he loses track of time in the evenings.

I sit in the hallway, waiting for him. It is a bitter cold night, and I can feel a draft of wintery air forcing itself under the front door. It is a shock to my whiskers.

When the show is over, I follow Father upstairs.

As he stands in front of his closet, sleepy, I settle down on the bed. He peels off his shirt and throws it in the hamper. Then he unbuckles his belt and hangs it on a hook in the closet. Father runs a hand over his chest for a moment, lost in his thoughts. He unbuttons his jeans, pulls them off, and hangs them up. Finally, he peels off his boxer shorts and socks and adds them to the hamper. Father is much more neat and organized than his children.

Father puts on a shirt and new underwear to sleep in, then lies down on the bed. Father pulls the sheet up over him first, and then grabs the blanket and Mother's comforter, smoothing them out on top.

At first, he lies still, and I know he is asleep by the even rhythm of his breathing. I listen to the clock chiming downstairs. But after a while, Father begins to toss. He moans in his sleep, and I wonder if it is a dream or a nightmare.

I hope it is a lovely dream.

I try to think good thoughts, about one of my favorite times with Mother.

I try to really remember every moment, every word, to figure out if there was anything I misunderstood. I desperately want to know if there was a clue that Mother was planning to leave us, something I might have missed.

I remember one night, perhaps a year before Finn was born, when Mother was telling Father one of her more exciting stories and Father let me sit on the bed with him. She acted the whole story out, pacing at the foot of the bed. I believe she was playing all of the parts, reliving something that had happened to her that day. Father had his pillow behind him and his hands behind his head, and he was very happy to listen. A few times, he laughed at her story. I sat and watched the two of them.

It was entertaining. Mother was so, so full of energy—almost bursting with it—and waving her hands wildly. She was in constant motion. And when Mother jumped on the bed, Father had his arms open, ready to catch her. She was soon on top of him and kissing him. If there's one thing you can say about Mother, it is that in those moments when she loved Father, she truly, passionately loved him and there was no doubt in it, not a shred of hesitation, not a moment of care for anything in the world but *Tommy Tommy Tommy*.

She leaned back to take a breath, gently running her knuckles over the scruff on his face. "Honey."

He moved a curl of her dark hair out of her face. "Baby," he said back to her. He was always hungry for more of her, when she was happy.

In those days, I was either jealous or bored when it wasn't my turn to get Mother's attention. I waited it out.

I longed for Mother to see me and give me the same loving embrace.

Looking back on it, of course Father didn't notice me very much in those days. He didn't need me. He had room for no one but her. She took up so much space and energy. I understand it better now.

I remember also what happened later that night, when Father had exhausted himself and passed out cold. Mother cuddled me awhile, but she never actually slept.

Instead, she snuck out of bed. I waited while she pushed her feet, one at a time, into her fuzzy slippers. Father never stirred. I followed her downstairs.

She went into the kitchen, flipped on the light switch, and peered into the trash bin. It was full of garbage. She carefully and quietly tipped the bin over and shook it, spreading the garbage out over the entire tile floor.

I know this game! I remember thinking.

She and I sifted through all sorts of interesting things: sticky Popsicle wrappers, coffee grounds, chicken bones, a stale roll, dirty napkins, a dead fly, an old sponge, two apple cores and apple seeds, torn envelopes, cold spaghetti with tomato sauce splattered everywhere, a newspaper circular, crumpled homework, a leaky pen, a banana peel, a few moldy grapes, the wrapper from a loaf of bread and the matching twist tie, and an empty cracker box.

So interesting! Full of great smells. I batted a dry piece of cereal, watching it skid across the floor.

Mother was hoping to find cans, accidentally placed there by one of her family members. But everyone was good about putting used cans into the blue bin out back. So, no luck.

She cleaned the whole thing up, using her bare hands to scoop the trash back into the bin. Mother used paper towels to pick up more of it, the smaller scraps. Then she wiped the floor with a wet sponge. Next, she sprayed the floor with a brisk cleaner and wiped it with a paper towel. Finally, she sprayed a foul-smelling liquid on the floor. After running the water until it got so hot that steam misted from the faucet, she ran the hot sponge over the floor one more time.

What a funny game. Mother was so much fun in the middle of the night! I was always happy to have a companion to prowl around with during my hours of nighttime adventure.

Having had no luck with the trash, Mother had to make do with what was available in the recycling bin. Opening the back door that led from the kitchen, she reached outside for the tall container as the cold buffeted her body, and she pulled the bin inside. It was disappointing to her, whatever she saw inside. I could tell by the look on her face as she glanced down.

"Oh well, Boo," she said to me. "Only a few cans tonight." Now that we had the cans, she smiled and relaxed a little. "Should we get to work?" Mother had a gleam in her eye, and she whispered sweetly to me. "You're my best friend, Boo. Want to help me? You're the only one who helps me."

Of course! I always wanted to help. Mother loved and appreciated me. Now that I had her undivided attention, all felt right in my world.

First, we had to wash the cans. I jumped up on a kitchen chair to watch. I knew the drill. Very hot, steamy water, and lots and lots of liquid soap on the scrubby brush. More spray, and a final rinse in the hot water. Then she dried the cans with a towel, shaking them repeatedly to get the water out of the nooks and crannies.

Next, the cans had to be reshaped. There were two soda cans that someone, probably Jimmy, had crushed with their hands. Mother tried to manipulate the cans back into a normal shape. Sometimes it could be done, sometimes not. She stuck a finger right into the can to try to push it back out to a circular form. Sometimes she cut herself and there was blood, so she needed a Band-Aid. But not tonight. The cans weren't perfect, but they were okay. Close enough.

Mother padded upstairs very quietly, the bin full of clean cans in her arms. I followed.

She did not turn on the hall light. We snuck into the guest bedroom. Only after Mother had closed the door, making sure my tail was safely inside, did she turn on the lamp in the room.

It was going to be a castle of cans. Cans already lined three of the four walls, several rows deep and as high as her knees. She added the new cans on top, one by one. It was a slow task, because one wrong move could potentially send several cans toppling over. I knew that

Mother wanted this to be a surprise for Jimmy and Mary. She told me so.

"What do you think, Boo? Is this enough? It's not enough, is it? We need more cans."

Mother looked over her creation and decided something was wrong. She began taking it apart, can by can. I got a little concerned as I realized she was going to dismantle the entire thing.

But it's so nice, I wanted to say to her. *Just leave it. It doesn't have to be perfect.*

But clearly, it wasn't perfect. There's a lot Mother knows that I don't, so I trusted her judgment. I watched as she took all of the cans down from their neat rows and put them behind her. I came to see that she wanted to group them by color: red, black, green, or silver. There wasn't enough room to lay them all out, because of the bed. As her movements became more frantic, I grew concerned. She was worried about her castle, and I felt terrible that I had no way to help her. But I stuck with her. That was the most I could do, stay with her and comfort her by just letting her know I was there.

Her eyes looked more and more tired as the minutes ticked by. She was beginning to squint at each can, as if the designs on the can were blurring before her eyes. I yawned. We were up such a long time. I wished Mother would go back to bed.

And then, I heard it: the heavy fall of feet on the floor. Father was up.

I heard him walking around, the weight of his footsteps on the floorboards, but Mother continued to work with her cans as if she had not heard and did not know that Father was coming. She must have known, but she was so very involved with organizing those cans that she could not stop. These cans were important, and her mind seemed to be consumed with it. They had to be just right. It was as if her whole life depended on it.

Let's go, I begged her in my mind. I suddenly knew that Father would be angry about this, all of this. *We have to go back to bed. You have to say you were just getting a drink of water. Or that we were checking on the children.*

I was filled with dread. I realized for the first time, now that I really thought about Father walking into the room, that he would not like this one bit. He never liked when Mother was consumed with projects that took all night, like the time she painted a rainbow of stripes that covered every wall in the basement, or the time she took all of the clothes and shoes out of her closet and arranged them by color all around the living room. Mother loved colors and had a very artistic eye. She also sometimes scrubbed the kitchen floor until the tiles were scratched and rough. She loved cleaning and putting things in order.

At the time, I just thought Father was selfish and controlling. That he wanted her to stay in bed because as her mate he thought it was his right to tell her what to do.

It didn't occur to me, the way it does now, that maybe something was wrong. And that, just perhaps, Mother wasn't building a castle.

"Carrie?" I heard him ask quietly in the hallway. And then I heard a slight rattle as his hand landed on the doorknob. The doorknob turned, and he slowly pushed open the door. Blinking in the bright light, he took a step into the room. He looked down at Mother, where she sat on the floor.

"No, no, no, no," she said, waving her hand at Father to drive him back. "Not now. I'm working."

"Working? On what?" Father looked around the

room, turning back and forth, in complete confusion. At first, he seemed merely curious. And then darkness came over his face.

"What are you doing?" he asked, and I heard it; I heard how his tone completely changed. His voice dropped and became more menacing, as if he were now speaking to a naughty child rather than his wife.

"I'm working," she spat back at him. "Get out. Out. OUT." She barely looked at him, turning back to her cans. She put red cans to the left, black cans in the middle, silver cans to her right. There was so much work to be done, and she couldn't waste a minute talking to him.

There was another shadow in the hallway, and then Jimmy stepped into the room.

Father spun around and grabbed Jimmy by the shoulder. Father demanded to know if Jimmy had known that Mother had been in the guest room, obviously for days now, piling up the cans.

Jimmy wrenched himself out of Father's grasp. "Don't you think I would've been the first to tell you if I knew?" Jimmy seemed bewildered, at both Mother's work and Father's attitude. "I'm the one who tells you everything."

A can hit Jimmy, and he looked up, startled. Mother had thrown a can at him. "Get out. Both of you. I have work to do. You have to go. Now."

"C'mon, Ma," Jimmy said. "What the heck are you doing? Why are you throwing a—"

"GO BACK TO BED," Father raged, wheeling around to face Jimmy. "DON'T MAKE HER TELL YOU AGAIN."

Jimmy slunk back, back into the darkness of the hallway. Father shut the door once Jimmy had gone. He turned and stared at Mother. The anger drained from his face until he looked tired and sad, his head tipped to one side.

Father bent down next to Mother, and she grabbed the sleeve of his T-shirt. She thanked him for getting rid of Jimmy, who was bothering her.

Father knelt on the floor. He explained that this was all trash, and it had to be thrown away.

But she just answered him with a long explanation of how she had carefully cleaned every can. Every can was like new.

What she was saying was true. I saw it. I watched her do all this. She worked so hard, my mother. She worked so hard to make nice things for this family.

Father explained it again. "We have to get rid of this," he said quietly to her. Mother wasn't listening. She turned away from him and started stacking up the cans.

"Go ahead, talk. I'm listening. I'll listen while I work."

"No," he said tenderly. "No, baby, no." He put his arms around her from behind and took a can out of her hand. For a moment, seeing her frown and wince, I thought she was going to elbow him in the stomach. But Mother surprised me and just went limp and leaned back into him. He told her again that this was crazy and they could not keep these cans up here, that the trash was not really clean and it wasn't good to have these things upstairs where the children slept.

Mother listened, but her eyes were glassy. She rubbed one hand with the other hand. I could tell she was itching to get back to work. "Why don't you help me?" she finally tried. "You can help me stack the cans. As long as they're straight. The rows have to be straight." She explained to him several times how to line them up.

Father took her hand in his and kissed it. Sometimes he fought with her, but other times he knew when to quit fighting. To just give up and start fresh tomorrow. Sometimes he would find a way to get her out to the doctor, and maybe she'd come back with pills of a different color, or maybe she wouldn't come back at all for a day or two. Sometimes he'd just give up and let her be. There were so many important things she needed to get done.

"What's the matter?" she asked. "Can't you leave me alone? Can't I be allowed to work in peace?"

"No," he whispered. "No, I can't leave you alone. Because look what happens when I do."

"Yes, a lot gets done!" She looked satisfied with herself. "Look at how many cans I cleaned. When this room is full, and everything is neat, with the right colors in the right place, I'll be done. You see?" Mother's eyes twinkled with new energy. "Won't it be beautiful? It will be just right. It's going to be perfect. And everything will be in its place. It's not my fault we're stuck here in your creaky, ugly, old house. Full of ghosts. But this one room will be very nice and complete."

"Okay," he agreed. "But just for a day. Then it all has to go. These cans can't stay here, and you know it."

"You're so mean."

Father wrapped his arms around her tighter. "I'm sorry. But you know I'm right."

She tried to squirm away from him, but he wouldn't let her. His muscles hardened as he held her in place. "You have to leave now," she said. "I only have a few hours left until daylight."

"Come back to bed. Please. Please. I'm so tired and I have to work tomorrow."

I could see the anguish in Mother's face. She just wanted to be able to lean forward and work with her cans. I don't know why he couldn't just leave her in peace and let her do her work. I got up to slink toward her on padded feet. I thought maybe if I sat in her lap, she'd find it comforting. But Father's big hand caught me on the hip as he pushed me away. "Get out of here," he snapped at me.

He wanted me gone, just like he wanted Jimmy gone. I thought he wanted Mother all to himself. I hated him in that moment.

Thinking back on it, perhaps he ordered Jimmy to leave because he wanted Jimmy out of harm's way. And maybe I was a distraction.

Mother gritted her teeth, angry. "Don't do that to Boo. Leave her alone. You're so horrible. Why did I marry such a mean person?" She tried to pull his arms off of her. "You don't appreciate what I do, what I create. You've got me trapped here in this old house. In this small town."

Father frowned, but he did not let go.

"You keep me here," she continued. "But the more you hold me down, the more I just want to run away."

Father buried his face in her shoulder. He was behind her, so she couldn't see his expression of grief. And now I couldn't see it either. A few minutes went by. Mother looked lovingly at her cans. She could see how wonderful it could be, if he would just let her finish.

"I'm not trying to be mean," he finally said. He sounded exhausted. "But this isn't right. Maybe you could do this in the basement, away from the kids."

"Oh." She thought this over. Maybe the basement would be a good compromise. "But it's dark down there."

"Yes," he agreed. "I don't want you there alone. But

maybe when I'm working out, with the weights. You could come down and do your work, and I'll be there anyway."

"That's not a bad idea. Because then they can't see me coming and going."

Father still hadn't lifted his head, and he talked into her back. But I could hear the tension creeping back into his voice. "Who can't?"

"The neighbors. They're watching me." Mother paused. She was speaking totally normally, not as if she was afraid of the neighbors. She was just telling it like it is. I hid behind the curtains with her many times, watching them. When she told me the neighbors were planning to take her away, I showed her how to be very still and keep a sharp eye on their movements. "They watch all of us. I know that." Mother reached back and patted his arm. "You're not smart enough to understand. Poor Tommy. But maybe someday you will."

She turned around in his lap. "Oh, you smell good." Father had to lift his head as she nestled onto his chest. His eyes were red. "Why do you always smell so good? Is this some kind of a trick? Is this a trick to trap me here? You smell like soap. And laundry detergent and I think toothpaste and oh my God Tommy you smell good."

Father stopped responding. He just sat, slumped over, holding her against his chest. Unable to let go.

Sometimes the humans couldn't get a word in edgewise when Mother was wound up. That may have something to do with why she loved to talk to me. I never interrupt. Father would also let her talk, when her words got jumbled up and didn't make sense anymore.

"Sweetheart." Mother sighed. "You have to leave now.

I have to get back to work. There really isn't much time. Do you realize how late it is?" She turned her head and looked right at me. "Boo understands. She's so wise. I don't even need to explain myself to her. Isn't that right, Boo?"

Of course! I lay nearby on the rug and looked right at Mother. We shared a special bond. I knew all about Mother's cans, and her special work, and all sorts of things that made her the most interesting human I had ever met.

"Such a beautiful cat. And you, my handsome husband." She turned and looked into his face. "Oh, sweetheart. Don't look so worried. Don't cry. All the time, so worried. You need to relax. Cheer up. Look. There's the guest bed, right there. Just lie down. I'll be here. I promise. I'm not going anywhere. There's so much work to do here. Please, just lie down on the bed. I swear, I'll work quietly. I just need the light on. That's the only thing. But you can turn and face the wall."

Father finally got up, and he did lie down on the bed. But he didn't face the wall. He kept his eye on her.

At the time, I remember wishing very hard that he would just go away.

Looking back on it now, I am impressed that he did not. And I am glad that he did not.

"C'mon, Boo," she said to me, using both hands to pull me onto her lap. I purred as she went straight back to work, and kept on until morning. She sang a pretty song, softly, and we both forgot that Father was even there.

In the morning, when the sun came up, Mother rose, leaving Father sleeping in the guest room. As I glanced back at him, his body looked heavy and still, like a rock.

Mother floated into Jimmy's room. "Good morning, sunshine!" she sang. "Time for school."

I ran after her into Mary's room. "It's time, love," she said with a kiss to Mary's forehead. She scooped up Jasper, who was looking like a brown ball of fluff, into her arms.

Before the kids came downstairs, Mother had fed me, cleaned my litter box, walked and fed Jasper, and made coffee for herself. Jasper barked excitedly as she floated around the kitchen.

As the children entered and sat down, Mother was efficiently setting out napkins, bowls, and spoons. She already had six boxes of cereal on the table, along with a carton of milk and a bowl of blueberries, and glasses of orange juice for Jimmy and apple juice for Mary.

When Mother had energy, things were wonderful. The house was clean, and she baked delicious treats.

When Mother got back from dropping the kids off at school, she slept all day. She didn't stir until long after suppertime. Father napped next to her on their bed, and I lay between them. It was heavenly. Anyone looking in on us would have thought we looked at peace.

Coming out of my memory, I realize I am on Mother's empty half of the bed and staring glassy-eyed at the wall in the darkness. Father is still tossing and turning, under the covers, stuck in his nightmare.

I realize now that this was a good memory for me because other times when she was full of energy, Mother got angry. She yelled and cursed. And all of those times I took her side. All of those times I assumed the rest of the family was wrong and she was right. She whispered to me that they were careless, and stupid, and hurtful, and I believed her.

She told me several times that she was sure Father

regretted ever marrying her. She said that the kids would be better off if she was gone. Mother told me that she just wanted to sleep, crying hysterically because she couldn't drift off like a normal person.

But when she said these things, I thought that the kids had upset her and that Father had been cruel. Now I wonder . . . When I think of how Father saw her project and first got so angry, and then so sad, how everything about her drained him completely and nearly broke him . . . I wonder if I misunderstood. Back then, I didn't understand Father the way I do now.

I still admire Mother for all of her hard work. And I feel bad about the fact that no matter what project she tried, Father never liked it and he always made her stop. Sometimes she would try the same project over and over, and he would ruin it time and time again. Father's temper was short in those days.

Yet now, looking back on how calm my family is without Mother here, I see that her activities and strange schedule were disruptive. She would go-go-go for four days in a row and then sleep for five. It didn't make sense.

I have to conclude that it wasn't normal human behavior.

Not that I expect all humans to be the same. And that's not to say she wasn't just a little advanced, a little ahead of everyone else. But looking back, I see how hard it was for everyone to keep up with her. How maybe it was too stressful, in the end.

Maybe, just maybe, my family will look back and wonder how they ever coped.

In the darkness, Father gives a shout, and his eyes flutter open. He stares at the ceiling, now awake. I don't know what is going through his mind.

He turns on his side, and we look at each other a minute. I get up, walk over, and curl up tight by his stomach. He pets me once on the head.

"Boo," he whispers to me. "Sorry. Go back to sleep."

Mother never went back to sleep when he asked her to, but I will. And I do.

18

Lonely Hearts

I take a nap under Finn's crib while I think about the night Father went out and brought Jenny home. I'm not sure how to feel about Father bringing another human female here. Now that Mother has left our family, I expect he needs a new mate.

While I am happy for him to complete this natural process, it makes me sad too. Because it is another reminder that Mother is off with a new family somewhere else.

But if it isn't Jenny, then who?

Of course, the answer has been right under my nose all along.

A few weeks later, Mary cuts strings of red hearts out of construction paper and hangs them in the dining room. She is having a party for her girlfriends. She is calling it the "anti-Valentine's" party for lonely hearts. She tells Jimmy that all of the boys in her grade are big, fat losers and so the girls must find their own fun.

Jimmy finds this enormously entertaining. He even

helps Mary decorate. They bake heart-shaped butter cookies, with cookie cutters that Mahmee has brought over for the occasion. And yes, I get a pat of butter in my dish.

Father walks into the dining room and admires Mary's work, the long strings of hanging hearts, with a wistful look on his face. I don't know if he is thinking about the past, or the future, but he stands and daydreams for a little while. I leave him alone.

The day before the party, Charlotte comes for her appointment. She admires Mary's handiwork with the decorations in the dining room. Mary offers her a cookie before sealing the rest up in a big, plastic bowl for the party.

As Charlotte and Father walk upstairs, Father tells her that Finn is sleeping. Charlotte says that it's okay as she nibbles on her cookie and wipes crumbs from her mouth. She suggests that she just work with Father instead. They sit right on Finn's rug like they usually do and talk quietly.

Charlotte sits opposite Father with her legs crossed and shows him many hand signals. Sometimes he doesn't get it quite right, so she takes his hand in both of hers and manipulates his fingers to correct him.

I see that Charlotte likes working with Father. She often touches him when I'm not sure it's really necessary.

But maybe she's just a touchy person.

Father and Charlotte seem to be having a nice time, and I am in a good mood too, so I get up to rub my head on Father's knee. Charlotte scratches between my ears and asks Father if he thinks I wouldn't mind being picked up.

Mind? I never mind.

Father puts his big hands under me, picks me up,

and places me in Charlotte's lap. He knows I'll be good. I am a floppy, friendly, lazy cat, just like Mother always said. I never scratch the humans. Charlotte's lap is just fine.

It's different from Mother's lap. Not better. Not worse. Just different.

I roll over, right in her lap. I stretch out my legs and arch my back while Charlotte strokes my soft belly. I know that if I look cute, I might get extra attention.

I look over to Father to show him that I am being good, but he's not looking at me.

He's looking at Charlotte.

He looks so keenly interested, his face flushed, his eyes wide and searching, and I—

Ohhhh, of course, I think. *Why didn't I see it before?*

But this just makes me very worried that Father has the wrong idea about Charlotte. I have come to understand that she is here to work with Finn. She is here to do a job. And she is a naturally friendly person.

Perhaps she doesn't think Father would be a good mate for her at all. Perhaps it has never even crossed her mind.

I have noticed Father taking Mary's advice and putting on clean shirts and combing his hair. He still shaves, about once a week, letting his whiskers grow in just enough so he looks impressive but also not too scruffy. That's a good thing, that he is taking care of himself. But still, it makes me concerned.

What makes me most apprehensive, as I lie there in Charlotte's lap, is that with a twitch of my nose I suddenly realize that Father is giving off the same pheromones that Jimmy is. I hadn't noticed, because it is so strong on Jimmy. Which means Father is definitely ready for a new mate, whether he realizes it or not.

I have grown fond of Father. I don't want to see

him rejected. I don't think he could handle another heartache.

Father mentions to Charlotte the new book he's been reading. Something about Finn and how to communicate with him.

"Well," she exclaims, "that's a great choice. A very smart choice."

Father is looking down at me at that moment, but his head turns up quickly to look at her. "What?"

"You're getting so smart on this subject. I'm impressed."

Father looks surprised. I have never heard anyone say anything like that to Father, or call him *smart*. I think Charlotte just took his breath away.

He sits up straighter. "I'm going to have it read by next week," he promises.

"Okay," she says. She has no idea what affect her words just had on him.

"I will definitely have it done by next week," he repeats, nodding.

Ah, poor Father. I'm not sure he is going to win over this one.

As Charlotte teaches him new hand signs, Father starts talking. And keeps talking. And doesn't stop for a really long time. I start to nod off, curled up on Charlotte's legs. He is quietly telling her about Carrie, and himself, and Jimmy and Mary and Finn.

Minutes, and then hours, go by. I lift my head when Mary peeks in the door to say good night. *Goodness,* I think, *Father is still talking.* He's never talked this much in his entire life. We must be Charlotte's final appointment of the day, because she makes no move to get up. She lets Father talk. She is a good listener, and when he asks her questions, she offers advice in an enthusiastic tone.

Finally, Finn stirs in his crib. Fortunately, he wakes in a good mood and not with a scream. I get up, and so do Father and Charlotte. I can't see Finn from my position on the floor, but I hear the baby gurgle when he sees the adults looking down at him.

Father is standing very close to Charlotte and sneaking glances at her, and I am suddenly afraid he is going to do something foolish.

My little heart seizes in my chest. I need to create a distraction. . . . I need—

Ohhhh, too late.

Charlotte has one hand on the crib railing and the other down by her side. Father reaches out and takes her free hand in his.

Oh.

I wait, frozen.

She lets him hold it for just a second, and then easily takes her hand right back and never stops smiling or talking.

Miss Davenport is a professional.

Father has no outward reaction. He just looks down and they keep talking about Finn. He seems to have no recognition of the fact that he just embarrassed himself. But I am angry for him.

He is such a fine man, how can Charlotte not even consider Father for one moment? How can she so coldly ignore his advances? I am outraged. I am—

But wait a minute.

Now I see she leans down toward Finn to say goodbye to him, and in doing so also leans closer to Father. Her arm brushes against his for a moment. She looks at Finn, and then at Father. Charlotte straightens up and teaches Father a few more signs, holding his hand in both of hers again to manipulate his fingers.

Father watches her, studying her. They are standing

so close that Charlotte blushes a little this time, unlike her confident manner when they sat on the floor. And when she is done showing him the last sign, she just stands there, with her hands still on his. This time she doesn't pull her hands away. She just looks down, as if she is afraid to make eye contact with him.

Hmmmm. Interesting. I realize Father understands something that I didn't, until now.

They just stand there, her fingers wrapped around his hand, so close to each other. I watch, whiskers alert.

They are so different, these two. I can see it, looking up at them. Father is a little older, and he is calm and careful in his approach. Father knows what he wants now and isn't afraid to show it. I think he would try to kiss her if she weren't so obviously skittish. But like I do when I am afraid of scaring away a bird on the windowsill, he waits with infinite patience and does not move. Charlotte starts talking nervously. She pulls away from him, finally, all fluttery hand gestures and feet shuffling. She cannot look up at his face, and her cheeks burn red.

I find this amusing! These humans.

Father walks her downstairs, and I watch from the landing. He stands in the doorway until her car pulls away.

After she leaves, Father absentmindedly wanders back up and into his bedroom. He sits on the edge of his bed, taking off his shoes and placing them neatly on the floor. Deep in thought, he twirls his wedding ring and pulls it on and off, on and off. I can tell he's thinking about taking it off.

He is still married, as far as I understand it.

This ring and that letter are what he has left of Mother. These two things, and their three children.

I know he will someday find a new mate, but I wonder

if his heart is ready for it now. I wonder if my heart is either.

The fact that Mother left still hurts me, and I can see it still hurts my family. Her spirit chases Father like a shadow in every room of this old house. Sometimes he turns a corner and lifts his head, and I could swear he thinks he has caught a glimpse of her from the way his eyes search the room, but she always eludes him. He is met only with empty spaces and dark corners.

She is gone. And we must move on.

I imagine that Father recognizes in Charlotte a kindness that I have also seen in her. The way she cannot help but smile when he enters the room. The enthusiasm in her voice when she talks to him. Warm hands that reach out to correct the hand signals he tries to make. A longing in her eye when she looks at him.

Father and I have each other, but I realize he must also desire a human companion who satisfies the needs of his head and his heart and his body. I must admit that Charlotte would be a good choice.

I jump up on the bed and roll over, next to Father. He places his hand on my belly and rubs gently.

The next night is Mary's big party. I have heard her say that Valentine's Day is not for a few more days, but Mary wanted the party to kick off the weekend so they can stay up late. Father makes a blazing fire in the fireplace and turns on the television to watch a game. Young girls, some willowy and others curvy—but all supremely confident—arrive in small groups. They are very excited and talkative. Soon there are nine girls in the decorated dining room, sparkly and glossy and working their small phones.

Jimmy comes downstairs to say hello. He is swarmed

and cannot stop grinning as all of the girls (except Mary) laugh at every little thing he says.

Father gets a call that causes him to jump off the couch. He writes down a few things on a piece of paper and then calls Jimmy over to him. I watch from a distance, on the stairs, as he explains it. There has been an emergency, and he must go put out a big fire. It is several towns away.

Father and Jimmy cast a wary eye over the girls, who are just standing and eating cookies.

Father has a few words for Jimmy, and then is gone.

"Where's Pops going?" Mary calls over her shoulder. She doesn't miss a thing.

"Fire," Jimmy answers. "Big one. Three-alarm fire. In Danvers."

"Danvers?"

My two siblings stare at each other a moment. And then both start furiously pushing buttons on their small phones.

The first one to arrive is Aruna, and I am glad to see her. Jimmy picks her up in his arms and carries her into the house while she laughs. Next is a skinny boy carrying a heavy backpack. Then four more boys arrive with cans and bottles. Jimmy is older and bigger than all of these other boys, but they travel in a pack and outnumber him, and I wonder if they will be trouble.

While I watch from the stairs, about twenty more kids arrive, a mix of boys and girls. Mary and her girl-friends seem to know all of them. "I thought you said these guys were all big, fat losers," Jimmy teases Mary, shouting to be heard over the music. "They're not so big. They're not fat either. Losers . . . well, yeah, I can see that."

After a few hours, I am curious and take a walk around the perimeter of the downstairs rooms. I am surprised to place my paw in a big, wet spot on the living room rug, and I realize someone has spilled a drink. I see the fire in the fireplace has gone out, unattended. In the kitchen, the back door is open, letting in freezing cold air. I hear voices outside. Smoke, similar to that created by the fireplace but sweeter, drifts inside.

I take a drink of water, but my food bowl is empty.

And then I hear it, in my big, wide ears. Finn is crying in his crib.

I pick my head up. The music and talking are very loud. Where are Mary and Jimmy?

I hear distress in Finn's tone. I'm sure he's okay, because he is safe in his crib, but it still makes me anxious. I begin to frantically dart from room to room, through a forest of legs.

Jimmy, where is he? And how will I alert him when I find him?

Just then, I see him. He is standing at the bottom of the stairs. I run right to his feet and meow with all my strength. He glances down at me, puzzled, and then tips his head as he finally hears Finn crying. Jimmy asks Aruna to go up and check on Finn. I follow her upstairs.

Finn is screaming, but okay. It takes Aruna a good, long while to settle him down. It's nice and cool and quiet in Finn's room, and I stay there with them.

When Aruna finally walks back downstairs, Finn in her arms, Jimmy is in a corner surrounded by young girls. He is telling a great story, the way Mother would at a party, and he has many enraptured listeners. I watch him a moment.

Let me tell you what I see: the curve of Jimmy's lips. The shape of his mouth. The dark mole on his cheek. His expressive face and the way he moves his hands in front of him to illuminate his story. He is just like Mother.

Jimmy breaks my heart all the time but doesn't know it.

I am glad he doesn't know it.

Aruna is angry. She pulls Jimmy aside and has many sharp words for him. He professes innocence, but they continue arguing. I notice now that Jimmy is holding a bottle just like the younger boys. Aruna clutches Finn tightly. Kids interrupt to ask if they can hold the baby, but Aruna won't let them.

There is a loud banging. Jimmy leaves his bottle on the dining room table and answers the door. It is the grouchy, gray-haired neighbor. Jimmy swallows hard and snaps to with a quick "Yes, sir" and "No, sir." When he closes the door behind him, he mutters, "Calm down."

Just like Father would.

Jimmy strides through the crowd over to the music machine and turns the noise down. He orders Mary not to touch the dial. "He's gonna call the cops if you don't get your friends to stop turning this up." Then he runs to the back porch and yells at everyone to get inside.

I am proud of him for taking charge and fixing the situation.

But the peace doesn't last for long.

Not twenty minutes later, there is another intrusive knock at the door. Jimmy sighs and lumbers over to answer it again.

But this time it is Sean's wife. Her eyes are red and her hands are shaking.

"Party's over, honey," she tells him.

19

The Jump

Something has happened to Father and Sean.

Sean's wife tells Jimmy to get the kids who live nearby to walk home in groups. Jimmy takes kids to the street, barking out directions. In the dining room, Mary helps her friends who live farther away call for rides home.

As the last kids trickle out, Mahmee shows up, looking exhausted and pale. She goes up to check on Finn and to find blankets and a pillow.

Poor Mahmee. I think this is very hard on her, having to worry about Father all of the time. He seems to be the most important person in her life.

Father has a younger brother, John, but he is not talked about. I have heard him mentioned only a few times. He did not carve out a straight path in life. He is in jail, which sounds like a cage for the humans who have done wrong.

Father also had a younger sister, Shannon, but she was killed not long ago in a car accident. It was called a "drunk driving" accident. I am not sure what that means, but Father said the persons who were drunk were Shannon and her husband. Shannon had no children, so Mahmee just has what she has: Father, Jimmy, Mary, and Finn. And she is devoted to them.

I know Father misses his siblings. Just after Shannon died, he started asking Mother for another baby. I heard him ask her often about it. She usually shook her head no.

And then one day, I realized Mother really was expecting a baby. That's when things took a turn for the worse.

Once the party guests have all been sent away, Sean's wife tells Jimmy and Mary they must go with her. I don't understand what has happened. She says something about "out of air" and I know Father and Sean "jumped." And that's all I know.

The house feels cold and empty once my siblings are gone. Mahmee comes down and sleeps on the living room couch, leaving the TV on low. The illumination from the machine flickers pale, ghostly flashes of light across the room.

I don't like it. Jasper doesn't like it either. He pants anxiously, sitting by the front door.

I think the fact that Father and Sean jumped must be a good thing. Usually when I jump, it is to get out of the way of danger. I guess the question is, Did they jump soon enough?

I'm sure I have nothing to worry about. Father and Sean are in good shape. I know their bosses make them exercise with all kinds of equipment down at the fire station, and they are tested on it, because Father and Sean complain about it, and also brag about what they accomplished. I know they are strong and agile enough to carry a big wooden dresser down the steep stairs, because I have seen them do it. They also have all kinds of protective gear for fighting the fires. Father once wore some of it home, and I didn't know who he was at first. He looked like he was ready for battle.

Still, shadows chase me all night. I am restless and skittish.

I want to be brave. But I am scared. I already lost Mother. I cannot lose Father too.

In the morning, Finn cries in a bitter tone, and Mahmee must get up. She takes a deep breath before using the railing to pull herself up those wooden stairs.

Later, she comes down and does a rare thing: She gets out a very loud machine and pushes it over the rugs. She pauses to pick up cups and bottles and throws them away. She opens the windows and sprays some kind of perfume into the air.

I think Mahmee is cleaning. Now, there's something you don't see every day.

Around lunchtime, I am happy and grateful to hear voices on the step. Jimmy and Mary are back, but they are not with Sean's wife anymore.

They are with Mother!

I watch from the stairs. I find it so curious. I am still mad at Mother. At the same time, my heart throbs with excitement when I see her. I feel as if I don't know her so well anymore, and it will take me a little while to warm up to her again. She has a small case with her, so I think she intends to stay a while.

Interesting.

Mother looks at me with those big, brown eyes, that soft and sympathetic expression, and I melt. *Ohhhh, okay*. I pad down the stairs and walk near her. I don't quite approach, but I get closer than the last time she visited.

She is my mother, after all.

Mary announces she needs a nap but first gives Mother a big hug. Jimmy excuses himself to call Aruna.

I follow Mother to the kitchen. She reaches up to a high shelf that the rest of the family doesn't use. She pulls out a little crinkly bag.

My cat treats! I haven't had one in many months.

Before long, I am rubbing against Mother's leg, and then I let myself be lifted into her lap. No matter how strong my resolve is to resist her, I cannot. It is a tremendous relief to have my best friend back here with me, no matter what she has done. Her touch is sensitive and careful around my ears. I absolutely cannot believe how long it has been and how much I have missed this. My purring revs up to its highest level. It's heaven. Mother doesn't smell quite the same, but I don't care anymore.

The children are also happy to have Mother here. Mary helps Mother cook supper and gives her mother many hugs and kisses. I catch Jimmy breaking out into a lopsided smile again and again as he watches his mother work at the stove. He eats every bite of the food she prepares for him, and asks for seconds.

That night, Mother gets right into her old bed without hesitation. She turns out the light, but I can see the outline of her body from where I sit on the hardwood floor. Mother calls for me.

It seems strange that she is back here and Father is not. Something in my gut says: *wrong, wrong, wrong.*

I don't understand everything about the humans. So much about them is a mystery to me. But I know a warm body is better than none at all. So I jump up and snuggle in next to Mother, just like I did many, many months ago when she left. It feels good now, just as it did then.

Still, I have trouble getting comfortable. I get up more than once to shift my position.

Mother is here. Her chest is soft to lie against, and her touch is gentle.

So why can't I fall asleep?

In the morning, Mahmee comes upstairs when she hears Finn crying. But by the time she gets to the top of the stairs, Mother has already fetched the baby. She has climbed back into bed, holding Finn in her arms.

From the hallway, Mahmee glances in toward us, confused. Then she scowls, but only for a moment. I'm not sure what she's thinking. She goes back downstairs.

I feel guilty. I look at Finn, and he is all smiles as Mother cuddles with him. Finn and I aren't doing anything wrong, are we?

Today, Mother, Jimmy, and Mary go out once again, and this time when they return, Father is with them. My little heart melts with relief.

Thank goodness he is okay. Somehow, I knew he would be.

The lower half of one of his legs is wrapped in a white, hard substance, and over that it is completely covered in a strange, bright green bandage. I see people have scribbled words on it with a black pen, and someone has drawn a four-leaf clover.

Later, I hear Mary say the clover has something to do with the "luck of the Irish," whatever that is. I guess we could use some luck, our family. I don't think we've been particularly lucky.

Father does not put pressure on that leg and uses supports, which I learn are called crutches, to walk gingerly up the steps and into the house. He goes straight to the couch and sits down, looking pale and exhausted.

It would not be an exaggeration to say that Father is in a horrible mood. Mahmee tries to get him to take some pills, but he refuses. He seems very angry about the whole situation. He complains that they wouldn't leave him alone in that hospital. He also complains that it hurts to breathe. Later, when I see the dark, mottled bruises up and down his side and over his ribs, I understand why. And when he gets up to go to the bathroom, he has trouble maneuvering. Father curses so much that Jimmy yells at him to *calm down*.

Father is a champion at cursing. Jimmy's been practicing, and someday he will be just as good as Father.

Father snaps back at Jimmy in a rage, yelling something about his children showing up drunk at his hospital bed. Jimmy backs away and makes himself scarce.

Mahmee apologizes for having to go home. She has two feisty Not Cats of her own: Seamus and Kearney. They have been here before, and I have seen that they are terribly spoiled. They must be fed and walked, preferably by Mahmee herself. Father is so upset she is leaving that he can't even look at her, but Mother walks Mahmee to the door.

When Father is lying down, I jump up onto the back of the couch. Even from up where I sit, he smells soooo good. I can tell he has bathed as I breathe in the fragrance of soap, and yet I can still smell the fire and the smoke on him. It's intense and wild. I'm sure it was a big fire. I want desperately to curl up next to Father, but I'm not sure he's ready for that.

Even in pain, once he sees me staring at him, he reaches up and scratches my head.

My tail shivers with delight. I love him. I'll admit it.

For supper, Mother makes spaghetti and meatballs. It's not something I can eat, but it still smells wonderful. My siblings are content and talkative. Father tries to sit at the kitchen table, but he's uncomfortable. He picks at his food, still miserable. When everyone has cleared out, he calls Sean, who I understand is in worse shape than Father. Father has many complaints about everything that was "screwed up" at the fire by foolish humans.

My siblings say good night, from a distance. Father is sitting up on the couch, staring at the TV, and they know he doesn't feel well. I perch right behind him, over his shoulder, on the back of the couch. I hope they are comforted knowing that I'm looking after Father.

When it gets late, Father tells Mother he cannot get up the stairs. He says he will sleep on the couch and she can have the bed.

Mother tells him she's already slept upstairs in the bed. She also mentions that Jimmy can help Father up the stairs if he wants to go. She can see Jimmy's light is still on in his bedroom. "Should I get him?" she asks.

I think it takes a moment for this to sink in, because Father doesn't move. He then turns his head toward her, but only slightly. I can see from my angle that his arms are crossed tight and his lips are pressed together. He doesn't look at her directly. Father tells her that's not a good idea.

She smiles and shakes her head, tired. "Don't you trust me? What are you worried about?" she asks him, as if he's being foolish. "Tommy, what's the worst that can happen?"

But I can think of plenty of things for him to worry

about. Things that could happen tonight, or tomorrow, or three months from now.

Like what if they both sleep upstairs and then Mary or Jimmy gets the wrong idea.

Or what if she gets into bed and then tells Father that she still loves him.

Or what if she gets into bed and doesn't talk to him but puts her hand gently on his arm.

Or what if she gets home and tells Robert that she slept in Father's bed with him.

Or what if Robert calls Father and says he can't do it anymore, that he needs help.

Or what if she feels better and stops taking the medication again.

Or what if she decides she wants Finn and me to come live with her.

There are a lot of possible upsetting scenarios where Father wouldn't know what to do.

"I trust you. I just don't trust myself," he answers quietly. He is being diplomatic. But also, what he is saying may be true.

Mother nods and accepts this. When she gets up, she reaches for me, but I move so that she cannot catch me. And then she leaves us alone.

The next day Jimmy and Mary go to school in the morning. I think Mother was planning to leave, but Father still refuses to take painkillers and is extremely agitated. He complains a lot, and Mother listens very patiently. She spends most of the day cleaning and food shopping and cooking a few meals for the rest of the week. And she is enjoying her time with Finn.

I have to admit, she is excellent with him. Mother has an expressive face and Finn enjoys watching her. She stays one more night.

On the following day, the kids are back off to school. They kiss their mother good-bye but don't bother Father, who is still asleep on the couch.

About midmorning, I hear a creak and run to investigate. The front door has opened, and there is Charlotte. She has let herself in, as she always does, and she is probably expecting to see Mahmee, although Father's truck in the driveway might have alerted her to the fact that he is home.

But I can tell from the look on her face that she wasn't expecting Mother.

They startle each other, and there is a long pause as they both struggle to remember names and faces.

"Oh, Carrie, good to see you," Charlotte gushes, recovering quickly, pulling off her wool coat and knit hat. Mother looks pleased to be remembered.

Mother explains about Father's accident. Father is now sitting up on the couch, reading the newspaper. He says hello as if he barely knows Charlotte, and only after she says hi to him first.

I wish I could tell him, *Relax*.

And, *Don't blow it*.

The women disappear upstairs for a long while. I wonder if Father is thinking what I'm thinking, which is that his bedroom door is probably open and Mother has clothes strewn all over the bed. Father has the paper open to the sports pages in front of him, but I don't think he's really reading much, because he never turns the page.

By the time they come down, Father has worked up his resolve and his courage. He is standing up and waiting for them at the bottom of the stairs, leaning on his crutches. He makes an imposing figure, standing there. I wonder what he is up to. Mother is holding Finn with her left arm, and she strides right up to Father and with her free right hand shows him all of the signs she has learned to communicate with the baby. She's a natural at it.

Mother raises an eyebrow as if to say, *Not bad, huh?*

A small smile comes to Father's face (I see he can't help it), and he gives a slight nod as if to say, *Not bad at all.*

Mother is beaming, holding her little boy.

"I'm so sorry I didn't call you," Father says quickly, turning to Charlotte. "It's been crazy here."

Charlotte puts on her friendliest smile and says it's no trouble at all, that it's good to have different people work with Finn. It doesn't always have to be the same people, she tells him. And she mentions that she was very glad to have the chance to work with Carrie, who did such a fine, fine job.

"No, not about the appointment today. About my accident," he persists. "It's been busy around here."

Charlotte just shrugs, biting her lip, and she looks a little bit nervous. I think Father is upsetting her.

"I'll call you later tonight," he says. "I promise."

Charlotte is now uncomfortable and gets her coat on as fast as she can, saying her good-byes as she does so. Father watches her walk to her car, standing in the doorway as he always does, this time leaning on his crutches.

When he turns back, Mother is still standing there. Staring at him.

She runs her tongue along the inside of her teeth. She shifts Finn so he is sitting on her other hip.

Mother pauses. "Ohhhh, Tommy," she says, exhaling. She turns away, as if she's suddenly exhausted.

There is still something unsaid between them. Something they need to talk about. But it's not going to get said now. Not during this particular visit.

Because after supper, Mother kisses my siblings and leaves, taking her case with her.

She never says good-bye to me.

And as much as I am still dreading the idea of having to go with her, and fear she may yet come back for me, the fact that she temporarily forgot about me—striding right past me without even a pat on my head—stings terribly. I run away from my family and hide under a table in the dark basement for hours.

I curl into a tight ball and bury my nose in my paws. It is a terrible shock. I thought I was past this. I thought her leaving wouldn't hurt me anymore. The heartache is tremendous, and I wasn't expecting it.

20

This Is the Easy Part

That night, and again the next day, Father calls Charlotte and asks her to please come over after work. He calls from the kitchen while leaning on his crutches. I don't think he is successful, because they are not on the phone for long.

Jimmy is also glum when he gets home from school in the afternoon. It's possible Aruna is still unhappy with him for asking her to care for Finn while he talked to other girls at the big party. Jimmy calls her, and like Father, he does not seem to get much out of his phone call.

"Beautiful, my sweetheart, my frosted cookie," Jimmy begs her, pacing in his room. "Sweetie, just listen. I want to sincerely apologize again for—" He gives it all he's got. "No, no, just listen. Please." But I guess she doesn't want to hear it.

Jimmy comes down to sit on the couch next to Father. They ordered a pizza for supper, and the empty box sits on the coffee table.

"I missed Valentine's Day," Jimmy complains, "because of the whole *insane-party-then-Dad-jumps-out-a-window-and-Mom-comes-to-visit* situation. I haven't even given Aruna her gift yet."

Father reminds Jimmy he won't be giving Aruna her gift any time soon, because he's grounded all week anyway over the whole *insane party* factor of the equation.

Mary has been standing in the doorway between the living room and kitchen, listening. She flops in the armchair. Turning to Jimmy, she asks, "So what did you get her?"

Jimmy shrugs. "A card, and her favorite chocolate bar, and earrings, and a cupcake . . ." He pauses. "But the cupcake wouldn't last, so I had to eat it."

Even Father has to laugh at that one. Jimmy smiles too, although he tries not to.

There is silence a moment, and Father mentions that he got something for Charlotte.

"What do you mean?" Mary asks.

He explains that he got her something for Valentine's Day. Just a card.

"What?" Jimmy snaps to attention and leans toward his dad. "You did what?"

Father repeats himself.

"Pops. Do you like her? I mean, do you, like, *like* her?" Jimmy is baffled, and he's speaking twice as loud as he was a moment ago. "What did you do? Wait. Start over. What did you do?"

Father sighs.

"Daddy!" Mary squeals. "Can I see it? Can I see the card? Where is it? When did you have time to buy it? You've been stuck here for days."

He admits he bought it last week, before the fire.

"Can I see it, pleeeease? Did you write something in it? What did you write?"

Father says no, she can't see it. I think he regrets bringing it up in the first place.

"Wow," says Jimmy, his big mouth hanging open. "That's . . . That is so crazy."

"Why?" Mary asks, with a shrug. "I'm the one who told Dad she'd be perfect for him."

Father interrupts, declares that's not exactly what Mary said, and says that they shouldn't get ahead of themselves.

When the hubbub settles down, Mary asks Jimmy to help her with something. He follows her upstairs and into her bedroom. I'm curious, so I follow as far as the landing, where I flop down and let my big belly spread out on the hardwood floor.

Mary has the big scissors in one hand and a box in the other. She gives Jimmy some plastic gloves.

"C'mon, help me with this."

Jimmy looks confused. "Help you with what?"

"C'mon."

"Nooooo . . . I don't think so." Jimmy starts backing away when he realizes what she wants him to do.

"I'll call Aruna for you, if you help me. I'll talk to her. I can smooth things out." Mary shrugs. "It was my fault and my stupid party. I swear, I'll call her. Tonight."

Jimmy looks skeptical, raising an eyebrow. But he follows Mary into the bathroom.

I hear them talking, and arguing, and complaining, and laughing, and fighting. It goes on for a good hour. There is the slicing sound of scissors, and an occasional shriek from Mary or groan from Jimmy. When they finally open the door, it looks like there has been an accident. There are drips of red on the white tile. And a lot of hair.

Mary's hair is half its normal length, cut so that it just brushes her shoulders. And the bottom half of her hair is dyed red. Bright red.

I know how important Mary is. Maybe like a bird with brightly colored feathers, she feels she must make herself stand out as a leader among the girl humans.

Jimmy sighs, looking around the bathroom, putting down the scissors. "You do realize that Dad is going to kill you. And then he's going to kill *me*."

"You're already grounded. How much worse can it get? He can't chase you while he's in a cast."

"Thank God for the little things."

They decide to show Father right away, to get it over with, as Jimmy says.

They enter the living room together. Jimmy's hands are stained crimson despite the gloves. Father isn't angry. Rather, he looks alarmed, sitting up straight.

"Is the school going to call me about this?" is the first thing he asks.

Mary shakes her head no. She explains that lots of kids do it.

"Are you . . . I mean, are you feeling okay, sweetheart?"

"Yeah, Dad." She shrugs like this is no big deal. "What do you mean?"

Father rubs his forehead with both hands. He could use Mother's help in situations like this. But tonight is probably not the right time to call Mother.

Mary gets up and leaves early the next morning. She is excited to show her friends her new hair.

Jimmy washes his hands repeatedly, but they are still

red. He finally gives up, grabs his backpack, and heads out.

Father has not been to work this week, stuck at home all day every day. He is bored and restless. I have heard him say that he is sick of wearing sweatpants, but they are easy to get on over his cast. So Father wears gray sweatpants and a white T-shirt. It's nothing special, but he looks comfortable and I think it suits him.

Father goes to the hutch in the dining room and pulls out the card he bought for Charlotte. He sits at the dining room table, pen in hand, alternately staring at it and looking at the wall. We listen to the grandfather clock tick as the minutes go by.

I can see how Father might find it hard to impress a woman like Charlotte. She seems very intelligent and fluid in her conversations. Father, on the other hand, is not the type to make a great speech. He never speaks with big words or poetic language. He is simple, but direct.

Finally, he writes something down.

Father makes a deal with Jimmy and Mary when they get home from school. He says he will lift their punishment of being grounded and give Jimmy money to take Mary to the mall and get supper at the food court. As long as they clear out for a while so he can talk to Charlotte and give her the card.

They are momentarily speechless. Mary's innocent face looks puzzled, a baby face framed by her newly shocking two-toned hair. Jimmy grabs the money from his father's hand.

"Thanks, Pops." He ushers Mary out before Father can change his mind. "C'mon, Mare. You'll be a big hit at the mall."

Not long after, Charlotte arrives. She walks in with caution, swinging the door open slowly.

Father is quick to meet her at the door, leaning on his crutches, and tells her again that he is really sorry for not calling her earlier in the week. He shows her that he's had Jimmy bring Finn downstairs. The baby waits on a blue blanket that lies on the living room floor.

It is hard for Father to lower himself to the floor, but he gets there. As soon as they are seated, he takes Charlotte's hand and apologizes again. He focuses all of his attention on her, telling her he is so sorry things have been strange this week. He tells her that he should have warned her Carrie would be here.

Finn plays with his toys, by their side. I sit on the far side of Finn, on the corner of his blanket.

While she would not talk to him long on the phone, Charlotte now listens to Father, looking back and forth from his cast to his crutches. She has on a pretty blue sweater and jeans with boots that come up to her knees. Charlotte's little hand, all pink fingernails and silver rings, fits into Father's hand, and she lets him hold it. She sometimes glances up to meet Father's gaze.

Father smiles at her as he talks, finally relaxing because he can see she is giving him a chance to explain. He gives her a blow-by-blow account of the whole weekend: the phone call that sent him running out, the kids' party, the big fire, the accident, the ride to the hospital, and Mother arriving and sleeping in his bed while he slept on the couch.

Charlotte listens carefully to the whole thing.

From the way her eyes flicker up to look at him— and rest for a moment before turning back down to Finn—I get the impression that it almost doesn't matter anymore what he is saying. Because I think I know how this will end. I think she has decided that she will let him kiss her.

I marvel at how different Charlotte is than Mother. The two of them are so, so different. Mother was soft and curvy. Charlotte is tall and thin, all angles. Mother's voice was loud and critical. In contrast, everything Charlotte says is soft and whispery, and infused with excitement. Mother filled Father's days with desire and drama and unpredictable turns. I think Charlotte, on the other hand, makes him feel safe and secure.

Neither is better or worse. They are just different.

Father doesn't mind that they are different. I can see it in his eyes and hear it in his voice, which is low and gentle as he talks to her. He wants this one now.

If I am honest with myself, I will confess that I still love Mother. I do. Something about this situation is confusing and makes my whiskers tingle.

But I know Mother is not coming back here. And Charlotte is a good human. If Father wants Charlotte, I want Charlotte to want Father back. That part of it is simple.

He gives her the Valentine's Day card. She reads it so fast that he can't have written more than a few words. I can only hope they are the right ones.

Charlotte glances up at him. "Tommy." That's all she says.

I wish I could read, I think. I am doomed to live my life not knowing some things.

From the look she gives him, her head bowed, I would say she is ready for him now. But she isn't like other women Father has known. Charlotte isn't like Mother or Jenny. She isn't going to make the first move.

Father looks back at her. He's waiting for her to do

something. And then, as his eyes widen slightly, I see it dawn on him that he'll have to do this.

It's funny. He has been confident all along. And yet now, for a moment, he freezes up, seemingly unsure of what to do.

I blink at him. I hope he can see that I am okay with this. I wish I could tell him: *Don't hesitate. This is the right time.*

Charlotte's hand moves just a few inches, to touch his cast, very gently. Just barely. I hope he understands now what I already know: He has permission to press forward. With a quick movement, as if he might lose his courage if he doesn't move right away, he takes her hand and puts it on his chest, right over his heart. By doing this, he pulls her an inch or two closer to him.

Father leans in, and then slowly, as if not wanting to startle her, he moves so his face is very close to hers.

I know I said Father is unable to give a speech, or tell a joke. There are many things he is just not good at.

But nature did not leave him without any evolutionary advantages. Now that he has her where he wants her, I'm confident he will know what to do.

Father's back is up against the armchair. He sinks his hands deep into her hair and pulls her to him, to hold her mouth right up against his for a kiss. He isn't giving her any opening to get away now.

Finn turns to look at me and smiles. I swear he does. He has a few more teeth than he used to, and he is developing a cute little grin to go with those big, round eyes.

Charlotte's arms encircle Father's waist, and she moves so close her hands slide up his back. She presses snugly up against him. After a while, Father moves back an inch to look at her. Her eyes flicker half-open, but she is in a trance now, her face flush and her mouth hanging open, waiting for him to come back.

"Tommy," she says again.

I see Father is overwhelmed. She is a sweet, delicate creature, and it is clear to him now that she wants him very badly. Whatever her reservations were before, including the fact that he is married, have been set aside because her heart has made the leap. He moves forward quickly to kiss her again, harder. He drops a hand out of her hair and lets it fall to rest on her hip. A few minutes go by, and they do not look our way. I close my eyes and purr. Finn sits and watches and chews his rattle.

Recently Finn has started crawling, and they're lucky he's not in a crawling mood. Sometimes, the baby just takes off.

Whoops—I spoke too soon. There he goes.

Father has a second sense about Finn. He extricates himself from Charlotte, although he stares at her as he pulls away, as if stunned, like he can't believe his luck. On two hands and one good knee, he catches up to Finn and grabs him. Charlotte is worried Father is hurting his leg, and she moves to take hold of Finn herself.

They end up sitting with the baby and talking, but with long pauses where Father just stares at Charlotte. I imagine he is not thinking quite straight. Once in a while, Father reaches forward to push hair out of Charlotte's face, tucking it behind one ear for her. He can't stop himself from touching her cheek, squeezing her hand, or rubbing her elbow.

While she is not dark and beautiful like Mother, there is something kind of adorable about Charlotte.

When my siblings walk in, Charlotte straightens up. Finn sits between her and Father on the floor.

Charlotte compliments Mary on her hair. Mary beams in response. They tell Father about their supper. Suddenly realizing what time it is, Father apologizes for not offering Charlotte any food.

"We have sliced ham," Jimmy offers, sincerely. "I could make you a sandwich."

When Charlotte declines, Father asks Jimmy if he could take Finn upstairs for a while. Jimmy gives Father a look while lifting Finn out of his arms.

Jimmy has seen the card on the floor with the heart on it.

If they were alone, I think Jimmy would make a joke about this situation. But since Charlotte is right there, he bites his tongue and just says, "Have a nice night," as he carries the baby upstairs.

Charlotte floats into the kitchen and pours a glass of lemonade. When she comes back to the living room, she clicks off the light switch, so the only light in the room pours in the window from the outside front door light.

Father has totally forgotten to make a fire, but it doesn't matter. The room seems plenty warm. He has turned up the heat for once.

They share the lemonade, drinking in turns from the same glass.

Once the glass is safely on the coffee table, Charlotte turns back to Father and throws herself on him with such enthusiasm that I scamper a few feet away. Father leans back to lie down on the floor, and he pulls her so she is lying on top of him, right on the baby blanket, his hand on her rump. Charlotte kisses him while moving her hands over every part of him she was only able to look at before: his arms, his shoulders, his hair. Her fingers trace a vein in his neck and touch his ear. Every inch of him interests her. They lie there for a while, and I start to drift off.

Suddenly, Charlotte lifts herself up. She says she forgot about Father's injuries and she's afraid she is putting pressure on his ribs and hurting him. He protests that he is fine, that his ribs are bruised but not broken. Father tells her he finally decided to take some medicine to help with the pain.

Straddling him, she won't lean back down to kiss him, no matter how he vouches for his lack of pain. Father relaxes and studies her.

Charlotte pushes his shirt up to his armpits and looks at his left side, purple and yellow from healing bruises. She frowns at his injuries. She pulls his shirt back down, smoothing it gently with her fingers.

Charlotte puts her head down carefully on his chest, away from his bruises and just over his heart. Father closes his eyes and plays with her hair, running a hand through the soft waves. They are very quiet.

They are still lying there when I hear footsteps on the stairs, and I know from the heavy thumps it is Jimmy. His hand squeaks against the banister as he stops himself short in the middle of the stairs. Perhaps when he noticed the living room light was off he decided he'd better speak first before coming down.

"Dad?"

Father picks his head up a bit. "Yeah?"

"I just got a weird call from Ma," Jimmy says, not moving from his spot on the stairs. I feel my ears instinctively twitch when I hear her name.

Now Charlotte lifts her head.

"What about?" Father asks.

"She wants to know if we can come visit this weekend. Stay overnight. And bring Finn too."

Father looks at Charlotte.

There is a long pause. I'm sure the idea makes him very nervous. I know the idea makes me very nervous.

Mother hasn't spent a lot of time with Finn. Will she be able to meet his needs? He is still small and vulnerable. I wonder if she might feed him the wrong foods, or put him down to sleep at the wrong times.

Even worse, she might ignore his cries. It is a terrible thing to say, but it did happen once before. Or if he does something naughty, she might get agitated and frustrated.

I have to assume that with Robert, Jimmy, and Mary nearby, however, these situations would turn out okay. Jimmy can take care of that baby just fine, if needed.

I think it is more likely that it will all come back to Mother, a mothering instinct that is stronger than any distractions. But what then?

What if she cuddles Finn and realizes she cannot let him go?

Or what if she takes him out and does not come back?

I suppose these risks flash through Father's mind as he lies on the floor. But just as there are risks, there are benefits.

If the three children go to visit Mother, then Father could have the house all to himself. He has no privacy when his children are here.

And the children have been missing Mother in a terribly intense way. They have been waiting a very long time for an opportunity like this one.

Father catches my eye. I wink in agreement, giving him my blessing. They will go. They will be safe. Then they will come back. Right?

Father tells Jimmy that if he and Mary agree they want to go, then they can go. He puts his head back down on the floor and squeezes Charlotte tight against him.

Father and Charlotte should enjoy it now, because this is the easy part.

I know that in the cold light of day, tomorrow and the tomorrow after that, this may not all look so easy.

21

New Flannel Sheets

There is a sweet smell of salt in the air.

Fog rolls past our windows, floating in from the shore. The snow is melting, and things are finally thawing out.

When I sit on the windowsill, I can look up and see that in the steady afternoon sun, the icicles hanging from the gutters are dripping and receding. Jasper is starting to shed his winter fur, and it's all over the house, brown hairs sticking to the couch and gathering in corners.

In the hallway by the front door, Father holds Finn tight, up against his shoulder. He won't hand the baby over to Jimmy until they've gone over several things.

"I don't want him ever left alone in a room," Father says.

Jimmy nods.

"If you leave the room, even just to go to the bathroom, remind your ma that she has to watch him," Father continues. "I don't want her taking him anywhere in the car without Robert. Robert has to go too, if they take him out."

Jimmy assures Father that he has babysat Finn many times and he knows what to do. He promises Father that he will call or text if there are any problems.

But Father won't drop it: "You know what to look for, right? You're old enough to know. If things aren't right. I wouldn't let you go if you weren't old enough to—"

"Pops. It's fine. I'll know if Ma isn't feeling well. She's not going to drop him on his head. She never dropped me on my head." He pauses, biting his lip. "Unless there's something you're not telling me."

Father sighs and gives Jimmy a small smile. He still hesitates.

As they stand there, I notice Jimmy's hand sliding up to rest on his opposite arm, right over the scar that is hidden by the sleeve of his shirt. "Pops," he says, almost in a whisper. "If something is off, I'll know. Trust me, I'll know."

"Nothing can happen to him," Father repeats, almost to himself. "If she's not acting quite right—"

"I know."

Father nods and hands Finn over to Jimmy. They all go out to the car, with two small bags and Finn's baby bag.

Father is back, alone, half an hour later.

After Father returns, he sits in the living room armchair. He just sits, not turning on the television and not reading a book. For a long while, he stares down at the old, faded rug. I can see the worry in the lines of his face. I jump up to sit in his lap. He pats my head while lost in thought, his eyes glazed over.

It will be fine, I try to communicate to him, a deep

purr erupting from my chest. Jimmy and Mary know how to take care of Finn. They do it all the time. They carry that baby around everywhere. Finn is always getting a ride to the different rooms of the house, squealing and chattering, perfectly content. Eventually I feel Father's muscles relax in his legs and hand.

Charlotte arrives with a big smile soon after my siblings leave, very happy to be here at week's end. I think she looks pretty in her pink T-shirt. Spring is coming, and this is the first time I have ever seen Charlotte wear a short-sleeve shirt. The skin on her arms is pale and lightly freckled. Father's mood instantly brightens. She and Father go out for several hours. I take a nice noontime nap on the couch and then slink upstairs to take an early afternoon nap up on the bed. The house is silent and serene.

The minute I jump up on the bed, a new scent tickles my nose. I remember that there are new sheets under Mother's old comforter.

Last night, Father and Sean went out. When they came back, they had new flannel sheets for Father's bed. He and Sean took everything out of the packaging and had a drink while waiting for the sheets to wash and dry.

Father has finally figured out how to use the washing machine without creating way too many suds.

I don't think Father had laundered the old sheets for many, many weeks. Possibly months.

Then Sean helped him put the new sheets on properly. Sean only had one working arm. The other was in a sling. But he did his best.

The first time they tried to put on the bottom sheet, it didn't fit. Sean asked Father if they bought the right size, and he swore they did. Then they realized they just had it stretched out the wrong way.

Neither one is a genius with bedding.

These new sheets are blue and cozy. So now it doesn't smell so much like Mother anymore. But the soft comforter is still here. I bury my nose in that for a while.

Father and Charlotte come back before supper, and I hear them downstairs taking off boots and coats and shaking off the cold. It would not be an exaggeration to say that Father has Charlotte up in our bedroom within ten minutes of their entering the house. The crutches do not slow him down on the stairs on this particular afternoon.

Charlotte climbs onto the bed with me, and Father stands at the foot of the bed, placing his crutches on the floor. He pulls his shirt off, over his head, and throws it on the floor. If his bruises hurt him, he is not showing it now.

Charlotte smiles and claps, like a child who is about to get a treat.

I told you she is a little silly.

Father looks at her blankly for a moment, not knowing what he has done to earn her applause. A smile widens across his face as he sees she is just very excited. Then he laughs.

He now carefully considers Charlotte on the bed, still for a moment. He is thinking about the best approach, like a cat stalking his prey. Finally, he crawls across the bed to her, eyes alert and muscles tense.

I assume he feels he must amaze her now with his mating abilities.

Charlotte beams at him. She is so, so delighted and cannot wait.

Regardless of his prowess, keep in mind that Father must impress Charlotte while wearing a bright green cast on one leg from the knee down. No disrespect to Father, but I find it a little bit amusing.

She shivers involuntarily when he gets very close. When his mouth is almost to hers, he pauses. Just to tease her, I think. To make her wait.

"Lay down with me," he whispers to her.

I jump off the bed, trying to avoid getting shoved accidentally onto the floor. I know the drill.

I lie on the floor by the window where I can't really see them. I hope Charlotte is satisfied with his performance.

Judging from what I hear, she is pleased. She says his name many times, as if she is calling him to her, but he is already right there with her. No man could be immune to that sort of flattery.

They are in bed the rest of the afternoon and evening. At one point Jasper comes scampering up the stairs, his claws scratching against the wood floor. Father gets dressed and takes him outside for a minute. Charlotte comes downstairs, and they have a small bite to eat. They watch the television for a short while. I meow, and this time Charlotte feeds me, for the first time. She knows where the cat food is kept now, on a low pantry shelf.

This must be love, if he is sharing with her where he keeps my cat food.

In the morning, Father sits up suddenly as he wakes, naked and disoriented. He looks around the room as if he is quite confused. I lie by his feet. Charlotte sees his reaction and puts a hand on his shoulder. He collapses back down by her side, throwing his arm and a leg over her. He gathers her in and holds her gently, his face up against her ear. He whispers things to her. She closes her eyes and listens.

At breakfast, they both seem tired out. I slink under their legs and rub against their ankles.

Today my siblings are coming back, which probably

makes Father a little anxious. He is not as relaxed as the day before.

I wonder what Charlotte thinks of all this.

I imagine Charlotte isn't sure if this is okay, this whole situation. She must wonder if she can truly love him. Father is strong and dependable, and she is attracted to him, but is that enough? He is burdened with many children, like a lion who already has a pride, and maybe she'd rather start new with a pride of her own. He has a difficult job, with strange hours, where he can get injured, as we all have been reminded. He could invite Charlotte to live in this big house with him, but it isn't clean and it isn't new, and I don't know what else he can offer her. Certainly not his sparkling conversation. Charlotte wears clothes that are silkier and finer than anything Mother ever wore. Perhaps they don't even like to do the same things outside of working with Finn.

These are unanswered questions that I imagine go through her mind.

Father goes out to pick up the children, and Charlotte waits here with me and Not a Cat. She showers and gets dressed and flits from room to room, looking over the whole house. She is thinking, thinking, thinking. Father is gone for quite a while.

When they get back, my siblings are happy to see that Charlotte is here. This has been a big weekend for all of us, in many ways.

Finn is wearing a new child-sized hat with a B on it, probably a gift from Mother or Robert. He looks very cute, a few white-blond, silky strands of hair sticking out from under the sides of the hat. I have to say he looks no worse for wear after being gone one night.

Jimmy and Mary take Finn upstairs. It's hard for Father to carry the baby anywhere with those crutches, although I've seen him tuck Finn under one arm and walk with just one crutch under his other arm. You do what you've got to do.

Father and Charlotte stand just under the stairs, Father holding Charlotte in his arms, and they talk quietly. She wants to know why he was gone so long.

He tells her he just wanted to hear all about how the weekend went. He needed to see where the baby slept and make sure everything had been good and safe.

I am not sure Charlotte fully understands why Father would be nervous about the children visiting Mother. She may not know how Mother treated Jimmy sometimes. She may not know about all of the things Mother did that made Father anxious.

And I believe Charlotte is afraid that he still loves Mother.

I have to tell you that in my opinion, yes, he does still love Mother. He will always love her. She was the love of his life. And she is the mother of his children.

But I don't think he is *in love* with her anymore.

I can see from the way he studies Charlotte that Mother isn't on his mind right now. Father smiles at Charlotte. He tells her he had a great weekend and kisses her cheek and then her neck, burying his face there.

He is marking his new territory, putting his scent on her so other men will know she is off limits. I give him some privacy.

I scamper upstairs to see how Jimmy is doing. It was a peaceful weekend, yet I missed my siblings terribly. So did Jasper, who is so excited that he runs up the stairs and leaps onto Jimmy's bed, where he usually never goes. He now is yipping his head off because he can't get down from the bed.

"Shut up, for the love of Christ!" Jimmy barks back at him. He lifts Jasper and places him on the floor.

"God, Jasper, you are *so small.* Where does all of that hellish noise come from?" Jasper runs out to find Mary.

Jimmy closes his door and phones Aruna. "Hey, sweetie," he says to her. He sits on the bed next to me and runs one hand down my back. He pets me too hard, but I let him get away with it. Just because I missed him.

"Yeah." He sighs. "It was fine. I had a good time. It was surprisingly normal." It seems that Aruna has forgiven him for his mistakes. "Yeah, I missed you too." He listens. "Mary? I think she had a good time. But yeah, she seems a little down. It's like, maybe if the winter would just get over with already we'd all feel better. I need some sun. I need the beach. We're going to have a great time this summer. I can't wait."

Aruna must be making a suggestion, because Jimmy cocks his head while listening.

"Hmmmm . . . that sounds like a good idea. A really good idea. I like it!"

Jimmy absentmindedly fluffs up the fur on my big stomach while pausing for a moment. There is a sparkle in his eye, which lets me know he likes whatever it is Aruna is saying to him.

"You see," he replies, "that's why I love you." He closes his eyes, and I hear Aruna squeal something in the background. A big grin spreads across his face. "Yeah, I love you. What did you think?" His eyes pop open as he listens. "It was the chocolate that tipped you off, wasn't it?" She says something, and he laughs.

"Yeah, let's have a big date next weekend," he continues. "Make up for lost time. I can't wait. So, speaking of dates, Charlotte is here. Oh my God. Can you believe that? My crazy dad?" Jimmy looks at me and ruffles the fur on my head. He winks at me. "I know. I know. It's, like, so crazy. So guess who is right here with me?" He pauses as she takes a guess. "That's right! Big Fat Crookshanks! Aruna says hello to you, Boo."

Huh? I still don't get why that's funny.

"Okay, sweetie, I'll see you on Tuesday. I gotta go with my dad to Finn's appointment tomorrow. Yeah, Boston Children's Hospital. Okay. Good-bye. Bye-bye. No, I can't. Okay, bye. Sweetie, no. Bye, sweetie."

This goes on and on for a good three minutes.

"Okay, seriously, I love you, good-bye." He hangs up. And then pretends to rest his head down on me, as if I am a big pillow. He doesn't put all of his weight on me though.

I ignore him. Because if I didn't ignore him, I'd have to swat him. And my paw might get stuck in his big mop of messy, black hair.

That would be a total disaster.

The next morning when Mary leaves for school, she gives Finn an extra hug and tells Father good luck. Father gets Finn dressed in a nice outfit, and Jimmy carries Finn out to the car. I assume they are headed for that hospital Jimmy mentioned.

I have a rare few hours when no humans are here at all. I listen to the dishwasher cycling, water splashing and draining. It's very calming.

I feel bad Finn will never get to hear the wonderful, comforting sound of a dishwasher gently splashing and draining.

When they come home, Finn is fussy. He cries and cries. The poor thing has little, plastic blue things behind each ear, and they are clipped to his shirt by strings. Finn pulls the blue things off his ears repeatedly, and Father and Jimmy struggle to get them back on him. They sit Finn down on the living room rug and try to distract him.

"Hey, buddy!" Jimmy tries with an expressive face. Finn's little hand moves up to paw at his ear. "No, look here. Here!" But Finn isn't having any of it. No matter how many times Jimmy puts the blue things back on his ears, Finn pulls them off.

"Maybe it's feedback?" Jimmy asks. "Or maybe he's actually hearing something and he's not used to it, so he doesn't like it?"

Father shakes his head. He's not sure. He reminds Jimmy that the doctor said these "hearing aids" might not help Finn at all. Father is worried that maybe these aids are just going to drive Finn crazy and make him uncomfortable for nothing.

Jimmy leans forward and gives Finn a hug. "Pops, we gotta talk more to him. The doctor said it's okay to talk to him. He said all parents should talk to their deaf baby." Jimmy pauses. "You know, Ma talked to Finn the whole weekend."

I can tell Father finds this interesting by the way he tips his head.

"Wait," says Jimmy, "I've got an idea." He stands and hustles up the stairs. When he comes back down, he's got the little B cap in his hand. Jimmy carefully puts the aids back on Finn's ears and then sticks the hat on Finn's head.

This time, Finn's hand moves slowly up to his head. And when his hand finds the cap, he is distracted. His blue eyes light up with amazement. I imagine Finn is remembering how happy Mother was to put that cap on his little head.

And his hand drops.

Father grins at Jimmy.

"Yeah, I knew it." Jimmy takes all the credit, as he should. "Yeah, that just happened. I outsmarted my baby brother. Deal with it."

I feel my purr increase to full blast. I can't help it. Jimmy beams like Mother used to when she was proud of herself.

Later, I follow Jimmy up to his room and we sit on his bed. I admire my big brother. He is an amazing human. Unlike Mary and Father, he is always cheerful. I can't believe I never appreciated this about him before Mother left.

It is like realizing that something I have been searching for has been right beside me all along.

My bond with Mother blinded me to the possibility of connection with other humans. Mother was the one who met all my needs, as powerful as the sun that warms me through the window. I took her presence here for granted. Jimmy and Mary were just other warm bodies circling Mother. We competed for her attention.

Jimmy is not exactly like Mother, but he has the same dark eyes, the same quick laugh. More than that, he is patient and brave. I think he has a good soul.

There is a photo of Mother on his bedside table, and it's one where she's cradling me in her arms. At one time, this was my favorite photo. Not anymore.

I slink onto the dusty table, which is covered in papers and cards and pens and electronics, all kinds of human junk. I purposely rub up against the framed photo, so hard that it falls off the table. Good riddance.

Jimmy turns at hearing the *thunk* and immediately reaches down to pick up the photo. He looks it over a number of times. I track his eye movements. I wonder how his weekend really went. I wonder how badly he misses Mother. I wonder if it was amazing to see her, or painful. Perhaps it was both.

"It's not her fault," he says softly, and I guess he is talking to me, but also maybe to himself. "It's not her fault she's sick."

I look away, pretending something outside the window interests me. I know now that Mother's actions were not normal at times, that she was full of too much energy and had some strange ideas. But *sick?*

I don't care if Mother is ill. I don't want to hear excuses for her bad behavior.

I turn back and give Jimmy a *yeow!* He needs to snap out of it.

But when I crane my neck to look up at him, Jimmy just glances at me and then stares down at the photo again. "You don't get it. She had to go," he continues, his voice barely a whisper. "Robert told me she had to go, to save her own life. He reached a helping hand out to her, and she took it. That's all. She just couldn't live here anymore." He sighs. "She misses you something awful, Boo. Believe me."

My fur bristles at this. Jimmy can tell himself anything he wants.

I am more worried about Jimmy now than I am about Mother. Those who are left behind need love too. Perhaps in some way we failed to take care of Mother. Perhaps Mother did have to go. But I feel betrayed and rejected. Now we need to take care of ourselves.

"Boo," Jimmy mumbles. "My stomach hurts."

I turn back to Jimmy and climb up into his lap.

Snuggling down, I rest my full weight on him. I will take care of him. I love my family. I don't want us to hurt anymore.

When I look up, I see tears starting to pool in Jimmy's eyes, but none run down his face. He is close to some sort of understanding, but not quite there yet. When he leans over and smothers me, putting his face right down into my fur, I allow it. I try to relax, feeling his breath hot on my back. I'm happy to help. My brother needs me.

22

Snap

The days keep getting a little longer. The sun feels warm through the glass panes of the old windows. I stretch out on the floor right in a square of direct light, feeling good.

I am being fed on a regular basis. I settle down at Father's feet every night, where I am welcome. So I can't complain.

But these have been a difficult couple of days for Father.

One night, he talks to Jimmy and Mary about Charlotte's visit, sitting with them on the stairs, where Mary paused to say hello to me. I like to sit on the middle stair to keep track of comings and goings.

Father clearly feels awkward, tapping his hand on his knee, stumbling on his words. My siblings are supportive and tell him they are okay with it. Father appreciates what they have to say, but at night he tosses and turns.

I think he is unsure about it.

But at the same time, now that Charlotte has gone home and he is alone in his bed, he aches for her. He stares at the wall, lost in his memories. Then he turns to grab the pillow she used and hugs it to his chest.

It's funny to think about Father being lonely in this house full of people and pets, but I know he has been. I understand.

As soon as Father falls asleep, Finn starts screaming and doesn't stop, all night. Father needs Mary's help to give Finn medicine. Father flips on the bathroom light, and it is so bright it blinds them. They can't figure out what is wrong. Finn grabs his ear. The hearing aids are off, but he still cries and pulls at his neck.

In the morning, my siblings have to go to school, but Father stays home. A trip to the doctor is fruitless, and there are twenty-four more hours of frustration and pain and crying and comforting and nonstop care. Father looks in his books but cannot find an answer.

I hear Father calling the doctor in the wee morning hours of the next day. "But he's still screaming. His fever is so high. I don't know what to do. You have to see him again." Father is very upset, pressing the phone to his ear. "No, something is wrong with him. I don't know what I'm supposed to do. Please, we have to come back in."

By the time they go back to the doctor, Father is exhausted and angry and at the end of his rope. I think he is ready to throw his crutches out the window.

He finally comes home with a new kind of medicine, but it takes another full day before Finn feels better.

Mahmee, while waiting for Father to return from the doctor, calls Charlotte to cancel her appointment, telling Charlotte that she doesn't need to come. Father, upon returning and hearing that news, is momentarily stunned.

He hasn't told his mother how he feels about Charlotte yet. So Mahmee didn't know Father might want to see Charlotte even though Finn is sick.

Father sulks and snaps at Mahmee whenever she tries to talk to him. He hunches over on the couch, massaging his temples, too tired to even raise his head. Father worries about Finn so much. I think his heart is heavy with it all the time, even when the baby is well. So having Finn in pain is too much to bear. He complains to Mahmee about how hard it is to raise a baby without Mother.

"Ah, c'mon, Tommy. Carrie's leaving was a blessing in disguise," Mahmee says, obviously frustrated. "She was more of a burden than a help to you."

Now Father's head whips up.

Mahmee shrugs. "What if she wasn't well and Finn was here alone with her? He wouldn't be able to tell you something was wrong, like Jimmy did. You wouldn't want that."

This doesn't sit well with Father. His face darkens. His hands clench into fists.

"OUT," he directs her, pointing toward the door. "Just get out, Ma. Go home. You're not helping me."

Mahmee is taken aback, but she sighs (just like Father does) and gets up to gather her things.

Father runs a hand over his face. "Don't talk about Carrie. You don't know what she went through as a kid, Ma."

"Like what?"

Father ignores this question. "She never . . . she never really hurt Jimmy," he continues quietly. "Nothing too bad. He's always fine. She just gets agitated. And scared.

Carrie's much more likely to hurt herself than someone else."

"Maybe physically," Mahmee mutters, digging in her purse for her keys.

"What?"

"I said, maybe she never really hurt him too badly physically, Tommy. Although I never liked her laying a hand on him, for any reason. But you don't think she's hurt him emotionally?" She shrugs. "Forget it. I guess you wouldn't know about that, would you? God help you. You keep yourself shut up so tight, you wouldn't know how that kid feels. As for me, I'm glad she's gone."

Father's face goes pale. He looks stunned. Before Mahmee can turn to go, Father snaps.

He grabs one crutch and stands up, yelling at the top of his lungs. "JESUS CHRIST, MA. Carrie is still the kids' mother. If it was up to me, she'd still be here."

And: "It isn't Carrie's fault that she's bipolar." I listen carefully, because these are the same words Jimmy said, that *something* is not Mother's fault. Perhaps Jimmy heard these words from Father.

And also: "Ma, you never made an effort to understand it, or help my wife, or help me deal with it. So you can just knock it off with that crap."

I don't think I've seen him this upset in a long time. His eyes are red, and he is shaking.

Mahmee has her coat in her hand, and she stares at the floor. "She should have told you she was sick before you married her. It isn't right what she did to you, not telling you."

Father just shakes his head. He says it wouldn't have mattered, and Carrie didn't know it herself.

I am confused. I have never heard them say things

like this about Mother before, and I don't know what they are talking about.

"You don't understand. I don't think of her as sick. She just has a problem. We all have problems. You never talked to me about it. You never asked me about it. I would have married her anyway. I love her, Ma. It's not a blessing that she left."

He demands to know what kind of blessing it could be to leave a baby—a little, helpless, deaf baby—without his mother.

And, he asks, didn't he try to protect Jimmy? Wouldn't it be worse to have no mother? Isn't this worse for Finn, to be stuck with no mother and a father who doesn't know what he's doing?

And Father says, "Don't you understand it's my fault she left? I have so much guilt. I don't know if I can live with myself."

Mahmee is badly shaken, and she says she doesn't understand. Trembling, she swears she doesn't understand it at all.

"Why would you say those things about yourself?" she wants to know. "You're a good father. What did you do wrong? You didn't do anything wrong."

"There's more I could have done," he says. "There's more you could have done too. But it's between her and me now. It's too late for you."

Clutching her purse, on the edge of tears, Mahmee looks at her son.

"I'm glad she's gone and I'm not sorry to say it. Goddamn it, Tommy. You're better off. Why can't you see that?"

Father will not talk about it anymore and insists that Mahmee leave. Which she does.

I don't worry about Mahmee coming back tomorrow. She will. She loves Finn. As I mentioned, my siblings are her only grandchildren. Father gets into his moods, and she understands that.

Although this is a worse mood than usual.

I watch as Father sits down again. And rests his head in his hands.

I am not sure what's wrong. I know there is something he did, or something he didn't do, that is eating at him. Something to do with Mother. Something that makes him upset. I'm sure he still needs to talk to her, but the opportunity to talk never comes up, and I know she won't take his phone calls.

It worries me. Like Mahmee, I haven't seen him do anything wrong.

I keep a close eye on Father all night, curled up behind his back, pressing my backbone against his. Sometimes I wish I could tell my humans that I love them. I can only hope that they feel it as I purr and stretch into them.

Father lies as still as a rock, sleep deprived from the past few nights of being up with Finn. Finally, everyone is sleeping in this house.

Mahmee comes again the next morning, as I knew she would. She hangs up her coat in the front closet and wanders into the kitchen. She kisses Jimmy and Mary as they take off for school. I walk up to her and rub my wide face against her ankles to show Father the proper way to greet her.

Mahmee is a good woman. She and Father have their fights, but humans do that sometimes.

Father sits at the kitchen table, staring into his coffee. Pale and bleary-eyed, he has both hands wrapped around his mug, and he slumps down in his chair. His crutches lean against the wall.

"I just want you to be nice, Ma," he says out of the blue.

Mahmee stands there, hands on her hips. She frowns, as if unsure whether to respond.

"I don't want you saying anything bad about Carrie. Especially in front of the kids. I did promise to take care of her, for better or worse. Remember, Ma? You were there." He doesn't sound bitter to me. He just sounds sad.

There is a long pause.

"I'm seeing Charlotte," he continues. "I mean, we're already . . . You know."

Mahmee shakes her head. She turns to pour herself a cup of coffee. I don't think she's that surprised. She knows Father very well.

"You're already what? Finish your sentence."

"Together, Ma," he says simply. "We're already together."

Mahmee scowls in disgust.

"You're still married to the first one. You have to jump right from one woman to the next one? You can't live without a woman for five minutes?"

He doesn't respond. He has no answer for that.

Mahmee sighs. She looks tired too, the wrinkles creasing her forehead.

"Don't even think about asking her to come live with you here in my house," she warns, as if she still owns the house. And then it occurs to me that even though Mahmee moved out, maybe she *does* still own this house. "You better start saving for a ring before you think about that."

Father just stares at his steaming cup of coffee. He doesn't look at her. "I'm not in a rush to get married again. I don't have any money for a ring anyway," he says quietly.

Mahmee takes a long drink of her coffee, standing there in the middle of the kitchen. She looks at Finn, who is quietly sitting in his high chair. The baby seems to feel a little better, because he reaches for a piece of cereal. Walking up to her son and putting her hand on his cheek, Mahmee rubs the short whiskers on his face. Finally, he glances up at her.

"There's no keeping the women off of you, is there?" She sighs again, studying his face. "Don't ask me for any more jewelry," she finally says. "Your grandmother's ring was buried with Shannon."

"Make up your mind, Ma. First you tell me to take a break. Now you want me to get married again." He pauses. "I need Charlotte, Ma. Let me just try this out. See how it goes."

Mahmee drops her hand. Father takes a drink of the hot coffee, and some color comes back to his face.

"You've already got three kids," Mahmee continues out loud. "You don't need any more. Make sure you're careful. We don't want any surprises again." She's thinking it over now, lost in her thoughts, glancing up and out the window of the back door. "I'm getting too old to babysit."

It occurs to me she may be remembering how quickly Father met Mother and married her and had Jimmy. How it all happened too fast, as I once heard her explain it.

"Don't you think Charlotte will be good for me, Ma?"

She turns away from him, bringing her coffee over to the refrigerator. Mahmee sets her cup down and opens the refrigerator to take out the milk. "I'll say this. She is a hard worker. Charlotte does know sign language pretty well. I mean, I've seen her. She works hard with that baby."

Father turns in his seat so he can hear what she's saying.

"She's a little . . . different, that one. A little different. But even so. She's nice enough. Nicer than Carrie, if you ask me—which you did, so don't yell at me for saying that."

Mahmee opens the cabinet to get out the sweetener. "Of course she'd be good for you. She'd be good for all of you."

When Mahmee starts pouring milk into her mug, and has no further warnings or criticism for Father, a little smile flickers over his mouth.

He's feeling a bit better, just like Finn.

But I am left puzzled.

Is Mother really sick? It was true what Jimmy said? What kind of sickness does she have? My heart squeezes behind my ribs, because this is something I did not understand before. And why does Father think it is his fault that Mother left?

My tail twitches furiously as I am left with more questions than answers.

23

Big Date

Father and Jimmy quarrel all week. Father suggests that he could call Mr. O'Callahan and try to get Jimmy a job at the beach club this summer. Jimmy isn't sure he is interested in that, but says he'd be willing to consider it.

Father pressures him to think about it "a little harder."

Jimmy talks for days about his big date with Aruna. Late in the week, Father starts frowning whenever Jimmy brings it up.

Charlotte has to cancel her appointment because of an urgent matter with another client. In the early evening, Father and Jimmy have supper together while Mary is out. Finn sits in his bouncy seat on the rug in the living room, where Father can see him.

Finn now has his appetite back. He picks a slice of banana up off his tray and tries to mash it into his mouth. He's making a big mess. Human babies are uncoordinated. I doubt you'd see a kitten making a mess like that. Father and Jimmy each have a big bowl of cereal with a lot of sliced bananas in front of them.

Father asks Jimmy why he keeps calling it a "big date."

"Because, Pops. We just made up after our first big fight. And I didn't see Aruna last weekend because I was with Ma." Jimmy shovels cereal into his big mouth with a giant spoon, milk dripping back into the bowl.

Father sits up straight and looks at him. He starts to reply, then stops. He can't quite find the words. He wants to know what Jimmy is planning.

Jimmy doesn't stop eating as he talks. "Maybe a movie, I guess. Then we'll stay out late, drive around and listen to music, go spin by the beach, I guess."

Father shakes his head. He pushes away his cereal and folds his arms. Father hasn't been doing that so much lately, so I am surprised. He says he doesn't know if that's a good idea.

"Wh—what do you mean?"

Father explains his concerns. He remembers what he was like at Jimmy's age. And he hopes Jimmy isn't pressuring Aruna to do anything stupid.

"Like what, Pops?" Jimmy's mouth hangs open. "Jesus. Pops."

Father leans forward, gripping the edge of the table. "You just have to be careful, Jim, because you slip up just once and the rest of your life goes in a different direction very quickly. Do you know what I mean?"

"Oh my God." Jimmy pushes his bowl away from him, his face turning red. "Really? You're serious? You think . . . Okay."

Jimmy gets up and leaves the kitchen. But he doesn't

go far. He sits on the living room sofa and stares down at his hands. I jump up into his lap to comfort him, and he pats me heavily, lost in thought.

Father doesn't apologize. But he comes in and sits next to Jimmy.

"Dad," Jimmy finally says with a big sigh. "I know you remember what you were like at my age. I've heard all about the beach club and the trouble you guys used to get into. But I'm not you." He pauses. "And Aruna sure isn't like Ma."

Father waits.

"I'm not going to mess up her life, Pops. Aruna is smart. She wants to be an engineer like her dad, and she'll probably apply to Cornell or something next year. And then I'll never see her again."

Father frowns. He asks why Aruna couldn't go to a school in Boston. And then something else occurs to him. He asks if Jimmy is supposed to be looking at schools for himself this year.

"Ma asked me the same thing," Jimmy admits. Sitting next to Father on the couch, he is just as tall as Father, possibly an inch taller. With that hair. "But Pops. I think I should to go to community college and stay here and help you with Finn. You don't have a lot of money saved up anyway, do you?"

There is a gentle orange light seeping through the front windows as the sun sets. Father thinks about it. I push my nose up into Jimmy's hand to show my support, and he absentmindedly scratches my head.

"I don't want you to have to do that," Father says quietly. "It would be really helpful, but I don't want you to have to do that." Father won't look at Jimmy now. Instead, he looks at me, and I stare back.

It's okay, I want to tell him.

Jimmy shrugs. "Pops. I don't mind."

Finn is in his bouncy seat still chewing on a banana slice. He paws at his ear. He pulls a hearing aid off and puts it in his mouth.

"Uh, Dad . . ."

Father closes his eyes for a moment and shakes his head. "I give up." He pulls the hearing aid, now covered in banana slime, out of Finn's mouth and hand. He also unclips it from Finn's shirt. Father takes the hearing aid off Finn's other ear too.

Finn gives Father his sweet smile, looking at him with those clear blue eyes. He has no idea of the stress he is causing, of course.

The next night, Mary helps Jimmy pick out a nice outfit. He showers and gets dressed, putting on too much of that bottled scent he likes. Mary doesn't tease him. The experiences of the past few months have made her kinder to Jimmy. They are getting older.

They are growing up, my siblings.

Mary goes to her room and puts on a short, twirly skirt and a sparkly top. I see that she, like Jimmy, grew a few inches this past winter. Blond hair still rings the top of her head like a halo, but the red on the bottom gives her face new angles. She has started drawing on darker eyeliner, like Mother used to do, and has a more relaxed stance, leaning back with a hand on one hip when she admires herself in the mirror.

I realize that Mary and Jimmy must be going out together.

Aruna arrives, with a hug for Jimmy and another for Mary. One of Mary's friends, a girl with big, brown eyes and dark ringlets of hair, follows close behind. They all talk and laugh, very excited.

When I rub against Aruna's leg, she picks me up and

slings me over her shoulder. This is something new. Now I can't see what's happening. I'm too fat to turn my head very far. But that's okay. It's kind of fun.

Father comes into the front hall to say hello to everyone.

"Pops, tell Sean I went out with three cute chicks tonight. He'll be jealous." Jimmy laughs.

It occurs to me that Jimmy may have invited Mary and her friend to come along to make Father feel better about his "big date."

Father promises he'll call Sean.

Aruna has a big surprise for Mary. She puts me down on the floor and then pulls out of her coat pocket four tickets to a concert this summer.

Mary is amazed. "I'm going to see Harry!" She and her friend squeal and scream and jump up and down. Aruna replies with her beautiful laugh.

Mary, who is still bouncing with excitement, says dramatically that she doesn't know how she will ever repay Aruna. But Aruna just scoffs. "Hey, I'm an only child. My dad spoils me. No worries, he can afford it."

The kids keep talking, thrilled and full of energy, not noticing what has been implied: that Father could not have afforded it.

No matter, I think. It is the truth. No harm was meant by it.

But I worry that it may feed his doubts about how happy Charlotte could really be with him. And how happy he can make his children.

Father holds the door open for them and says good-bye, then retreats to the kitchen. I walk into the dark dining room and jump up to the window seat to watch my siblings out the window. Mary and her friend walk ahead to Father's truck, which Jimmy will drive.

Jimmy stops Aruna on the top step by the front door.

He turns her coat collar up against the spring wind, and when doing so he leans forward to give her a kiss on the mouth, lingering there for a moment, reluctant to turn away from her. He does it again, more insistent the second time.

Well! I haven't seen that before. Maybe Father was right to worry a little bit.

Father calls Sean on his little phone. He tells Sean about Jimmy's date, and Sean responds with something that makes Father laugh. The two of them complain about their injuries and talk about how goddamn boring it is to be at home. Father suggests he is just going to cut his cast off with a knife because it itches him and he can't stand it.

Father and Sean always find something to complain about. They seem to enjoy complaining very much.

Father then asks Sean if he'll come over next weekend to meet Charlotte. It sounds like Sean agrees.

The next call is to Charlotte, which I know because Father's voice gets low and soothing and calm. He apologizes for the short notice, but he wants to know if she will please come over. He tells her the kids are out and Finn is asleep.

"No, not for that," he says in response to her question. "Well, yes, for that, but not only that." He tells her how much he misses her and that he can't stand it. He is going crazy from not seeing her.

She is there within an hour, and they sit on the couch, sharing a can of soda. I curl up on the armchair next to them. Father is transformed; his face lights up as he looks at her, and he holds her hand. Always, always, he clings to her small hand.

He says they should probably talk about the—*not the rules, but the*—he can't find the right word.

"Parameters?" she suggests.

There is a long pause, and Charlotte and I both realize he might not know what that word means. I don't know either.

"Guidelines?"

Okay, he agrees. In case this works out and they move forward, they should have guidelines. Just to know where they stand.

He looks down at her hand in his and comes out with it: He's not sure he wants to have more children. Maybe, but he's not sure. He needs her to know that. He's just too exhausted to do it again. At least, right now.

Charlotte nods *okay,* and he is relieved.

I wonder if she agreed to that a little too quickly.

He also needs her to know that between Finn's therapy and doctors, and Jimmy's college and then Mary after that, he is broke. Plus he needs to think about Carrie's medication and therapy, which he will pay for forever because he promised to take care of her. Sometimes that includes an expensive overnight hospital stay. And sometimes that includes paying off a manic spending spree that they can't reverse. So that's his financial situation.

Charlotte gives him a patient smile. "It's okay. I do all right for myself." She shrugs. "It's not like I hang out with millionaires. Everyone I know is drowning in student loans." I listen carefully, but I don't know exactly what she means by all this.

Father squeezes her hand. He tells her it's easy for her to say that now, while she's sitting on his couch. But he's worried about her friends, and especially her parents, and what they'll think when they hear he has three kids—

Charlotte interrupts. "You let me worry about them. You have enough to worry about."

Now it's her turn.

She wants him to know that she realizes that he and his family eat very badly, but she does not cook. She has liked salad since she was a child, and this is mostly what she eats. She doesn't want to feel pressured—or even be asked nicely—to make meals for everyone, because that is not something she wants to do, and it would upset her if it came to that.

He agrees immediately.

I wonder if she should trust him to stick to that one.

Also, when he takes Finn to the beach this summer, Father has to promise to keep his head down. She says a cute dad with an incredibly sweet blue-eyed baby will attract trouble, and it makes her nervous.

I can see from the look on her face that she is teasing him now, and Father laughs. "Okay," he says. "You should come with us to the beach."

But there's one more thing.

Charlotte puts both of her hands on his and says, "Tommy."

In her tone is something that makes both Father and me sit up straighter.

"You have to decide what's happening with Carrie. You're still married. I know—I know you don't want to upset her. But you need to tell me if you're going to let her go. Not just a divorce. That too. But I mean, in your heart."

Father takes a deep breath. I think it is hard for him to explain what he's feeling. He may not even understand it himself.

I need to tell Father that we will all support him, whatever he decides to do. And show Charlotte that this could all work out.

I jump up to the couch and climb right onto Charlotte's legs. I calculate very carefully, and then I reach my paws up to climb onto her shoulder. I've never done this before, and I know I must be heavy. But I want her to hold me the way Aruna did, to see how much fun we could have together. Frankly, I don't fit in her arms quite as easily as I did in Mother's. This is a little awkward. Still, I hang on for dear life. Not letting go.

"Ah, Boo," Charlotte says in surprise, gripping me with two hands so I don't slide off.

I hear Father promise Charlotte that he's going to think about what to do. He says he will ask Carrie for a divorce very, very soon. Father explains he was just with Carrie for so long that he doesn't know anything else, and he worries about her, but he's trying really hard to get past it. He knows Carrie is living her own life now.

Charlotte puts me down gently into her lap, and I see Father squeeze her hand when it is free. "I love you," he says to her.

Charlotte nods. She is cautious about being too quick to reply, just like Mother was so many years ago. She does not say "I love you" back to him. Not yet. It doesn't seem to worry him at all.

It doesn't really worry me either.

But Charlotte is softened by his speech. He moves much closer to her, and before she can think too much about it he has one hand sliding behind her back and the other hand on her face, and he is about to kiss her. I jump away as quick as I can.

She teases him that she just came over to talk, "so don't get excited, Tommy Sullivan."

"Too late for that, Charlotte Davenport," he says softly back to her.

Father kisses her, using his weight against her mouth and the hand supporting her back to lay her down on the couch. Charlotte wraps her arms around him. She is quickly and effortlessly positioned beneath him as he moves her legs. She loves to touch him, squeezing his shoulder and stroking his hair. They easily fall into a rhythm as she arches up into him.

I'm glad at least something is easy for Father.

Father has missed Charlotte desperately all week. He napped and daydreamed every afternoon, as I believe he is still not working. Then at night he tossed and turned in bed, accidentally nudging me with his foot sometimes. I have seen him sending her messages on his little phone, and I know the notes are going to her from the way he rubs his forehead and takes a deep breath in and out. He is lovesick, I think.

Later, Charlotte goes home. Father is already in bed and asleep when my siblings arrive. Usually he waits up for them, but tonight he is too tired.

That's okay. I greet them instead. I can do that for Father.

Mary and Jimmy come up the stairs very quietly, without turning on the hall light. I walk upstairs with them. They brush their teeth and get into their pajamas.

Jimmy seems to pass out as soon as his head hits the pillow. Mary stays up late, reading and writing in a notebook. I visit her, lying myself down next to Jasper.

Jasper completely ignores me. As far as he is concerned, I am a loaf of bread.

Mary's eyes are gleaming and her face is calm and satisfied. She pins the four concert tickets to her bulletin board.

Like a ghost, she silently pads her way over to Jimmy's dark room. I follow her, thinking it is time to make my nighttime rounds of the house anyway.

Mary leans over Jimmy. He doesn't stir. "You're a

great brother," she whispers to him. And then she is gone.

After she has left, I sit on the rug watching over Jimmy. My eyes adjust to the darkness, details and shadows sharpening as they come into view.

And then, although his eyes do not open, I see a small smile curl on Jimmy's face.

24

Woman in Blue

When the alarm goes off, it takes Father a few minutes to open his eyes and rouse himself. Outside the bedroom window, the day looks gray and gloomy. The sun seems to be struggling to break through the clouds.

After pulling on sweatpants, Father barely looks at anyone, including me. When Mahmee arrives, he hands Finn off to her with barely a grunt. He works out in the basement while the kids get ready for school, showers after they leave (turning the water as hot as it will go and neglecting to turn the fan on), and gets ready to go out. I don't know where he is going today. We exchange a look as he passes by where I'm sitting, right by the front door.

I jump up to the windowsill to watch him go.

Mahmee throws a treat my way after she drinks her coffee and eats her toast with strawberry jam. Then she gets Finn ready for a walk in the pushcart. Finn gets a nice warm sweater, a thick coat, and a snug hat that must be pulled and stretched to fit onto his round head.

Finn's eyes are gentle and soft blue in the golden glow of the lamplight. Little mittens go on his baby hands. Mahmee decides to take Jasper along for the walk. She whistles for him, and hooks up the red leash to his harness. Even on the mornings when it is very cold, they bundle up and go out.

Sometimes when I am left alone in this big house I experience regret, and I cannot stop the bad thoughts from coming.

You see, I have a secret.

Far under the oven in the kitchen, I have hidden one of Mother's most precious things. I wonder if she ever misses it, or wishes she had it. I feel terrible for stealing it.

But it seemed to bring bad luck to this house, and get Mother into trouble, so I hid it. Perhaps I should never have messed with it in the first place.

It's so hard for me to know. I try to help, but I wonder if I made things worse.

The item that sits in the dust, out of reach, is a simple, thin gold disk. It is a fake, dull coin, and I think it used to belong to one of the children's games. But that coin gave Mother special powers.

Mother told me all about ghosts. She used that coin to speak to the dead, which is an ability most humans don't possess.

The night I stole the coin, many months ago during the hottest time of the year, when baby Finn had just been born, Mother had been carrying the coin around for days in her pocket. When no one was home, I saw her take the coin out and talk to it. She was communicating with those ghosts. I was always nearby, watching and studying her. Mother always operated on a higher plane than other humans. She was in touch with other souls, even ones we cannot see.

She was agitated. Pulling at her hair. Rocking gently back and forth.

Mother kept peeking out the window at our new neighbors, standing behind the curtain, rubbing the coin in her hand. Something about the neighbors was bothering her, and I had come to hate them. I hated what they were doing to her. While watching out that window, she bit her fingernails until they bled. The fingers that pulled aside the curtain were covered in Band-Aids of all sizes that she fetched from the kitchen.

Finn was upstairs in his crib, not a week old. Jimmy was upstairs in his own room. Father was also upstairs, taking a nap, having been up with Mother and the tiny baby a long time the night before. Mary was out with a friend.

Although Mother had spent most of the last months of her pregnancy in bed, ever since the birth of the baby, she had been up and about, pacing and unusually distraught. She didn't seem to concern herself much with the baby, so I didn't either. It worried me that she wasn't resting enough. I realized that the situation with the neighbors was making her anxious.

A sticky heat permeated the old house, settling into the cracks. Everything my paws came into contact with felt too warm and too damp. Father had all of the fans going, but they only pushed the hot air around, providing very little relief. A musty scent tickled my nose every time I entered a new room. The baby periodically screamed with discomfort.

Finally, Mother went down to the basement and came back with an ax in her hand.

Without bothering to put on shoes, she went right out the front door, into the night. When she came back, without the ax, she looked exhausted.

She shut the door behind her as if it were very heavy

and went into the living room. When she sat in the corner, on the floor, I climbed into her lap to calm her down. I watched a bead of sweat roll down her neck. We were quiet and still for a long while.

But then, suddenly, there was a sharp, insistent banging on the door. Jimmy came running downstairs.

From where I was sitting, I heard voices. Jimmy's voice sounded full of surprise. He was soon yelling for Father to come down: "Dad! Dad, get up." It sounded like Jimmy was trying to block people who were attempting to come in.

I caught only a glimpse of Father as he hurried down the bottom stairs and flew to the front door, looking disheveled. A woman's voice said something I didn't catch. I strained to listen as carefully as I could to the humans, because I was afraid they were threatening my family.

"No, Ann, everything's fine. I don't understand," Father begged.

I heard the woman's voice again. "I'm sorry, Tommy. They called 911. We have to come in."

"Who called? No one called. We're fine here. You don't need to come in."

"Your neighbors. They saw her on their property with an ax."

"What? A what? No, she—" There was a pause, and then Jimmy came in to check on Mother. Perhaps Father was stalling. "No, no. She's here. She didn't go out."

"Yeah, she's right here," Jimmy called out, standing over us.

Mother just hummed to herself and turned the gold coin over and over in her hand. She was perfectly still, and I turned my head up to look at Jimmy. At the time I remember thinking what a fool he was, what a fool all of these humans were to bother us. Mother and I were just sitting and thinking.

"I'm sorry, hon. We have to come in. They called 911."

"No, no, I don't think that's a good idea. You'll upset her. You're going to make it worse."

"Tommy, you know the rules. They called. Emergency call. We have to come in, hon."

Finally, they were all in the room. A woman dressed in midnight blue stood with her hands at her sides, one thumb tucked into her belt. She wore a short-sleeve shirt with a badge on the arm, and there was sand on her shoes as she stood on our rug. Her blond hair was in a tight bun on top of her head. A young man, taller and skinny, waited behind her. His hair appeared to be shaved under his hat.

Mother and I faced the wall. Jimmy hovered near us, and then sat to join us. Father also stood close by, as if shielding us from these strangers. There was a long pause. Mother did not acknowledge their presence.

Finally, the young man cleared his throat. "Ma'am?"

"DON'T TALK TO HER," Father exploded. "Who's he?" he asked the woman in blue. "Where's Jack?"

"On vacation." She held her hand up to the young man. "He's right. Don't directly address her."

"Is he trained? Step back. Step back. Don't let him near her." Father pointed at the tall man. "Don't go near her. Don't touch her. Don't even think about it."

Father was enraged, and I got a bad feeling in my stomach. After all, everything was fine. There was no need for this fuss. I sometimes don't understand human reactions to my beautiful mother. But I understood why Father wanted to protect her. I agreed they might make her upset.

The woman in blue crouched down near Jimmy. "Hey, Jim," she said softly. "What's your mom been doing?"

"I don't know," Jimmy admitted quietly, the tears coming to his eyes now that the woman in blue was being so kind to him. "I wasn't watching her. It was my turn to watch. I'm sorry."

"Did she go outside?"

He shrugged, a tear falling down his cheek. "I don't know. I don't know. I'm so sorry."

"It's okay, hon." The woman looked at Mother. "Carrie? Hey, it's me. Carrie? It's Ann. How are you feeling tonight?"

Mother turned her head now. I wondered why this woman with her blond hair in a bun, wearing midnight blue, was intruding on our family. She seemed to hold some power over everyone in the room, and I felt it.

"Fine. Great. Thanks, Ann. It's just this," she said, holding up the coin. "It helped me contact my grand-mother yesterday, but it's not working tonight. The thing is, Tommy promised me he would call Father Boyle. He promised that he'd invite Father Boyle over so I could explain to him all of the things that God has been telling me, but Tommy of course never called. He fell asleep. Because when you have a lazy-ass hus-band, nothing gets done, and I'm sure you know ex-actly what I'm talking about, because obviously he called you and never called Father Boyle."

"Hon, Tommy didn't call me. Your new neighbors called me."

"Oh!" Mother's voice was chipper and bright. "Oh, that's great. That's right. They've been watching me. They watch me come and go. They watch me out the window. Those people called you, and they called the town hall, and they called the governor. And I'm sick of it. I should have called you myself, because they've been harassing me. I told Tommy, but of course he never did anything about it, although you'd think if your husband was really worth something he'd take care of it. He thinks he's a tough guy, but he's not. I'm sure you think he's really brave and handsome. I guess you're together now, is that right? I know the police station is right next to the fire station. You think I don't know what goes on over there on your lunch break? You think that I don't know? Clearly he called you and not Father Boyle."

"Carrie, Tommy didn't call me. I only talk to him when I need to come here to talk to you. Your neighbors—"

"Frankly, you can have Tommy. I don't care if you do. He's lazy, he's stupid, he doesn't listen, and he doesn't do what I ask him to do."

The woman smiled mildly at Carrie. She blinked, barely breaking a sweat. "Carrie? Can I ask you a question about the ax?"

"What?"

"Where is the ax?"

Mother shrugged.

"I'm going to send my partner out to get it back for you. Where did you leave it?"

"In the tree."

"Which tree, hon? In the neighbors' yard? Or your own yard?"

I held my breath. I understood that this was an important question.

"I don't know," Mother said.

"Okay. That's fine." The woman turned and said over her shoulder, "Buddy, go out and get the ax. If the neighbors come out of their house, tell them we'll be over there next, but come right back. Don't get sucked into a long conversation with them yet."

"Please," Father implored, "don't talk to them at all. Just let Ann talk to them."

"Um, yeah, he's right. Just go get the ax." Ann nodded at Father, then stood up. "Tommy, do you want us to call an ambulance?"

"No," he said. "No. Definitely not. Look at her. She's okay. She's just sitting there. For Christ's sake."

Jimmy wiped the tears off his cheek with the back of his hand. He straightened his back. I watched as his hand slowly slid up to where his sleeve covered the X scar on his upper arm. "Yeah, she's been real quiet," he chimed in.

"Shut up," Mother whispered to him. "No one asked you." She looked up at Ann, her eyes fierce and shining. "No one asked you either. Get the hell away from my husband. I know you called him. Here you are in my goddamn house. You're out to get me too."

Father frowned. His mouth opened, but he hesitated. I think he was afraid that no matter what he said, he would make her worse. "Stop, Carrie. You don't want to go to the hospital, do you?" Father's hands were on his hips. He had rings under his eyes. The baby had been keeping all of us up at night. His voice shook with the effort of trying very hard to stay calm.

"Of course not, you idiot."

"Then you'd better be nice."

"Nice. Great. I'm done talking to you people anyway. I was having a good conversation before you showed up."

"But Ma," Jimmy interjected, "who were you were having a conversation with?"

Ghosts, I wanted to tell him.

Ann stretched. "Hey, Jim. Why don't you give me and your dad a minute?"

Jimmy glanced at his mom, slowly getting up. He looked scared out of his mind, pale and shaken. I wasn't sure why. Mother seemed fine, and this strange woman in uniform had been very reasonable. He walked out of the room and up the stairs.

"She's not having a good week, Tommy," Ann said very quietly to Father. "I asked around, and she was down at the bar last night. Did you know that?"

Father folded his arms very tightly, a vein in his bicep pulsing out against his skin. "Yeah, someone called me. I know she had a few." Father frowned. "I picked her up."

Ann raised an eyebrow. "There were a few guys from Gloucester down there who thought she was very entertaining. You gotta watch that. You gotta make sure—"

"Jesus Christ, you think I let her go down there? You think I wanted her there? I had a call. I had to work."

There was a pause. Ann pressed her lips together. Her finger tapped on her belt. "Didn't Carrie just have that baby about a week ago? I'm surprised she felt well enough to go out. Is she having some kind of postpartum breakdown?"

Father was very still. "We did. Have a baby. Obviously she shouldn't have been out." He was holding his elbow so tightly that his arm was turning red.

"I assume someone was watching the baby. If you were working. And she was out."

Father glared at Ann. She, in turn, looked cool and calm, as if they were just chatting about the weather. Father's shirt was getting soaked with sweat.

"Someone is always here with Finn. Sometimes my

mother. And Jimmy or Mary are always here," he said through gritted teeth. "They're always here if I go out."

"Okay." Ann just nodded. "I'm going to go talk to the neighbors. We better hope that ax—"

The young man breezed in, looking proud of himself, ax in hand.

"In the driveway!" he announced.

Father and Ann just stared at him. The young man was momentarily confused, and his cheeks turned pink. The hand holding the ax dropped by his side.

"I mean . . . good news. It wasn't in their tree. It was in your own driveway."

Everyone exhaled.

"Okay, then. I'll go see if I can explain the situation, ask them not to press any charges."

"But . . ." Father's eyes betrayed how worried he was. "Ann, why would they press charges? You can talk them out of that, can't you? They just moved in. They don't want to start off this way, do they? I mean . . ." He wrapped his arms around himself. I could see that he was just barely holding himself together. "Can you please explain that she's not . . . she rarely leaves the house these days."

"Rarely. Yeah, I hear you. But rarely isn't never."

"Ann, you know her. C'mon."

"I'm sorry, Tommy." I saw Ann reach out as if she was going to pat his arm, but with a quick glance at Mother she thought better of it and pulled her hand back.

I felt Mother's gentle hands firmly on my sides, so I stood up and climbed off her lap, because I knew Mother wanted to stand up. Everyone's head turned when she stood. Mother was wearing shorts and an old T-shirt. Her bare feet were dirty. I wondered what the neighbors thought when they saw her out there with that ax.

Despite her dirty clothes, Mother looked luminous, with a dewy sheen of sweat on her face. She was beautiful and radiant, her face flushed with the heat of the night. She stared at the young man, who still held the ax in his hand. I have seen men get flattered and excited when Mother turns her attention on them, at parties and cookouts here at the house. They smile back at her and enjoy her rapt attention, the way her eyes never stray from the man she is talking to. But now, the young man with the ax looked more nervous than anything else to find himself the object of her gaze.

"Are you the one who has come to take me to the hospital?"

"Me, ma'am?" He looked left and right, as if Mother must have been talking to someone else. "No, ma'am. Not me." I saw his throat waver as he swallowed. "We didn't come here for that. I mean, unless you need a ride. We could take you there."

Mother raised her head and looked down her nose at him, sizing him up, as if she was evaluating him for an important task. "You're very nervous, aren't you? Don't worry. You seem like the right type. Should I go with you now? I don't mind. I'm really tired. I need rest. You look very kind."

I could hear Mother's words and thoughts and phrases starting to jump out of order, like a jumble of nonsense. I know Father heard it too, from the way he tipped his head.

Mother smiled sadly and continued, "There's something that was said to me that seems wrong. You're a good young man and you've worked very hard. You've spent many years listening and listening, and sometimes I'll listen and sometimes I won't. I can't promise

I will always listen, but I see that at least you're trying. Are you going to take me away now?"

"No, ma'am." The young man suddenly looked much younger, putting an awkward hand out in front of him quickly. "Not at all, ma'am. I'm not taking you anywhere."

Mother's face fell in disappointment. "I need water," she stated. "Tommy, will you make them go away?"

"I'll get you water. C'mere." Father came and took Mother by the arm, holding her too tight, leading her into the kitchen as if she were a naughty child.

Ann and the young man exchanged a look, standing there in the stuffy living room. I stared at them, trying not to move too much in the heat. My fur coat felt like an extra layer of insulation that I didn't need on top of my fat.

Ann adjusted the clip holding her hair as she walked toward the window. "I hope for Tommy's sake that baby starts sprouting some blond hair," she said under her breath to the skinny man.

The young man immediately bowed his head, hat still in place despite the heat, looking down as if to inspect his shoes. He wrung his hands together in front of him.

"Oh don't look so shocked," she whispered. "You work in this town long enough, you'll learn some things. You'll see some things you won't even believe."

Father came back out of the kitchen without Mother. "You don't need that, do you?" Father interrupted, gesturing toward the ax. "Can I have that back?"

"What? No. I mean, yes, you can have it."

Father took the ax. "Ann. We're all okay, aren't we? Can you guys get out of here now so I can talk to her? You're going to make it worse."

"Tommy, I'm sorry about this. We're going to go.

But if she gets more agitated you have to promise me you'll take her right to the ER. Or call 911." Ann looked directly at him, but Father was staring down at the ax, weighing it in his hand. "You've got two kids here. And a newborn baby. An ax is not something you can fool around with. Someone could get hurt. And you shouldn't be letting her out of the house."

Father suddenly lifted his head and scowled at Ann with such furious intensity that I was sure he was going to curse her out or scream at her, but he did neither. He just didn't respond. Father never "let" Mother out of the house, like she was an animal that wasn't capable of operating a doorknob. Mother did whatever she wanted to do. Father's arm holding the ax was shaking slightly. For a moment, I almost thought he was going to take a swing at Ann with that ax. But he didn't move a muscle.

Ann returned his gaze. "All righty, then. We'll let you know if we need you again."

We heard the door shut. Father and I didn't move from our spots in the living room. There was no need to see these people out, these people who came in uninvited.

After a moment, Father walked into the kitchen. A glass of water rested untouched on the table, and Mother sat silently in her chair. The lighting in the kitchen was eerie and unnatural.

"God help you, if you ever pick up this ax again . . ."

"What? You'll kill me? You'll murder me with it?" Mother didn't sound afraid. She looked right at him. "Go ahead."

Now, I know something about predator and prey. I have a powerful instinct for self-preservation. I avoid pain and I despise heartbreak. But I have no fear of death, or blood and guts. I have killed two mice that found their way into this old house, and I ate their hearts out.

Father is so much bigger than Mother, I could see that with one or two swift blows of the ax he could kill her. It would be quick, and it would be easy.

But Mother was not afraid of death, I believe, and certainly not by Father's hand. She had some interesting and strange ideas, but that wasn't one of them. She was never afraid of Father. On the contrary, he had protected her for many years.

"Jesus Christ," is all Father said, and he left the kitchen swiftly. I assumed he was going to hide that ax somewhere she couldn't find it. I jumped up into Mother's lap. Her touch was light and lovely, as always.

Father came back in a few minutes later, rubbing his eyes. "God give me strength."

"God give you patience," Mother corrected him, holding up one finger, echoing what she'd heard him say many times before.

That earned her a little smile from Father. "Yeah. That too. I need that too. By the way, I got you something." He hunted around in the kitchen, opening cabinet doors and looking on one high shelf and then the next. It was clear to me he bought something for her a long time ago, in case of a situation like this one. Finally he found it. It was a bag of her favorite candy, caramels.

She took the candy from his hand, bewildered. Pinching it in her fingers, she checked to make sure it was soft enough to eat. I had seen her do this before.

"This is good," she declared. "This is good enough."

He sat down next to her. "It better be."

Mother nodded. "God told me you were watching out for me. So I know all about it. I've heard a lot about you, and you don't need to worry, because things could be a lot worse." She sighed, and whispered, "I know I ruined your life, Tommy, and you don't need to tell me. You know how sorry I am, and I know that you'd all be better off without me. I wish I could stop it, but I can't. I told you to call Father Boyle, but you never did. You don't listen, and that's the problem with you."

Father just shook his head. "Please don't say things like—"

She continued without pause: "There's a lot of other things that I can't tell you about, Tommy, because there's too many and Father Boyle is a very busy man in the order of that he doesn't have time for me when you walk into the kitchen and my problems other than they told me what to do."

I knew she was talking nonsense now, but Father still listened as if it all made perfect sense to him. "I know, sweetheart."

"You haven't been listening to me."

"I know. And I'm sorry." He had one hand on the back of her chair. His voice was softer, the energy sapped out of him. "Carrie."

Mother looked at him. "You're just doing your job."

"I am." Even now, even after all this, it is hard to describe the look he gave Mother.

He loved her like I did, which is to say: completely.

We both thought it would be forever.

Father pulled her hand to his mouth and kissed her knuckles. "I'm so grateful for that sweet little baby upstairs you gave me. He's such a blessing."

Mother reached down and scratched between my ears.

"Care, are you listening to me? Thank you for that baby. He's going to be okay."

Mother smiled down at me, and I winked back.

"Listen. Carrie," he tried again. "That baby needs you. I need you. You need to stay home, not go out anywhere, and take care of—"

Mother lifted her head, and her expression changed, turning perfectly cold. "No, you listen. The baby is absolutely not going to be okay. And neither am I, trapped here." Upstairs, as if on cue, Finn began his shrill newborn scream. Father winced, as if the sound was painful to him, but Mother's face never changed. We soon heard footsteps on the old floorboards above us, and then we heard Jimmy cooing at Finn. "You wanted that baby. So now you've got him. But it's not going to help. You're better off without me," she whispered. "That baby is better off without me. I'm a bad person. I'm not going to be here much longer. I'll do you a favor and go."

"Don't say that. Please. Please don't say that."

If we knew she was just a few months away from leaving us, maybe Father and I would've paid more attention. But at the time, it just seemed like the sort of thing Mother would say when she was having a very bad day.

"I don't feel well. Tommy—"

Mother, who had been holding the gold coin this entire time, let it slip from her fingers, and it dropped to the floor. Father jumped forward and caught her as she slumped into him. You see, I think Mother knew something was horribly wrong, and she was fighting it. Father helped her up and carried her into the living room.

He brought Mother to the couch and laid her down with her head propped on a pillow. First Father brought her pills and the glass of water. She took them without question. Then he lay down next to her on the old sagging couch, as if shielding her from the world, even though he could barely fit. He wrapped his arm around her and held her tightly.

Thinking back on it now, I think this was Father's greatest fault: He didn't like asking for help. He never spoke with anyone about Mother's behavior that I knew of. I think he was afraid of losing her forever. Maybe he was afraid that if they came for her, they would not bring her back. Sometimes she would go to the hospital for a night, but he always made sure she came right back home. He wanted her home and nowhere else.

Even after she cut the Xs on Jimmy.

Even when she carried an ax in the house where that newborn baby lay crying in his crib.

He loved her too much, and that was a problem. Without realizing it, perhaps he was stopping her—and everyone else—from getting the help they needed.

I loved her too. I am guilty of the same things. Father and I are very much alike.

While they were sleeping, I paced back and forth, watching them. And then I noticed the gold coin, sitting on the kitchen floor. Unattended.

Maybe, I thought, that coin was the source of the trouble. After all, the voices came from the coin, didn't they?

I padded into the kitchen and tapped the coin with my paw. It was lightweight. I tried picking it up with my mouth, but it was too difficult. I couldn't get it to tip up enough to clamp my teeth onto it. So I batted it once, twice, and on the third try it went skidding under the stove.

Success!

The evil coin, the one that brought bad luck to this house, was hidden. I congratulated myself on my efforts. And I hoped Mother would not be too upset.

By the time Mary got home, Mother and Father were both fast asleep on the couch, and Father was snuggled up behind Mother. One of the lamps was still on, and it took Mary a moment to even notice them there. She tiptoed in with a big smile and looked at me. I sat in the armchair, half-asleep myself. "They're so cute together, aren't they, Boo?" Mary asked me with a soft laugh. "New parents. Always so tired."

Mary didn't know that upstairs Jimmy waited for her, rocking newborn Finn in the dark, keeping the baby quiet. I had heard Jimmy weeping quietly and considered going upstairs to comfort him, but I didn't want to leave Mother.

Mary didn't know that Jimmy waited for her with a scary story. A story about ghosts, and the neighbors, and an ax.

And a woman in blue.

I wait under the stairs, hoping Mahmee returns soon with the baby. My body feels tired and achy, heavy with memories. When Father and Jimmy said Mother is sick, this must be what they meant, that her ability to talk to ghosts is in fact an illness and not a gift.

I don't care what the humans call it. To me, Mother always seemed wise and magical. Maybe that is how I should choose to think of her, no matter how angry I am. My memories are my own.

25

Empty Closet

Father wakes up early on his day off. He seems full of energy and purpose.

After starting up a pot of coffee, he takes Jasper outside. When he comes back in, he has the newspaper with him. I get a glance of the sky as Father walks in the front door, and it's barely light out, the sky pink and white. Father isn't usually up this early, so I think he must have plans for the day.

He skims through the newspaper and then brings his coffee upstairs. He is still wearing flannel pajama pants and a T-shirt, with a ratty old sneaker on the foot that is not in a cast. Once the hot coffee is safely on his dresser, on top of a napkin, he goes back downstairs and right outside to his truck. It takes several trips for him to carry in a bunch of cardboard boxes from the back of his truck and up to his bedroom. He still has his crutches, but sometimes he only uses one, or none at all. I guess his leg is feeling better.

Soon, there are boxes all over the floor. Father leans

on his dresser and surveys the room. Finally, he picks up the biggest box and puts it on the bed.

I sit next to the box, with my paws tucked under me.

Father keeps a big fan in his bedroom, which he mostly uses in the summer. Even though it's early spring, he cracks open the windows and turns on the fan, which rests on the floor. A crisp breeze is soon circulating around the room. The blades of the fan turn quickly, in a blur. Sometimes I like to sit right in front of that fan, to feel my whiskers tingling from the wind. The cold air filters right through my thick fur and down to my skin, a cooling sensation.

But today I stay on the bed so I can watch the proceedings.

After opening the middle drawer of Mother's dresser, he looks inside. Father gently drags his hand through the clothes he finds there. I stand up and stretch my legs for a better view. He picks up a handful of clothing and looks closely. These are Mother's things. I recognize her blue underwear and a lacy purple bra. I remember her wearing the white socks that he moves aside. Finally he scoops it all up in his arms, brings it over to his box, and dumps it in. It takes three armfuls, but he fills the box.

He doesn't stop there. The next drawer Father opens is the bottom one. Shirts, shorts, exercise clothes, bathing suits—he gets it all into a second box.

His persistence reminds me a little of the times Mother was working on an important project. He is very focused. Some natural instinct in him has kicked in and seems to be pushing him to get this done today, for some reason.

Finally it is time for the top drawer. This one takes longer. It is full of jewelry. I know Father gave some of it to Mother, because I remember the occasions. At one point he takes out a necklace. It is a little gold bird, and it must mean a lot to him, because he sits on the bed just holding it. The chain is sparkly and snakes around in his palm. I bat at it with my paw. "No," he says mildly, moving it away from me. "It's mine." But he drops it into one of the big cardboard boxes, watching it slip through the pile of clothes and disappear.

Then he pulls out photos and papers. Some of it appears to have been made by Jimmy and Mary. A card that says "To Mom" in scribbled crayon. A picture rendered in colorful markers showing Mommy, Daddy, My Brother, and Me. A pencil drawing of an orange cat that does not appear to be me.

Were there cats before me? I've never wondered about it before.

Father places these things into a neat pile and stacks them into a box. He drinks more coffee. Everything seems to be going well. He has slowed down a little in his work, but he has accomplished a lot, and Jimmy and Mary aren't even awake yet.

He stops to take a shower. I take a quick nap.

Once he is dressed, Father recommences his work. He cleans out the drawers with a wet paper towel.

And then, with a deep breath, he opens the closet.

Shoes go in one box. Shirts in a second box. Then skirts, pants, dresses, belts. Father soon runs out of boxes. A trip downstairs yields large, green bags. He fills up four of these before he is done.

Who knew Mother had so many things stuffed in that closet? I've been in there many times. I liked to hide in the darkness, squeezed between shoes, slinking under hanging fabrics.

Father does not open his own closet. Everything in there is his. But now, Mother's closet stands perfectly vacant. He and I stare into it, the gaping emptiness of it. It's like a hole in my heart, to see it. But we have to see it. I understand. I know why Father must do this, and why we must look at it and accept it. But it's terribly hard.

Father fetches Finn, who has started to stir. He lets Finn sit on the rug and chew on a toy. Father sits next to him on the rug and reads a book, waiting for the teenagers to wake up.

Jimmy wanders in, finally awake, hair askew. "What're you doing?" he asks, rubbing his eyes.

"When you're ready," Father explains, "I need you to take all of this to Robert's house. We'll load up my truck. Then I need you to drive over there and leave this stuff for your ma. They have to take it. Don't take no for an answer. If they aren't home, you have to leave it on the porch."

Jimmy's face falls as he looks into Mother's closet and realizes what is happening. "Oh," he says quietly, choosing not to say more. Jimmy leaves to go get dressed.

After he has eaten breakfast, Jimmy helps Father load up the truck, carrying many heavy boxes and bags down the steep stairs while Father holds the front door open. They wake up Mary to watch Finn. She holds the baby in her arms to keep him out of the way.

"This is all Mom's stuff?" she asks repeatedly. "Everything? Her clothes? Her shoes? Her jewelry?"

"Yes," Father explains. "I can't keep it here forever. I just can't. I'm sorry, Mare."

"But . . . why didn't you ask me if I wanted some of it?"

"Jesus, Mare," Jimmy complains. "She's not dead. Ma needs her stuff."

Mary's delicate face crumples. "Sorry. You're right. Sorry."

But I know what Mary is feeling. In a way, it does feel like Mother has died. It feels like we should keep a memento. We don't really know when we'll see Mother again, or how often we'll see her. It hasn't been made clear yet.

Mary wanders upstairs and into the bedroom. I follow. "Wow." Mary notices the open closet door. "Oh my gosh. Now that it's empty, that closet looks so big."

Funny, I thought the opposite. I thought it was amazing that all of Mother's clothes, a lifetime of items, fit into that small closet.

I go back downstairs to find Father pacing a trail in the living room, waiting for Jimmy to get back from his task. Father walks from the kitchen, to the dining room, to the front hallway, and back. I don't think he is feeling any pain in his injured foot today. He occasionally looks out the window.

Father is making me nervous. I jump up on the couch, hop back down to the rug, dash under the dining room table, and run back to the couch. I can't stop my legs from moving.

When Jimmy gets back, he looks tired.

"How'd it go?" Father asks.

Jimmy avoids Father and heads to the kitchen. "Fine," he says.

"Was she there?"

"Yeah."

Father stands, looking worried. I think he doesn't understand why Jimmy won't tell him more. He just stares as Jimmy grabs the bag of bread and takes out a slice to place into the old toaster. When the button won't stay down, and he realizes he can't make toast, Jimmy gives up and just throws the bread into the trash can with a sigh. He turns and sees his father watching him.

"I don't want to talk about it."

Father frowns.

"Trust me, Pops, you don't want me to talk about it."

Father just nods.

Jimmy and Mary go out. Father is restless for a few hours. He is still full of energy but doesn't seem to know what to do with himself. At one point, he sits on his bed and types into his little phone. The machine pings now and again, and he smiles.

I know what that phone is for, and I know he is receiving messages from Charlotte from the look on his face. I enjoy studying human faces lately, because I've realized I can learn a lot from watching them. I love the way Mary's face opens and her mouth gapes when she gazes out her window at the stars at night. Like she is seeing something amazing. Father looks fondly down at his phone, with a small smile, and I can see it provides something that makes him warm from the inside out. I imagine that Charlotte is crafting messages that are just for him.

A loud banging at the front door makes us both jump. Father and I make eye contact quickly, and his face goes pale before reverting to a scowl. We both get up and quickly descend the stairs.

When Father swings the door open, Mother breezes in. She shakes out her long black curls and lifts her chin to look Father in the eye.

"The door wasn't locked—" he starts.

"Thank you," she says, "for having Jimmy bring my things over." Mother puts her hands on her hips and takes a step closer to him. She studies him from head to toe. "You could have warned me you were going to do that."

Although Father is a head taller than Mother, he flinches and looks down at his feet. "Carrie," he says quietly. Her effect on him is startling and immediate. I see his chest expand and contract as his breathing gets more rapid, and as I watch I feel my fur bristle along my spine. It's almost as if I can hear his heart beating faster from my spot on the stairs. Mother glares at Father and gets very close to him.

"Tommy . . ." she begins, her tone sharp and unforgiving.

"I'm sorry," he whispers, still unable to look at her. I watch his hands clench into fists. "I'm really sorry. I should have had Mary call you."

"Yes. You should have." She tips her head, searching for something in his face, but he stares at the floor. "You send poor Jimmy to do your dirty work for you? Honestly."

Wiping her mouth with the back of her hand, Mother turns around and sees me. When she takes steps toward me, I cannot move. She's mesmerizing. I feel just as trapped as Father. "Boo," she coos, and I allow her to lift my plump body up with her hands and rest me against her chest.

"Is Boo happy here?" I hear her ask, her voice softening. "Are you feeding her?"

I see Father's shoulders relax a little. "Of course. You see how fat she is?"

"Well, yes." Mother carefully sits down on a stair and allows me to settle comfortably in her lap. It's a sturdy place to sit. Mother has never once in her life leapt up without warning and sent me flying.

Father approaches and leans on the banister. "Do you . . ." He hesitates, and then stops, his mouth closing quickly. By his frown, I think he regrets saying anything.

"Do I miss her? Of course I do," Mother says with a sigh.

Me? I feel my eyes open wide. *Are they talking about me?* I stare at them, curious.

Mother looks up at Father and smiles at him, her big, wide smile an echo of Jimmy's crooked grin when he's very happy. "Do you think she misses me?"

Father pauses again. He and I make eye contact for a brief moment. Did she really just ask that question? "Yes," he answers, almost a whisper.

"Do you think she'd be happier living with me?"

Father clears his throat, but his voice is still hoarse as he says, "I know she's always made you feel better when you're down." His forehead creases together as he speaks. It's that look he gets when he's very worried.

No, I start to think. *Wait.*

I freeze up. I look quickly back and forth between the two of them.

Of course I still love Mother. Deep in my heart I will always love her. But I also don't want to leave this family. Doesn't Father feel the same way? Does he think I belong with Mother?

I am not something that can be traded away, or a peace offering. Do I need to prove to him that I am part of this family, that I want to stay here?

I start to panic, and I get to my feet, all in a rush. I can't lie still. I hop out of Mother's lap and tear up the stairs at a gallop, my back legs kicking out behind me. I'm not sure what else to do, so I run into Finn's room, leap up to his high dresser, and then plop down with a thud into the crib. I snuggle right down near the baby's feet, defiant.

I belong here. I am furious, and I feel wild in my anger.

Mother was right: Father is stupid sometimes. He

offered her the baby at the holidays. Now he thinks he is going to let me go? I will not go.

It is not long before they come and find me, peering over the crib railing to watch me with Finn. The baby is asleep, and Mother runs her hand through Finn's hair.

I hiss at Mother, and she draws her hand back in surprise.

"Boo," Father commands, a hard edge in his voice. "No."

The two of them. The two of them! Doesn't either one understand me at all? Don't my wishes count in all of this?

Father watches Mother, and she returns his gaze for a moment.

I remember:

When she ran the back of her knuckles over the scruff on his face.

Honey.

When he moved a curl of her dark hair off her neck.

Baby.

How when she loved Father, she truly, passionately loved him and there was no doubt in it, not a shred of hesitation, not a moment of care for anything in the world but *Tommy Tommy Tommy.*

How he was always hungry for more of her, when she was happy.

For a moment, I think—

For a moment, I worry that—

For a moment in time, I can see that there is a chance he will do anything in the world for her, anything she asks, and—

He leans in toward Mother, speaking slowly and softly. "If you need Boo, I think you should have her. She used to follow you around this house, day and night. You always held her when you were under a lot of stress. It might not be a bad idea."

My resolve melts away when I see his face. When I realize how hard it is for Father to say these words. But he means every word he says.

Oh dear. I fear he is right.

Someone must look after Mother. I am ready to do what must be done.

Mother watches him. I wonder if she can see what I see, how much strain he is under himself. His tired eyes. How tense his arm is as he grips the side of the crib. She pats his hand and shakes her head. "Yes, but . . . I don't know." With a wave of her hand toward me, she asks, "I think the kids would miss her, don't you?"

Father's mouth opens slightly, but he doesn't respond. He freezes for a moment.

I realize she is offering him an opening. *Take it,* I think.

"Well . . . yes. The house would feel wrong without the cat," he finally says, breaking the silence, standing up straight. He clears his throat and glances at me, seeing the way I am guarding Finn. "Finn loves the cat. And it would be very quiet without her. The house would feel so empty."

I'm not sure what Father means by *very quiet,* because I make no noise.

I think he just means he cannot bear to lose anything else.

The important thing is that he understands. I comfort Father now, not Mother. I want to help with the baby. I belong with my siblings. I'm an important part of this family. And he knows it. He knows it. He has found his courage, and he is able to say it.

Thank goodness!

Mother studies him carefully. She moves her hand to rest briefly on Father's arm. Rubbing his elbow, she nods. "Then don't worry about it. Boo should stay here, of course."

"The kids would be mad at me if I let the cat go," he goes on, his voice breaking.

"I understand. It's okay. Don't get upset. Tommy, don't—don't fall apart."

"I can't expect you to take on extra work right now." He stumbles over his words as they spill out. "I don't want to ask too much of you."

"I'm okay, Tommy. I'm fine. I'm better. It's not hard to take care of a cat." She raises an eyebrow, I think to try to make him laugh. But Father is upset and not in a laughing mood. "Oh, Tommy. I'm sorry. I think you're right."

Mother continues to rub his forearm until he glances up. Finally, he gives her a small smile.

I meow my approval. Mother strokes my head, and this time I let her. She is a strong woman. Not afraid of me, not afraid of Father, not afraid of anything but those pesky, horrible neighbors.

And suddenly I come to see that the most astonishing thing is not that Mother disappeared one day.

It's not that she up and left all of us without warning.

No, the most astonishing thing is that between Mother and Father, *she* was the one who was strong enough to make a change that may improve life for all of us. When she first disappeared, I thought she was injured or kidnapped or killed, but she was none of these things. She left because she needed to leave.

She is happier and healthier than she was before. Mother found Robert, who is helping her get the care she needs. And Mother is showing Father that it is possible for them to live apart and go on with their lives. To start over.

Mother clears her throat. "I'm glad you cleaned out those drawers. Did it feel good to clean them out?"

Father's face darkens, and he looks away. "No. But it was a relief, to be honest. I needed to do it."

"Okay. Then I'm glad you did it."

Finn stirs. His eyes open wide when he sees Father and Mother both looking down at him.

"You didn't do me—or yourself—any favors by hiding me away," Mother whispers, smiling down at Finn. "Keeping all of our problems shut up in this house."

"I didn't—" Father frowns. "I just didn't want anyone to—" He presses his lips together tight, unable to go on for a moment, but then bursts out with: "I don't trust doctors. I don't like any of them. They don't really fix anything."

I notice Father is looking at the baby when he says this.

This much is true: The doctors don't seem to be able to fix Finn's ears.

Mother pauses, thinking this over. "I don't like them much either. I know you were trying to protect me. But it wasn't good for any of us."

Mother picks up the baby and takes him into her arms. She kisses Finn on the cheek. He laughs and then wiggles because he's ready to visit Father next. Father lets Finn pull on his sleeve.

I wonder if Father ever waits for Finn to say his name. I wonder if he ever thinks about that baby looking at him and saying, "Daddy" like Mary does or "Pops" like Jimmy does. He must realize it may never happen.

I guess Finn will find a way to say Father's name using his hands. I wonder how they will figure that out. I don't understand human hands very well, although I can see they are quite complex and can accomplish all kinds of tasks.

To me, Father still looks worried when he gazes at Finn. I suppose it is hard for him not to worry. It may take years for him to stop worrying.

He may worry long past my lifetime. About Mother. About Jimmy and Mary. About Finn.

It's just something that Father must live with. There will be no end to it, I see that now. But maybe his burden will be just a little bit lighter, now that Mother has found the help she needs.

Mother notices the gloomy look on Father's face. "Finn is so happy," she remarks. "Have you ever seen such a happy baby?"

"You're right. He's always happy." Father takes Finn and holds him close, but Finn is squirming and wants to be passed back to Mother again. He enjoys this game.

But the time for games is over.

I am staying, for good!

Later, after Mother has gone, Father sits on the couch in the living room. I flop down right in his lap and rest a paw on his strong arm. I arch my head all the way back so he can scratch under my chin.

I have never been so relieved in my life. When Father lies down, I climb up on top of his chest and lie there. When he closes his eyes in exhaustion, I do too.

26

Drawing the Line

Father sits in the dining room, the afternoon sun filtering through the sheer curtains to give the room a golden glow. The window is cracked open, and a sweet, spring breeze flows through the screen. A few weeks have gone by, and Father's cast is off. He is incredibly relieved to be rid of it.

Occasionally I see him limp a little out of habit, but he now puts weight on his leg again, and he moves around without pain. He especially loves jogging up the stairs to bed at night after he's walked Jasper.

I know he loves the feeling of the new sheets on his bare legs and feet, now that the cast is off. Every morning he wakes up and stretches against the downy flannel. I do too. We lie there in bliss for a few minutes, loving the softness of the bed.

The nights are getting warmer. It's actually almost time to switch to the cotton sheets. I wonder if Father knows to do that. I suppose when he's sweating at three in the morning and has the ceiling fan cranked on high, it will occur to him to go dig the cotton sheets out of the closet.

Now, he has his jeans on and an old T-shirt, with bare feet. He sits in a dining room chair with something on the table in front of him. I jump up on the window seat to see what it is. It's a pad of blank, unlined paper, and Father holds a pen. Finn is asleep in his car seat on the floor, which is where Father sometimes parks him at nap time because Finn seems to like the security of the way the seat wraps around him. It gets him to sleep faster than the crib.

Mary walks in. She was doing homework upstairs and has come down for a break. "What are you doing in here, Dad?"

Father stutters at first, but then explains he's going to write Mother a letter.

Mary sits right next to him, interested. "You mean . . . You mean, like the one she wrote you?"

Father presses his lips together. Maybe he forgot that he mentioned the letter to Mary late one night, a few months ago, after the holidays. "Yeah, kind of like that." He scratches his head. "It's just . . . She doesn't want me to call her too much. But I really need to talk to her. And this way, I can think about what I want to say."

"Oh."

Jimmy walks in, puzzled, holding a bottle of water. "Why are you guys in here?" He tips back the bottle to finish it off.

"Dad's writing Ma a letter." Mary turns to him. "Why, Pops? What do you want? I mean, why do you need to talk to her?"

Father puts his hands in his lap and stares at the blank piece of paper. He pauses as if he has no idea how to answer that question.

Finally, he explains that he needs to figure out what's going to happen next.

"Happen next?" Jimmy sits across the table from Father and Mary.

The grandfather clock clicks off the seconds as my family sits and thinks about it.

"Pops, what is it that you want to happen next? I mean, you don't still want Ma to come back, do you? Is that what you still want? I mean, no, right? Because you're with Charlotte now?" Jimmy runs his fingers over the label that is peeling loose from the empty water bottle still in his hands. "You want Ma to come back?"

There is a hint of hope in Jimmy's question.

I understand. We're talking about his mother.

Father shakes his head. He says he knows that Ma isn't going to come back. He thinks maybe it's time they all moved on.

Mary sits up straighter and puts her hand on Father's shoulder. "It's okay, Daddy. It's okay to feel like that. So, tell her. If you want a divorce, tell her. She can handle it."

Father looks at Mary and makes a face. He is skeptical. I can see he doesn't know if that's true at all, that she can "handle it."

"Robert will be there," Mary suggests. "How about you give the letter to him? And he can give it to her. They can read it together."

I can see Father doesn't love that idea either by the way he winces at Robert's name. He hunches over the paper and stares at it again.

"Pops." Jimmy leans across the table. "You want me to call her?"

"No." Father is adamant. "No, Jim. I've got to write it. You see, it's my fault that—"

Jimmy throws his hands in the air. "JESUS, POPS. FOR THE LOVE OF OUR GOD IN HEAVEN STOP SAYING IT WAS YOUR FAULT." Jimmy runs his hands through his hair and then rubs them over his eyes and face. "Mary and I have been here the whole time, and there is nothing that was your fault in particular. You guys fought all the time. It just happened."

Father takes in a deep breath.

"Pops. Pops," Jimmy continues. "I am not letting you say that it was your fault again. I DRAW THE LINE." Jimmy dramatically draws a huge imaginary line in front of him in the air.

It is so much like something Mother would do that I hold my breath in awe.

Father is startled also.

In fact, I think Mother literally spoke those words— "I draw the line"—in one of her last fights with Father.

And she made the same exact gesture. And everyone saw it.

Father suddenly starts breathing very hard. I think he is having the same kind of panic attack he had months ago in front of the fireplace when he first read the letter from Mother.

Mary stands up quickly, hunching over him as he gasps to try to catch his breath. Father presses his hand to his heart and winces with pain. Jimmy is also alarmed and moves around the table to the other side of Father.

"Are you okay?" Jimmy asks, sinking into a seat, his hand lightly on Father's back. "Dad. You're not having a heart attack, are you?" Jimmy looks scared, his face pale and his confidence drained away.

"Should I call 911?" Mary demands.

Father shakes his head no, vigorously, and slowly he catches his breath. A long minute goes by where my siblings wait and make sure he can breathe. My whiskers twitch as I watch.

"I'm okay. It's just anxiety. I'm fine. Just—I'm sorry. I'm fine."

Mary slowly lowers herself back down into her seat, frowning. "You don't look fine." She rubs her fingers together, a nervous gesture. "Dad. Seriously. I don't think you're fine."

Father takes a deep breath. "I am. I'm okay. I'll live." He looks from Mary to Jimmy. "I'm sorry. I'm fine. But I want to tell you guys something."

It's quiet in the room. I listen carefully. The big clock in the hall counts off: tick-tick-tick.

Father tells my siblings how when their aunt Shannon died in that drunk driving accident—right after their uncle got sentenced to five years in jail—Mahmee started asking Father if he and Mother might have another baby. Mahmee was depressed and missed the daughter she had lost and the son who could no longer be with her. She had expected to have many grandchildren, and she was starting to realize that her dream was never going to come true. Father thought about it more and more, until it was all he could think about. He missed his brother and sister too. And he decided another baby was a good idea.

He thought maybe it would make things better with Mother. He was worried that Mother was thinking about leaving him. All they did was fight, and make up, and then fight again.

Father was right. I remember. Mother either *passionately loved* or *absolutely hated* him, and there wasn't a lot in between.

Mother was against it, but Father pressured her, and she finally said okay and got pregnant. But then the baby doctor said he thought Mother should stop taking all of her pills. The doctor handed Father a brochure that explained all the horrible things that could possibly go wrong if a pregnant woman took medication. It was a small risk, but still. A risk.

But Mother wouldn't stop. She wouldn't even consider it.

So Father took the medication for her bipolar disorder and threw it all away. And he knew. He knew what was going to happen. He knew how terrible and empty and scared she was going to feel.

Mother was angry at him, at first. And then she sank into the lowest form of misery and hopelessness. She just wanted to die. "The highs could be upsetting," he explains. "But the lows were worse, and she spent more time that way. You remember how bad she got. I kept telling you guys it was okay, but it wasn't okay."

Father saw how she couldn't get out of bed. At the same time, he was scared for the baby and he didn't let her take any more pills. He didn't want something to go terribly wrong with the baby and then they'd live their lives never knowing if it was because of those medications she took.

And then, of course, the baby was born and it made no difference that she'd stopped taking the pills, because Finn was born with a problem anyway. He was deaf, which would have happened whether she took those pills or not.

Mahmee had never mentioned that she had an uncle who was born deaf. It wasn't until Finn's doctors started asking questions that Mahmee told Father for the first time about her uncle, who was sent away as a child.

So Father felt he had made Mother suffer for nothing.

And, Father tells them, "This poor kid didn't have to

be born at all. It was my idea. And now he doesn't have his mother anymore and he needs her so much. He's just a baby. It's my fault she left."

And: "Sometimes I don't know if I can do it, take care of this kid for the rest of my life. Because he reminds me of how your ma suffered, and I know he'll suffer too without her. I can't live with the guilt."

Father puts his hands over his face, his elbows on the table.

There is a moment when Jimmy looks down at the rug, thinking. And then he takes his hand off Father's back.

"I can't believe you just told me that." Jimmy looks confused. "What is wrong with you? Why would you even tell me that?" He stares at Father, appalled.

And then Jimmy stands up, tall and imposing and angry. "I hate you *so much* for doing that to Ma. And saying that about Finn. What kind of a person are you?" He paces back and forth for a moment, thinking.

And then, unexpectedly, Jimmy starts to cry.

It washes over him like a wave and catches him by surprise. His body, tense since Father's panic attack, now folds in and crumples as the tears well up in his eyes. He begins to shake and puts a hand up on his eyes.

I realize, as I watch him, that I never saw Jimmy cry after Mother left. He has been calm, and resigned to the way things are, and even upbeat on many days. Maybe he hasn't really allowed himself to think about it too hard, until now.

Mary cried many nights, and cut up things with scissors, and dyed her hair, and did what she had to do. But Jimmy never fell apart like this.

Jimmy walks a few paces away from the table. Father drops his hands from his face but doesn't look at his son. He just listens, staring down at his lap.

"What kind of person does that, Dad?" Jimmy whispers. A tear rolls down his face. "You pressured her to have a baby? That was the last thing we needed. You took her medicine away from her knowing she was going to get *worse?* While she was pregnant? What if she had . . . ?" He winces, and I can see he doesn't want to allow himself to complete that thought.

Mary frowns at her brother. But she doesn't correct him.

Jimmy turns around in a complete circle, hands on his hips, as if searching the room for something that's missing. "What if she had hurt herself?" he finally blurts out.

"I'm sorry," Father whispers back, his throat hoarse.

"Yeah. Great." Jimmy frowns, gasping to catch his breath. "I offer to go to community college and stay here and *help you,* and you don't say one goddamn thing to stop me. Knowing this is partly your fault. You let me think it was all *her* fault. You let me think she did this herself."

"I'm sorry."

Jimmy's face is red as he cries harder. "Jesus, Dad. *Dad.*"

Father doesn't move. He can't watch Jimmy cry. He can't face it. Jimmy looks like Mother, and talks like her, and there is only grief in it. Father is helpless in front of his son.

"You are incredibly STUPID." Jimmy says this knowing it was Mother's favorite insult, knowing how much it is going to hurt. "And careless. And mean."

Father turns his head away from Jimmy, unable to face him. He speaks softly, his voice now a whisper.

"I'm sorry. I didn't want her to leave. But I messed up. She left anyway. I love your ma. I tried to take care of her. But I screwed up. And I'm sorry. I don't understand it. I don't understand it at all."

"I hate you." Jimmy stands very still.

Please, Jimmy, I think. *Please don't do this.*

"Jimmy," Mary scolds him, a sharp tone in her voice. "Stop."

Mary's voice seems to snap Jimmy out of his tirade. He finally sighs, a heavy sound, and rubs his forehead. "All right. Okay. Fine. The truth is, it's not all your fault. Don't forget she left me because of me too. It's my fault too."

Father immediately turns and looks at Jimmy. He gets up and walks over to his son, grabbing his shoulder gently. "It has nothing to do with you. You should never think that it did. Why would you think that?" he wants to know.

"She didn't like me either, Dad. I messed up too." A thought washes over Jimmy, and I can see the shock in his face. "Oh my God. I made it worse. I didn't help her at all. I drove her crazy." Jimmy convulses in tears all over again.

"Jimmy, none of this is your fault. Your ma loves you. Don't—"

Mary is still sitting at the table. She finally leans toward them and interjects. "Guys. Please stop. Please, come sit down."

A bird calls loudly from a tree branch just outside the window. The air drifting in is warm, fresh, and light. It's like nature is reminding our family to start over.

Jimmy thinks about it. He looks at Mary. The tears still well in his eyes, but he takes a deep breath, in and out. He and Father come back to the table and sit.

"Okay." Jimmy is drained now, his face mottled and pink. He wipes off his cheeks. "I said what I had to say. I said it. So that happened." Jimmy glances over at Mary, and they exchange a look. "But now. Now, Pops, you can—"

"Apologize," Mary finishes the sentence. "See, now, Daddy, yeah, that's horrible. You were horrible. Maybe we all were. But now you can apologize, and write Ma this letter, and wish her a happy life with Robert. You see, that's what you can give her now. You can do this."

Father puts his hands over his face. He takes a deep breath and then forces himself to sit up straight. His eyes are very red, and he wipes his nose with the back of his wrist.

"I'll get you a bottle of water," Jimmy offers, and gets up. He shakes his head. "No wonder you feel guilty. No wonder you've been acting so . . . Jesus, Pops. I don't know who's worse, you or Ma." He walks out to the kitchen.

Jimmy is angrier with Father than Mary is. Regardless of how Mother treated him, Jimmy is the oldest child and he is very close to her.

But Jimmy's a good boy. I believe that by tomorrow he will have slept on it and have decided to forgive his dad. That's just how he is.

Mary leans her head on Father's arm. "It's okay, Daddy. We all love Ma. And we all wanted her to come back. Yeah, you did a bad thing, but so did she. She didn't have to run off and live with Robert."

Father glances down at her.

"She hurt you back already, right?" Mary turns so her forehead is right up against Father's shoulder. "She already got even. You said she was thinking about leaving anyway, no matter what you did. And if she had taken her medication while she was pregnant, maybe Finn would have been born with more problems than just being deaf. Who knows. There's a lot of *what ifs*."

He kisses the top of her head. Father says he's sorry because she and Jimmy and Finn are the ones who are paying for it now, with their mother gone.

Mary closes her eyes. "She can see us anytime she wants, Daddy. Anytime. How often she sees us is her choice now. Just let her go, Dad. That's exactly what you can do for her. Let her go and live her life. And you know we're going to help you with Finn. Finn is going to be okay."

When Jimmy comes in with the water, Mary exits. Jimmy sits in the same seat, right next to Father, turned to face him. Father dries off Jimmy's cheek with his thumb. Jimmy just looks exhausted now, his eyes swollen.

Mary comes back with a book and sits in the window seat with me. She strokes my back.

"You need any help writing that letter, let me know," Mary offers to Father, sitting in a spot of sun. I get up, stretch my legs, and climb in her lap.

Father looks at me. My eyes start to close as I soak up the sun.

Write it, I think, hoping he can read my thoughts. *It's a good idea.*

He taps his pen to the paper.

"Start with *Dear Carrie,*" Jimmy jokes, wiping his face again.

Father returns a sad smile and starts writing.

27

Dance Party

After Charlotte has worked with Finn one night, Father tells her that Sean is coming over for supper in a few days. Father would like Charlotte to meet him. Sean's wife has offered to bring fish chowder.

Father asks Charlotte if they could possibly make a salad together. "After all," he tells her, "you like salad."

I assume Father remembers Charlotte's "no cooking" rule. But he probably doesn't think making a salad counts as cooking.

She agrees, but adds: "Tommy Sullivan, if you walk away from that kitchen counter for even one minute . . ."

He promises he won't.

Of course, when the day of the dinner arrives and they have returned from the supermarket with oyster crackers and drinks and vegetables, Father is useless with the salad. He doesn't even know how to peel carrots. And he does walk away from the kitchen counter, to talk to Jimmy, and then he has another pressing chore to do, and then he has to check on Finn.

Charlotte lets him get away with it, biting her tongue.

Charlotte Davenport, you should know better, I think, watching from the kitchen floor with curiosity. *You're setting a bad precedent. Start as you mean to go on.*

When Father comes back into the kitchen and the salad is done, Charlotte wipes her hands on a towel and just looks at him. He takes her in his arms and tucks a hand under her blouse in the back. When he moves his head forward to kiss her, she turns her head away from him. But he persists and gets his mouth on hers, and she doesn't really resist very hard.

Suddenly, he has all the time in the world to kiss her. I guess it's more fun to kiss than peel carrots.

I never said Father was perfect.

He did, in fact, drive Mother crazy all the time.

"I love you," he says to her.

"Yes, I know," she answers. "I love you too." She whispers this last part, as if she is confessing something that's been a secret all along.

She is weak to his charms. I am thankful for that.

Charlotte is funny. She is still shy with him. I know Father's gaze is intense, but sometimes she acts as if she has never kissed him before. Every time he touches her, it is new to her all over again. Maybe she's not used to another human looking at her like that.

Sean and his wife are polite and kind and so happy to meet Charlotte. The only criticism I hear all night is when Sean is helping his wife out of her coat. She whispers to Sean, "She's a little young." But they are turned away from the others, so Father and Charlotte do not hear her.

"Look at that," Sean remarks. "Look at Carrie's cat.

She heard you." Sean's wife turns to look at me as I continue staring at them.

They think I'm hilarious.

Jimmy takes Mary and Aruna out for a bite to eat, but Finn stays at home with us. Charlotte carries Finn into the kitchen, and the others follow.

This group does not stand on ceremony. The table is set in the kitchen. No one in this family actually uses the dining room for dining.

Sean's wife brings a big pot over to the stove to re-heat her chowder.

Father quietly gets Sean's attention, and then motions toward Charlotte while her back is turned and she is fussing with Finn and the high chair. Father puts up his hands as if to say, *What do you think?*

Despite all his talk about being loved by the ladies, Sean blushes and awkwardly shuffles his feet. He tips his head to one side and looks Charlotte over, as if he's contemplating buying a piece of furniture and isn't quite sure if it will fit in his living room. He gives Father a thumbs-up and a nod.

Father smiles. He looks . . . he looks . . . I haven't seen this look on his face in a while.

Happy?

Really happy.

While they eat, I linger under the table with Jasper, waiting to see if anyone furtively (or accidentally) drops us any scraps. But it's chowder and salad, so there isn't much to drop that would interest us. Maybe I'll get a little piece of fish later in my bowl. During supper, the humans play songs on the radio, and Sean makes several trips to the refrigerator to pull out more drinks. Everyone seems relaxed, and I'm pleased to find that Charlotte is doing okay with this bunch.

Toward the end of the meal, I hear Sean's wife talking, and her voice is getting shrill and tight. I realize that she and Sean are getting into an argument about something. Sean asks Father for his opinion. "Tommy, help me here," he says.

I expect Father to jump in and defend his friend, but something surprising happens. From my vantage point under the table, I see Charlotte reach over and put her hand on Father's thigh and rub gently.

Father, who was tapping his foot, stops moving. It completely catches him off guard. He does not respond to Sean, because his brain is momentarily distracted. There is an awkward silence. Charlotte then asks Sean's wife a question in her chipper voice, changing the subject.

I find this soooo amusing. Charlotte is smart. And intuitive. I give her credit for that.

A song comes on the radio, and Sean is suddenly snapping his fingers and getting to his feet, pulling his wife up. I don't know if it's an old song they've known for years, or a brand-new one they all like, but it's got Sean moving and dancing right in the kitchen, and his wife joins him.

"C'mon, Tom. C'mon!" It's funny to see Sean shake his butt.

I move out from under the table and jump up to watch from the armchair in the living room. Music and loud noise are not my thing.

Father laughs at Sean. He looks down at his soup bowl and then over to Charlotte.

I know what he's thinking. He'd like her to join in. I haven't seen him dance in ages.

But this is something he used to do with Mother. It feels suddenly wrong, or strange, and fraught with the possibility of failure. Charlotte might refuse. She might not like to dance. Or she might feel unsure about it.

Father leans in and whispers to her, and then I see them both slowly standing, cautiously, as if being careful not to step on each other's feet. Father leads her away from the table, and I realize I am holding my breath watching them.

But I exhale as I see Father has figured it out. He puts his hand around her waist and pulls her hips up against his, and he puts his forehead right up against hers. She smiles, shyly. Father has always been a good dancer, and I quickly see Charlotte cannot dance at all. But he leans into her and leads her, so there is no way she can feel awkward or excluded. Father mouths the words of the song to her, and Sean sees this and cheers him on.

Charlotte's face is red. The words of this song must be somewhat embarrassing, I think, but I think she looks very happy too.

Jimmy, Aruna, and Mary have just walked in and heard the music. They appear in the doorway of the kitchen.

Jimmy stretches to take off his sweatshirt, surveying the scene. "It's a Sean Murphy and Tommy Sullivan dance party," he says dryly, looking at Aruna.

The kids laugh. The girls strip off their spring coats and throw them on the couch. Then they start dancing too, in the living room. Jimmy dances with Aruna, heads nodding and their hands in the air. Mary picks up Jasper and bounces and twirls him around.

Finn and I are the only ones not dancing. But let's be real. He's a baby who can't hear the music.

And I'm just a cat.

28

A Sweet Life, Again

Let me tell you about my father.

He has a firm hand, but he is not too rough. Father is a quiet human most of the time, which I appreciate. He's comfortable just sitting with me on the couch for a long stretch while he watches the television.

Sometimes he will read a book in bed while lying on his stomach, and he has a warm, strong, broad back that I like to climb up and sit on. Otherwise, I usually sleep by his feet. I enjoy our nights alone, when Father and I can really stretch out.

On the nights that Charlotte sleeps over, sometimes I get to snuggle between two humans. It is a great feeling, being sandwiched between them. Other nights, I find space on Father's pillow. I am a fat cat, but there is occasionally room for me behind his head when he nestles up close to her.

Father likes to whisper in Charlotte's ear in the morning, before he gets up. He always listened very carefully to Mother, but now he is the one talking.

I think he is talking because he has been through so much, and life is short, and we need someone to listen to our stories.

When Father goes out, he always comes back. He is always here because there are three children and a cat and a Not a Cat who depend on him.

Little Finn is walking now and needs extra attention. Father has built a gate at the top of the stairs, so sometimes I get accidentally trapped up there with Finn. But I don't mind. Someone is always up there with us.

Father calls me Boo, or Fat Cat, or Fatty. Sometimes he scratches between my ears, especially when I am sitting up on the back of the couch and looking down at him.

I catch him looking at me on occasion. When Mother lived here, and he looked at me, I was never sure what he was thinking. But now I think he remembers. *There's Mother's child. There's Mother's cat. These are the creatures I need to take care of now.* We are familiar to him, and he takes comfort in us.

Before, with Mother, he was always worried. He still worries, but maybe a little less.

I keep an eye on him. He's my best friend, after all.

Finn is a sweet baby. He looks at me with a friendly face, just like Father does. He likes to pet me and see how it feels to sink his tiny hands into my silky fur. I can't wait for him to get a little older.

I worried about Finn when he was very small. I thought he would not thrive, like the runt of a litter. He has surprised me. He is a big, strong, handsome, and bright-eyed baby.

Sometimes in the morning, Father brings Finn into our bed with a little book that has fabrics he can touch. Father will put Finn's hand on me, and together they will stroke my soft back. Finn may not be able to hear my purring, but I'm sure he can feel it. Finn smiles his toothy grin and looks happily up at Father. Father puts Finn's little hand up on his face to feel his own whiskers, and Finn squeals.

Father also keeps a ball on his bedside table. It is a hard, white ball with red slashes sewn through it. He runs Finn's little fingers over the seams. The ball is kept right next to the wooden cross.

Both of these items seem to hold some mystical meaning to them. They certainly worship that ball.

When Mother visits every now and again, I let her pet me. I enjoy her exquisitely gentle and precise touch, while it lasts. But I also have Mary and Charlotte and Jimmy and Finn and Mahmee and Aruna, and all of my humans are good to me.

When the afternoon sun comes through the front window and makes a bright square on the floor, I lie down, spread out my fat stomach, and purr.

Yes, life is short.

My life will be the shortest of all, but such is life for a cat.

Acknowledgments

Thank you to Michael, Hunter, and Summer. They allow me time and space to write. It is nice to live with creative people who are full of ideas and encouragement.

A huge thank-you to my super-smart agent, Stacy Testa, at Writers House, for holding my hand every step of the way and answering all of my questions. I am also very lucky to work with editor John Scognamiglio and an amazing team at Kensington Publishing. Their enthusiasm is contagious! I appreciate their hard work and dedication to the book.

I have appreciated all of my writing teachers along the way, including Tim Averill and John Stuart at Manchester High School, Tufts professor Jay Cantor, and my Creative Writing professor E. L. Doctorow at NYU.

Thanks to my early readers, editors, and supporters of this book, including Susan Breen, Brenda Windberg, and Debbie Goelz. A shout-out to all of the wonderful writers in my author groups, the Algonkian Round Table and '17 Scribes.

I'd like to thank The Avengers, code name for my mom friends who force me to leave my computer once in a while and get out of the house. Thanks also to my mom and dad, who nurtured my love of cats and books, and made sure I always had both.

My big, black cat Winnie was my muse for this book. I imagine she thinks she is Bagheera to my Mowgli as she follows me around the house. She guards me carefully.

I love hearing from readers! You can find many ways to connect with me on my Web Site: www.sandiwardbooks.com.

Thanks for reading!

THE ASTONISHING THING

Sandi Ward

ABOUT THIS GUIDE

The suggested questions are included to enhance
your group's reading of Sandi Ward's
The Astonishing Thing!

Discussion Questions

1. Were you as surprised as Boo was to find out where her mother, Carrie Sullivan, was living after she moved out? What did you think had happened to Carrie? Did your guess change over the course of the story, until you learned the truth?

2. Like a child, Boo had some understanding of what was going on in her family but didn't always have the full picture. Was Boo a narrator you empathized with? Did you agree with her judgment most of the time?

3. Did your opinion of Carrie change as the book progressed? Did it change more than once? If so, how?

4. Which teenager did you think was more resilient after Carrie left, Mary or Jimmy? Did either of them react the way you think you would have if your mother moved out when you were that age? Jimmy and Mary continue to talk on the phone to and text their mother after she moves out; does today's technology make it easier for kids to keep in touch with their parents? Do you think they would have kept in such close touch with Tommy if he had been the one to leave?

5. Do you know anyone like Tommy Sullivan, who felt he needed to hide family problems from the outside world? Why do you think Tommy was so distrustful of people who weren't in his immediate

family? Was it primarily due to a misunderstanding of mental illness, or the stigma attached to it, or a fear of doctors and hospitals that stopped him from getting more help? Were his fears justified? Would you feel the same way in his situation?

6. When a family member has mental illness, it is important to "see the person, not the illness," even when the person's words and behavior are hurtful. How hard do you imagine it is to do that? Was Boo able to do that? Were the other members of the Sullivan family able to do that?

7. Families and caregivers of persons with an illness often forget to—or don't have the time and ability to—take care of themselves. What could the Sullivan family have done better to help Carrie, and to help themselves? Do you and your family have anything you do to alleviate stress during tough times?

8. Do you think Tommy's relationship with Charlotte will last over time? Why or why not? Why do you think Charlotte does not say "I love you" back to Tommy when he says it to her for the first time? Have you ever been in a relationship where you felt the other person was rushing into things? How did you resolve it?

9. Was Tommy's mother helpful to him, or did she make things harder for him? In what ways? Is there anything you think she could have done differently?

10. Do you think part of Tommy's desire for Carrie to come back was driven by his insecurities as a parent? Do you know anyone who has unexpectedly become a single parent and experienced similar doubts? Does Tommy provide his children with the love and support they need? Do his children to some degree end up parenting him?

11. Do you think pets provide comfort and stress relief in families? How so? Have your pets ever helped you through a tough time in your life?

12. Discuss the novel's title, *The Astonishing Thing*. What was the most astonishing thing that happened in the story? Does more than one thing come to mind?

Turn the page
for an exciting Q&A
with Sandi Ward!

How did you come up with the idea for *The Astonishing Thing*?

The idea of writing from a cat's point of view came to me after I read *The Curious Incident of the Dog in the Night-Time* by Mark Haddon. *The Curious Incident* is an amazing book that allows the reader to get inside the head of an autistic young man who looks at the world from a unique perspective. I loved the idea of using an unconventional narrator.

I decided to write a story from a cat's point of view as she tries to solve a mystery. In this case, Boo's mother goes out one day and doesn't return. Boo wants to know: What happened to my mother?

As I wrote more of the story, I realized that Boo's point of view was similar to that of a perceptive child. She understands a lot of what's going on with her humans—but not everything. Boo doesn't know much about mental illness, or divorce, or what exactly is wrong with baby Finn. So the reader must go on a journey with Boo, piecing together clues until the story becomes clear.

How easy was it to write a novel from a cat's point of view? Did you have to do any sort of research?

It was easy to write scenes where Boo is observing her family interacting. I just had to get her down on the floor, or up on the back of the couch, and make sure she was physically located somewhere a cat would want to be. It was a little harder to make sure Boo was a character who had an active role within the bigger story. Let's face it—cats are limited in what they can do. Boo is not a big golden retriever who can pull a drowning boy out of a lake. But Boo can climb into a lap to comfort her humans and give them unconditional love when they experience emotional highs and lows. She can demand to be noticed, tipping over a photograph to get attention, or hiss and scratch to make her opinions known. Boo considers herself to be an important member of the family, no matter how small she is.

My only "research" was observing my cat Winnie. For example, the *boom boom boom boom* sound Boo makes while going down the stairs is the noise Winnie makes when she's bounding down our stairs in the dead of night.

As far as Boo's personality goes, I think most people imagine their cats to be devoted and affectionate at heart—but with a little bit of attitude. Boo loves her family, but she's also sarcastic and judgmental at times, and that gives her voice some humor.

How long did it take you to write the book?

I wrote the first draft quickly, in a few months, but it was too short to be a novel. I then took a few additional months to expand the story to book length. I always spend more time editing than writing, so I went on making revisions for over a year while at the same time starting new projects.

Were any particular parts of the book easier to write than others? Harder?

Tommy's scenes were the most emotionally draining to write. Carrie's medications don't always work well. Her words and behavior sometimes break Tommy's heart. But Tommy doesn't blame Carrie for being ill. Instead, he blames himself for being unable to manage her better. And he definitely doesn't like talking about it! So I needed to portray how trapped and hopeless he felt, and sometimes I felt like I was stuck right there with him.

I enjoyed writing scenes with Carrie, because she brings a certain energy with her when she enters a room—she's often very up or very down. It was important to me that readers see her as a complete person, to get a glimpse of her strengths as a wife and mother as well as her more challenging behaviors. I hope that comes across.

The easier scenes to write were those involving the two teenagers, Jimmy and Mary. They were the most fun to spend time with. Readers often tell me that Jimmy is their favorite character. He's easygoing and funny, and handles his problems with a lightness and grace that I think people would like to have themselves. I have teenagers at home, and I know from experience that they can be very resilient.

The ending was also satisfying to write. While the novel explores the darker ways mental illness can tear a family apart, I hope it also sends the message that families can repair themselves. It's a story about being strong enough to get help and make changes, even when those changes are painful.

Are you working on a new novel? If so, can you tell us anything about it?

My next novel is also told from the point of view of a cat! But it is a different cat, named Lily, and tells the story of a different family.

Just as Mother was Boo's favorite person in the world, Lily has a best friend: a sensitive, fourteen-year-old boy named Charlie. Lily sees that Charlie has bruises he hides from his family, and she assumes that he is being bullied in school. She makes it her mission to find out who is hurting Charlie and help him put a stop to it. But along the way, Lily discovers that her family has even more pressing issues to deal with.

Like *The Astonishing Thing,* it's a story about a family that falls apart and must figure out how to put itself back together. There will be drama, romance, and I hope a few surprises along the way.

So, the most important question: Are you a cat person or a dog person?

Ha ha. This is, of course, the most important question!

I grew up with cats. Unfortunately, the woods of northern Massachusetts are not the most hospitable place for cats to live. We had one cat killed by a neighborhood dog, and another who fell through thin ice. But our next two cats lived many years.

Right now we have one cat, Winnie (who stays indoors), and one dog, Jasper. I don't want to insult Jasper by saying I'm a cat person. Yet the truth is, Jasper is a small, fluffy lap dog and a couch potato. He's about as close to a cat as a dog can get.

Author's Note

According to the National Alliance on Mental Illness (NAMI), one in five American adults experiences some form of mental illness in any given year, and one in every twenty adults lives with a serious mental health condition like schizophrenia, bipolar disorder, or long-term depression. Yet less than half receive mental health care.

If you are one of the millions who face mental illness, or you care for someone who does, you know that it can be hard to talk about. Everyone's journey and experience is different. It might feel like no one else could possibly understand what you are going through. But you are not alone.

Help is available, not just for those with mental illness but also for their loved ones. Please take care of yourself. It's important to manage stress and find support. NAMI provides information and suggestions on their Web site and may be a good place to start:

www.nami.org
NAMI helpline: 800-950-NAMI

Sandi Ward's shrewdly observed, funny, and wonderfully touching novel tells of a fractured family, a teenage boy, and a remarkable cat whose loyalty knows no bounds . . .

A boy and his cat. It's an unconventional friendship, perhaps, but for Charlie and Lily, it works beautifully. It was Charlie who chose Lily from among all the cats in the shelter. He didn't frown, the way other humans did, when he saw her injured back leg, the legacy of a cruel previous owner. Instead, Charlie insisted on rescuing her. Now Lily wants to do the same for Charlie.

She's the only one who's seen the bruises on Charlie's body. If she knew who was hurting him, she'd scratch their eyes out. But she can't fix this by herself. Lily needs to get the rest of the family to focus on Charlie, which is not easy when they're wrapped up in their own problems. Charlie's mother kicked his father out weeks ago and has a new boyfriend who seems charming but is still a stranger. Oldest son, Kevin, misses his father desperately. Victoria, Charlie's sister, also has someone new in her life, and Lily is decidedly suspicious. Even Charlie's father, who Lily loves dearly, is behaving strangely.

Lily knows what it's like to feel helpless. But she also knows that you don't always have to be the biggest or the strongest to fight fiercely for the ones you love . . .

Please turn the page for an exciting sneak peek of Sandi Ward's SOMETHING WORTH SAVING available wherever print and e-books are sold!

1

A Boy Named Charlie

I worry most of all about the youngest boy.

Bad things have been happening lately. Unpredictable things that I don't see coming.

And someone has been hurting Charlie. I've seen the bruises.

Who would do such a thing?

Charlie arrives home at the same time every afternoon. Usually, I hear his footsteps on the outside stairs, and then the front door swings open. Most days, the doorknob clicks when it shuts behind him, and Charlie is already on the move—flinging his sneakers off, dropping his black backpack in the middle of the hall. He always heads straight for the kitchen to make a snack.

But today, he is early. Charlie opens the door cautiously, looking left to right. He steps into the house and waits on the mat, listening, clutching a strap of his backpack with one hand.

I watch from the middle of the stairs. I startle when I first see him, and scamper back up a few stair steps.

He has changed in a most peculiar way, and I hardly recognize him!

This morning, the hair on his head was dark, and he looked very much like Dad. But now his hair is light, reminding me of the snowshoe hare kept in a crate by a girl down the street. What in the world happened to him?

He sees the way I arch my back, whiskers spread in shock. "It's okay, Lil," he whispers. "It's just me."

Why yes, it is. I would know that smooth face and those green eyes anywhere. I feel foolish for scaring so easily. Bending my head, I lick my paws to cover my embarrassment. My feet gather dust from the floors, which the humans rarely sweep. I reflexively clean myself whenever I don't want to be the focus of attention.

When I look up again, Charlie is leaning back against the front door, taking in a deep breath. Okay, so maybe he looks different. But I'll get used to it. Charlie shrugs his backpack off of his shoulder and lets it fall to the floor with a thud.

I hear Gretel, the big family dog, barking in the backyard. She's probably wasting her energy chasing a squirrel, and so Charlie and I will get a nice quiet moment together.

Charlie is such a sweet boy. He comes up to sit beside me. His hands always smell like peanuts and pencil lead, although today a strange scent coming from his hair also tickles my nose. Charlie whispers in my sensitive ears: "Lily, Lily, Lil-Lil. Sorry if I scared you." His touch is gentle and soothing, and I lean my head into his fingers. "You're so beautiful," he coos.

I know, I know.

"Look at you. You're gorgeous. All that fluffy fur."

You're not so bad yourself. And I'll learn to love your hair. Just give me time.

Charlie likes to flatter me, but I think Charlie is good-looking too, compared to other humans. I would tell him so if I could. Charlie has grown several inches this past year, and he is getting stronger. He is almost a man. His long legs stretch out over many stairs.

I suspect that this change is something that Charlie did to himself, and it was not a sudden illness or an accident that lightened his hair. He is healthy and has a good appetite. Charlie is at the age when the teenagers start to preen and groom and try to make themselves attractive to other humans. I remember when Kevin and Victoria went through the same change.

Before long, we hear a bus rumbling down the narrow road in front of our house. It is big and yellow, so you can't miss it from our windows. A group of teenage boys ride on the bus in the afternoons to get to the sailing club across the street, and then they go out in boats on the river.

The humans enjoy living on the river, but I stay away from it. When I was younger, I would sneak through the fence across the street and pad my way under the boat trailers to get to the water. But the salt marsh is pungent and wet, not a good place for a cat. One time I accidentally fell into the river. The water was cold and dark, with no bottom. My feet flailed in nothingness and I barely managed to scramble out, my claws sinking into the mud. My fur was so heavy when wet! I still have nightmares about that day.

Another time, there was a red fox hiding in the marsh, and I had to run for my life. It was terrifying. Not that I had a doubt I could outrun that fox, because I'm fast and nimble. But the river doesn't interest me much anymore.

The teenage boys go out in their boats every day, until spring turns to summer. But before they do that, they run. They sprint right past our house. It's part of their routine.

"Here they come," Charlie whispers to me, shifting to get a better view out the big picture window.

Most days, Charlie will make himself a peanut butter sandwich and then watch the boys from the safety of our home. He can be shy, cautious about who he talks to. But maybe it's just curiosity. Perhaps Charlie wants to observe without being seen.

I would understand that. I know a little something about curiosity.

Two years ago, I think Charlie hardly noticed the boys at all. Last year, he started watching from an upstairs bedroom.

This year, he usually stands behind a sheer curtain in the living room, stuffing his face with his sandwich. And he watches. I suppose that he is now the same age as some of the boys that sail on the river. I wonder if he knows any of them from school or the neighborhood.

The boys run together, like a pack of dogs. For the first couple of weeks, the days are so cold they can see their breath in the air. The boys jog past in sweatshirts and sweatpants, wearing hats that cover their ears. But now that spring is breaking, they wear shorts and thin jackets. There are usually a few big, strong, older boys in the lead. Then comes the middle of the pack, and there are always some stragglers at the end. They run around the block repeatedly, circling three times, before heading to the boats. Charlie is usually done with his sandwich, taking the last bites of the crust, by the time they are on their final round.

Sometimes he frowns, watching them. He occasionally moves away from the curtain, as if afraid someone will see him.

Other times, he looks wistful. As if he wishes he could join them. He seems lonely sometimes.

I have never seen Charlie run in my life. So this may not be the right activity for him. I wonder if he will ever try it.

Today, as soon as we've watched the boys run past, Charlie stands and heads upstairs. "C'mon, Lil!" he calls to me, and I follow.

First he walks into the bathroom. I jump onto the toilet to watch him. When he lifts up his shirt, I see it: faded bruising, turning from purple to green. On his side, by his ribs.

I have seen this kind of thing twice before, both recently. I know it means he has been injured. But I haven't seen Charlie hurt himself here at home.

It's truly terrible. The bruises on his body have convinced me that someone must be hurting him. But I don't know who to blame.

I tip my head to ask: *What happened to you?*

Charlie sighs, and stares at the mirror. I sometimes puzzle over why humans look into the shiny wall, but I have concluded they see a reflection of themselves. And in that reflection, they find the answers they seek.

I don't see anything but a silver sheen when I look at the wall. It's something of a mystery to me.

Charlie takes both hands and messes with his newly lightened hair so it stands up every which way. I blink. I would find it very uncomfortable for someone to push my fur around like that. But it doesn't seem to bother him.

We both flinch at the same time as we hear the front

door open again. Charlie straightens out his shirt. I know he won't show anyone that he has been hurt.

When he is injured, he hides it.

"Charlie!" we hear from the front hallway. It's Kevin. He is bigger, older, louder. He gives Charlie all kinds of advice and orders. I think Kevin often feels the need to confirm his place as a dominant human in this house. His voice booms up the stairs. "I know you're here. I see your backpack. What the hell's going on? The principal stopped me in the hallway to say no one could find you. He was about to call the police, but I told him you probably went home, and I'd check." There's a pause. "Hey, Charlie. Answer me."

"SHUT UP," Charlie yells back, not leaving the bathroom. "It's none of your business. You're not Dad. So stay out of it."

Oh dear. Did Charlie leave school in the middle of the day again? I always worry about Charlie getting himself into trouble.

"CHARLIE." The voice gets louder, and we freeze. Heavy footsteps let us know Kevin is coming up the stairs. Charlie's face creases in concern. "Mom and Dad are too busy at work to keep getting calls from the school." There are three hard knocks on the door. "I'm coming in."

Kevin has to push to get the sticky door to open. All of the doors in the house get jammed in their frames. Nothing quite fits as it should.

Charlie and I both take a step back. The bathroom is small, and Charlie is up against the shower curtain. "Stop," he begs. "You're not Dad. Stop shouting at me."

I wish I could say: *I agree.*

I don't like it when humans yell. It makes my fur stand on end.

Kevin's eyes open wide. "Holy hell. What did you do?"

Charlie shakes his head. "I just missed a few classes. Gym. And study hall. No one cares. And maybe math—okay, I missed math too."

"No," Kevin interrupts, "your hair."

Charlie looks over at me, but there is nowhere to hide. Nowhere to go. I don't know what to tell him to do.

Kevin starts to move toward Charlie, with his hand up as if he wants to touch Charlie's hair, and Charlie flinches. I instinctively *hiss!* I spit like a sparking blaze in the fireplace. Just a warning: Stay away from my boy.

Kevin moves back to where he was.

"Kev, please. I went to Karen's house and we dyed my hair. It's not a big deal." Charlie tries to move, but his legs are up against the tub and there's nowhere to go. "Please just leave me alone."

Kevin steps out of the bathroom, hands up in surrender. "Wow. Dad's going to love that. I don't even know what to say, just—wow." He backs up slowly, as if he's afraid I might attack him. "Okay. Good luck when the principal calls Dad. He's gonna love this. Really. Dad will love it. Skipping school for *that*? Man. Good luck, buddy." He turns and heads down the stairs, shaking his head.

Thanks for nothing, I wish I could call after him.

Charlie and I look at each other. I don't think the hair change is so bad. It's already growing on me. I think Charlie looks rather interesting.

I let Charlie pick me up, going limp in his hands. I'm not a small cat. But he places me carefully on his shoulder as if I'm delicate cargo, and carries me to his room. We both lie down on his bed, right on top of the red wool blanket. Charlie and I enjoy lounging in his bedroom upstairs, staying away from activity. The afternoon sun peeks through the slats of the blinds and casts a warm light. We don't have a view of the river since his bedroom faces the backyard, but through his window I can see down into the garden lined with bright pink rugosa and the woods beyond. Charlie sighs and puts his big blue headphones over his ears; I hear a beat playing. I curl up near the bruise on his side.

Poor Charlie. He is the youngest in this family. He often seems sad and I wish I could do more to make him feel better.

Charlie is my favorite human. He's the one who chose me. He walked up and down the long hallway full of hundreds of cats where I was waiting to be adopted, and as soon as he saw me, he pointed me out to Dad. I was the only one left of my litter, and I missed my siblings terribly, living alone in a cage. As soon as our eyes met, I knew I'd found my soul mate. Charlie has the most amazing human eyes, and they lit up when he looked me over.

There is a reason I was the last one chosen in my family. It is something unimportant—something that makes no difference to me—but the humans notice it.

I was injured when I was young. My siblings and I were born in a cold house, and a human who I can hardly remember liked to move us out of his way with a kick. I was only a kitten when I unexpectedly received a hard jolt from a heavy boot one night, and my back leg was broken. The pain was horrible. My siblings were in no position to help me. There was nothing any of us could do but stumble to get out of the way when we heard the human coming. Finally, one day we were put into a bag and the next thing I remember is waking up in a cage.

Humans smile when they see my face, but frown

when they first see me walk. My gait is not graceful, because my back leg never healed quite right.

But rest assured it does not slow me down. No—just the opposite. I take pride in my speed. I have worked hard to become as strong as any cat who lives on the river.

When he saw me in the cage, Charlie lifted me carefully with two hands and told Dad, "I want this one. Look at her long fur. Why hasn't anyone adopted her yet? She's so cute." He laughed. "She's practically hugging me. Look at her, Dad. I love her already. She wants to go home with me."

When the woman in charge of the cages put me on the ground and had me demonstrate how I walk, I looked up at Charlie and Dad to watch their reaction. And I tell you this: They did not frown. No.

In fact, Dad gave a small smile and nodded, as if I were exactly what he wanted. Charlie looked up into his father's face, and that was that. Their minds were made up.

"She's a little different," Dad said quietly to Charlie, his hand on the back of his son's head. "I like that. You know, it's okay to be a little different."

Charlie bit his bottom lip, and I knew that he agreed. And I guessed that, perhaps, Charlie was a little different himself in some way.

So they brought me home and named me Lily. Dad found a nice bed for me, which I appreciate and sometimes use during the day. But at night I sleep with Charlie on his bed.

Now that I am older, I appreciate Charlie even more. I know who looks out for me. I know who loves me best. We are as close as animal and human could ever be. So I wish I could do more for him.

No creature should be mistreated. I did not deserve it, and neither does Charlie. I remember the fear, the constant knot of anxiety in my stomach that I felt when I heard the bad man coming. And I recall how humiliating it was to be too small to fight back. It makes my eyes sting and nose quiver when I think about it.

Believe me, if I knew who was hurting Charlie, I would scratch his eyes out.

I am sound asleep when the doorbell rings. Charlie jumps up, and I scramble to my feet. It is a loud musical chime that always makes my heart leap. We hear Kevin's footsteps clomping down the front hall, and the door creaks open. Gretel's nails click on the wood as she follows Kevin, and she gives a sharp *woof woof woof!* Her bark of warning echoes up the stairs, but Kevin scolds her, telling her to quiet down. Adult voices murmur, and Charlie puts a hand on my back.

There is a long pause. "Charlie," Kevin calls up the stairs, his voice breaking. He does not yell this time, which almost makes it worse. "The police are here to talk to you."

Like I said, bad things keep happening.